'Phil Whitaker uses email, letters, diaries, newspaper clippings and first- and third-person narrative to construct a convincing reality in _Triangulation_, which cuts assuredly between the Directorate of Overseas Surveys in the late 1950s and a slow journey across England in the late 1990s. The metaphor of the title involves not just a three-way relationship in which nobody accurately assesses what the others think or feel, but also, more ambitiously, the mapping of a changing Britain, from an empire with a purpose to an agglomeration of suburbs with no role. The drabness of office life and the vehement colour of east Africa during the struggle for independence are caught with impressive skill. Whitaker makes ignorance itself a theme for knowledge and compassionate understanding' _Sunday Times_

'This summer's must-read has to be _Triangulation_ . . . it is sumptuous' _Tatler_

'An effortless, rewarding read' _Glasgow Sunday Herald_

'[_Triangulation_] attempts to travel to the core of a certain kind of sepia Englishness . . . Whitaker gradually unfolds an involved tale of several betrayals . . . The machinery of colonialism is delicately examined in this distinguished, resonant novel' _Spectator_

'Conspicuously well done . . . _Triangulation_ is absorbing stuff' _Independent_

'It was very brave of Phil Whitaker to site so much of his novel in the consciousness of a dull, ungifted semi-civil servant, and very clever of him to smuggle so much passion and tragedy past the filter . . . Well-crafted and ultimately moving' _Time Out_

Triangulation

PHIL WHITAKER

PHŒNIX

A PHOENIX PAPERBACK

First published in Great Britain by Phoenix House in 1999
This paperback edition published in 1999 by Phoenix,
an imprint of Orion Books Ltd,
Orion House, 5 Upper St Martin's Lane,
London WC2H 9EA

A CIP catalogue record for this book
is available from the British Library.

ISBN: 0 75380 770 X

Printed and bound in Great Britain by
Clays Ltd, St Ives, plc

For my parents, Bridget and Derek Whitaker.
And, of course, for Lynn.

SURVEY

1 To determine the form, extent and situation of any portion of the earth's surface by linear and angular measurements, so as to construct a map, plan or detailed description of it.

2 To look at from a height or commanding position; to take a broad, general or comprehensive view; to examine the whole extent.

Surveying from Air Photographs, Captain Martin Hotine, Constable & Co., London, 1931

TRIANGULATION

A survey method in which an area is divided into triangles. In essence, the unknown distances between fixed points can be calculated from the observed angles. The mainstay of geodetic and topographical survey prior to the development of electronic distance measurement (EDM) and satellite global positioning systems (GPS), triangulation is now of historical interest only.

Mapping in Modern Times, Anthony L. Howell, Pinches & Tate, New York, 1996

PROLOGUE

My final project was the stewardship of a tourist map of the Falklands – around seven thousand people visit annually, so there is a market. There was no new air survey to arrange. We used the original maps produced by the Directorate of Overseas Surveys in the early sixties, reduced the scale, took off extraneous detail such as fence lines, marked in the battlefields, and added penguin and seal symbols at the sites of breeding colonies.

The Falkland Islands Development Corporation in Port Stanley supplied the coordinates for the cemeteries, military convention dictated the colour scheme: red for Argentine, blue for British. Our art people designed the cover. The accompanying text – hotels, tourist attractions, that sort of thing – was written by the Falklands' trade representative in London. It was a close-run thing – it often is when drawing together the efforts of various far-flung agencies. But after a fair amount of chivvying on my part, I was in a position to send the final four-colour screens to the production department on the morning of my last day. My swan-song sung, so to speak, I set about clearing my desk, intent on an early departure so as to save my colleagues from awkward goodbyes and the need to stage some sort of embarrassing gesture to commemorate my reluctant retirement.

Ordnance Survey has embraced the technological revolution and paper memos have been replaced by e-mails, so there wasn't much in the way of tidying up to do. I transferred the contents of my drawers to my briefcase and returned a few aerial photographs to file (Tanzania, coastal region, 1964, recently lent to the university in Dar-es-Salaam for a study of changing land use).

If OS has embraced computers, my relationship with them

might best be described as a formal handshake. Once my things were stowed in my case, I logged on to check mine for the last time. I was half-expecting another memo from the marketing department, the next in its long series, 'What *now* with the Falklands?'. I would have taken great pleasure in sending it straight back with a succinct postscript to the effect that, as of an hour ago, the project was out of my hands. (The people who sell our products these days seem to me to have little appreciation of the complexities of map-making. They do the rounds of industry, staying in one company only a few years before moving on to enhanced salaries elsewhere.) However, the item in my in-box was not from them.

!	⊠	✂	From	Subject
	⊠		Tom O'Dowd	The centre of Great Britain and 401 associated islands

The author's name was unfamiliar, but in an organisation of several thousand people one can't expect to know everybody. However, as Special Projects coordinator in OS International, I was unaccustomed to receiving memos relating to domestic mapping matters. Puzzled, I double-clicked on the little envelope, the screen blanked briefly, then the message appeared.

From:	Tom O'Dowd, Digital Database > t_odowd@ordsrvy.gov.uk
Sent:	28 November 1996 16:53
To:	John Hopkins, Customer Services > j_hopkins@ordsrvy.gov.uk
Cc:	
Subject:	The centre of Great Britain and 401 associated islands

I didn't read any further. This sort of thing happened to me from time to time, ever since someone by the name of John Hoskins joined Customer Services. Computers have come too late in my day for me to be capable of more than the basics. I know there is a way of forwarding misdirected messages, but I've never got to grips with it. So, I drafted a reply, explaining to Tom O'Dowd that *my* name is John Hopkins, that I work in OSI not

Customer Services, that the person he wanted was John *Hoskins* and would he like to try again.

When I'd finished, I moved the cursor to the Send button, but hesitated. This was the last act in a forty-year career. It seemed rather pathetic to go out with a single click of a mouse. As my finger hovered, my gaze drifted down to the text of the original message.

John

The hunt for the centre of Britain does seem to be hotting up. There's been talk of a lottery grant in connection with the millennium celebrations and I suspect that's what's brought all sorts of contenders out of the woodwork.

I've studied the claims you sent me. The case for Allendale in Northumberland seems to rest purely on the declaration inscribed on a sundial mounted on St Cuthbert's church. Whoever placed it there probably did so in good faith and I guess the notion of tourism, and the revenue it brings, was unheard of 150 years ago, so it was never challenged.

On the face of it, the other Northumberland contender, Haltwhistle, is using a more objective method: civilisations as far back as the Ancient Greeks found their centre points by means of bisecting north–south and east–west lines. However, Haltwhistle appears to have been a little selective. To start with, if you use a different map projection, you get a different result. And in choosing their longest north–south line they've conveniently ignored the Shetlands. Extend the line up there and the centre of Britain lies in the sea!

Avebury in Wiltshire was something of a surprise and, to be honest, the whole concept of Neolithic miles is rather baffling. Sounds a bit New Age, if you ask me.

The Newcastle University study cites Short Heath in Derbyshire on the grounds that 50% of the population live north and 50% live south of it. Though interesting, I don't think this is a valid centre point. As they say, throughout the century the population mid-point has shifted south – at least when there's a Conservative government. Two whole miles during the eighties.

So we come back to the centre of gravity method, which most people agree is best suited to such an irregularly shaped land mass. A few years ago, we calculated this on the Digital Database to find a site for BT's 100,000th phone box. We came up with a village called Dunsop Bridge in Lancashire. I'm sure the debate will run and run – at least till the lottery funds are allocated – but if OS has to endorse any of these, then, for my money, Dunsop Bridge is the centre of Britain.

Hope this is helpful. If you need more information, do wonder over some time.

Yours, Tom

I sat there, staring at the screen, a peculiar, cold sensation afflicting my insides. Helen Gardner, The White House, Dunsop Bridge, nr Clitheroe, Lancs. For a good while, all I seemed able to manage were some oddly detached musings: incredible that, in some long-forgotten corner, my mind should have preserved something so perfectly – albeit something once so familiar. And then for it to leap to life like that, crisp and clear, as though it were only yesterday when I last wrote that address.

I've no idea how long I remained stuck on that thought. All I know is that at some point something gave and the impasse was broken. Then, entirely without warning, I was struck by a memory from nearly forty years ago. A baking hot day in a thoroughly unusual summer, the continental weather inviting departure from the work-canteen-work routine. Walking back from lunch at the Toby Jug, turning the corner into Kingston Road, the Directorate up ahead on the left, and just beyond it the bridge carrying the line from Waterloo to Chessington. And the way, in those days, tyre manufacturers – without a hint of irony – used to paint their advertisements on the sides of railway bridges. Huge, dark red lettering on a white rectangle spanning the road: GOODYEAR TYRES. Helen, walking jauntily along at my side, the hem of her cotton dress dancing, pretending to take her own pulse, laying a hand on her own forehead, laughing, *There, not a trace of homesickness. I told you I don't miss Lancashire.*

Thoroughly unsettled, I sat myself perfectly upright in my chair, thinking it might help. A swift survey of our open-plan office: colleagues bent in concentration over their everyday tasks, the gentle patter of fingers on keyboards, a loud sigh of exasperation from Kieran Kirkby at the next desk, the chunter and whirr of the departmental fax on the receiving end. These things acted rather in the manner of an antidote.

Eventually, feeling considerably straightened out, I turned my attention once more to my computer. I reread the e-mail, as much to convince myself that I hadn't been mistaken as anything else, then I sent it back to Tom O'Dowd, after adding a line to the effect that it was wander, not wonder. That done, I logged off and, without a moment's hesitation, got to my feet. I left the office, speaking to not a soul, briefcase in hand admittedly, but otherwise to all intents and purposes embarking on a trip to the loo. I made my way straight out of the Ordnance Survey building, walked for the last time through its grounds, and emerged on to Romsey Road to commence my life of leisure.

Tuesday 4 March 1997, at home

By the eve of my departure I had come to regret ever having taken Mrs Bryant into my confidence. What with one thing and another, I found I had rather gone off the whole idea. Mrs Bryant, on the other hand, remained convinced that it was exactly the sort of thing a person in my position should do.

We were talking in the lounge. I was sitting in the fireside chair, she was behind me, over at the desk. She wanted to know whether I had yet got around to discovering the time of my train. After a certain amount of flannel I confessed, in as nonchalant a way as possible, that I hadn't; that I was, in fact, starting to have second thoughts. There was a pause in her activity, then a drawn-out hiss, followed a few seconds later by the sweet, waxy smell of Pledge (slogan: *Cares for all your furniture*). The sound of rubbing resumed.

'Don't be like that, Mr Hopkins, it'll do you the world of good,' she told me, her voice slightly tremulous with the effort of her polishing. 'I'm sure it's meant.'

Mrs Bryant has endured considerable misfortune in recent months and, in my opinion, the stoicism she's displayed has its roots in that simple philosophy: if things happen, they are meant; if they don't, they aren't. As far as I am concerned, the stray e-mail arriving when it did was nothing more than a coincidence. But, given the still delicate nature of her feelings, I decided against further discussion. Instead, I took the cup of coffee which she'd made me over to the telephone table. There seemed little harm in going through the motions, if only for her sake.

British Rail is no longer British Rail in the phone book, but no matter, there's a helpful entry, just below the number for the

British Psychodrama Association, referring the prospective traveller to Train Information instead. Turning to the Ts, I found a full-page advertisement detailing all manner of ways of enquiring into the various rail services. While I pondered the selection, Mrs Bryant stopped work and brought her elevenses across to the sofa. I opted to call the twenty-four-hour enquiry line at Paddington, the phone squawking musically as I tapped in the digits.

I waited for some considerable time, listening to the ringing tone, thinking that at any moment I would put the phone down and have done with it. Periodically, a recorded voice interrupted to remind me I was in a queue and that calls would be answered in strict rotation. Outside the window, naked trees shivered in the March wind. A light shower started to spatter against the glass. I gave Mrs Bryant a wan smile, which she acknowledged by taking a bite of biscuit. Eventually, an operator answered. London accent: *My name's Ian, how can I help?* I told him that I wished to travel, off-peak, from Southampton to Dunsop Bridge in Lancashire, but that I didn't think there was a station there. Neither did he; the nearest one is in Clitheroe, he told me. We agreed that in all likelihood this was going to be my *best bet* and he proceeded to use his computer to define the route.

I won't go into the twists and turns. Suffice to say that the only way of completing the journey in the space of one day is by a complicated process involving four trains running a sort of relay up the west side of the country, with myself as the baton. After noting the details, I put the receiver down, more convinced than ever that I couldn't go through with it.

'Well,' I said to Mrs Bryant, shutting the phone book and sliding it back on the shelf. 'It looks as though I'd have to leave at nine-forty-seven tomorrow morning, arriving Clitheroe at quarter to six.'

If I'd imagined that my housekeeper, who had been sitting patiently on the sofa listening to my half of the ten-minute conversation, would be as put off as I was by the length of the journey, I was soon disappointed. She gave me a funny sort of look and adjusted her position, cup clinking on its saucer.

'But Mr Hopkins, how ever are you going to get to Dunsop Bridge from there?'

The question gave rise to a certain feeling of stupidity. I am not what one would describe as a seasoned traveller. Though I've known many people who've lived and worked overseas, never once in my sixty-one years (less two days) have I set foot outside the country. I can't even remember the last time I left South-ampton. It is perhaps paradoxical that someone whose whole working life has been concerned with far-off and exotic lands should be so stay-at-home, but there you have it. Anyway, this seemed the only possible explanation for the fact that, as it stood, I'd arranged to arrive tomorrow evening in a strange town, quite probably after dark, with little idea how to complete my journey.

'Good point,' I conceded. 'It can't be far, though.'

My housekeeper joined me at the table, peering over my shoulder as I located Dunsop Bridge on the northern England map, No. 5 in our Travelmaster series.

'Too far to walk, anyway,' she said, as we examined the single B road and associated minor lanes which together constitute the somewhat straggly link between Clitheroe and the tiny grey blob representing my destination. 'Can't she come and pick you up?'

'There's bound to be a bus,' I told her. (If my tone was a little brusque, it was simply because I didn't want to admit that, despite having written some ten days ago, I had yet to receive a reply.)

I returned to the phone. Mrs Bryant took her seat again and, to be honest, as I tried to extract a number for Clitheroe bus station from directory enquiries, I began to find her continued presence irritating. I admit this was uncharitable; nevertheless, irritated was how I felt, and that's all there is to it. When I was at work, of course, I never witnessed her time-management at first hand. There's never been cause for complaint – the house is always scrupulously clean and the meal she leaves for me in the evening is invariably delicious. But in the months since I retired I have begun to notice quite how much of her time – time for which she is handsomely paid – she spends sitting around drinking my coffee.

Anyway, whatever dusting or vacuuming was being neglected, she seemed determined to remain there for the duration of my subsequent calls. Eventually, I got through to a company called Ribble Stagecoach. The way the woman there kept repeating, *Dunsop Bridge?* you'd have thought it was somewhere in Kenya, not just up the road from her. I was as helpful as I could be, Travelmaster balanced on my lap, trying to pinpoint features which might ring some bells.

'It's near a place called Newton on the B6478.'

'Newton? No, we definitely don't have anything going out that way.'

I almost gave up – only the presence of Mrs Bryant on the sofa prevented me from doing so. But after a long, muffled, hand-over-receiver conversation with a colleague, the woman discovered that there is in fact a service. It is infrequent to say the least, and the last bus leaves Clitheroe uncomfortably soon after my train is scheduled to arrive. But the woman gave me detailed instructions for the walk from the station, assuring me it would take five minutes at the most.

'There!' I pronounced, laying the phone to rest. 'I told you there'd be a bus.'

Mrs Bryant confined herself to a nod before taking her things through to the kitchen. I stayed where I was, finishing my drink, feeling strangely exhilarated. I remain uncertain quite how this polar change in mood came about. Ever since the idea first took root, I've been nagged by worries and doubts as to the wisdom of the enterprise. Sleep, never my friend at the best of times, has been fitful and fractured; most nights I've lain awake, sheets and blankets rucked into uncomfortable ridges. I can only put my reticence down to the distance involved. I am naturally disin-clined to travel, always have been. I think perhaps I'd been experiencing foreboding at the prospect of undertaking what would surely be the journey of my life.

Still, at that moment, when I successfully slotted the final piece of my route into place – at that moment I had no misgivings whatsoever.

PART ONE

The greatness and prosperity of Britain are due in no
small measure to her advantageous position. If we turn
the globe into the position in which the maximum
amount of land is visible at a glance we shall see that
Britain is almost in the centre of this land hemisphere.

The British Isles, Thomas Pickles, J. M. Dent and Sons Ltd,
London, 1958

Wednesday 5 March, on board the 09.47 CrossCountry train to York

I've found myself a window seat complete with table and have elected to sit facing backwards, so to speak, the landscape unfolding as we progress. The train is far from crowded. There's only one person in my immediate vicinity, a young woman. She's sitting just across the aisle, also in a window seat but facing the direction of travel, perhaps preferring to see what's coming rather than what has passed. Leaving aside the question of leg room, this paucity of fellow passengers is a definite bonus. I've brought quite a bit of reading material to help me while away the hours and I shall be able to spread it out on the table without it getting in anyone's way. Nor will I need to worry about a curious neighbour casting sideways glances at my personal correspondence, some of which is somewhat sensitive in nature.

Our guard has just been using the loudspeaker system to detail the long list of stops which this train will make on its journey north, although I am going only as far as Reading. I am quite sure my day's travelling will ultimately prove to be tedious: long stretches of boredom made bearable only by losing myself in my reading, interspersed with anxious flurries of platform-hunting at stations along the way. Thus far, though, the experience has been quite enchanting, largely because of the view out of the window.

It took no time at all to clear the suburbs of Southampton, the rows of houses, the high-rise flats, the telescopic reservoirs of the gas works. But even this undifferentiated urban vista contained moments of interest. At one point we passed a sewage plant and I admit to having been somewhat taken with the strange beauty of the long rotating arms, trickling their untreated waste on to the circular sewage beds below, each looking like a giant second hand sweeping steadily over the face of an electric clock. I realise it was an odd thing to find appealing, but appeal it did. For a time, as we cut our way through the suburb of Swaythling, the River Itchen meandered companionably alongside, a little tract of nature in the heart of the city. Ducks and coots bobbed about; reeds crowded together on the banks like bathers cautious about taking the plunge. Without warning, the river suddenly widened, turning into a marina, dozens of canvas-covered boats mounted on blocks, patiently awaiting better weather. I've lived in Southampton for fourteen years but I've never before seen these things. To travel by train is to observe familiar territory from a new and unexpected angle. We made a brief stop at the airport and I was struck by the packed car park, the numerous small aeroplanes ranged around the runway, so many people travelling. I've never flown and for a moment I was curious to know what the view from the air would be like.

Anyway, Southampton is gone now and we're out in the Hampshire countryside, fields rolling and undulating, grazing animals dotted about, a farmer unloading a trailer piled high with hay from the summer before. As we forge ahead I can see behind us the effects of our passing. A flock of gulls – Great Black-backeds, from the look of them – rises from a freshly ploughed field, startled no doubt by the noise. A small child, residing in a tree house in the garden of what might very well be an old rectory, rushes to the edge of the wooden structure, waving frantically. I have a fanciful vision of our train, looked down on from an aeroplane perhaps, inching across the land, ripples of perturbation in its wake. As we travel, it seems to me, we cannot help but disturb the world through which we pass.

I find myself wondering what the countryside ahead will be like. Wartime excepted, I have never been north. Mrs Bryant, far worldlier than I in this respect, assures me that the north of England is very picturesque – she and her husband enjoyed many holidays in Yorkshire and the Lake District in better times. She has no opinion of Lancashire, however, having spent no time there. Helen is the only person I ever knew from that part of the country and her attitude towards it underwent a sea-change over the years. When I first got to know her, in 1959, shortly after she started as a trainee cartographer at the Directorate, she couldn't put her home far enough behind her. She was excited by London, by what she termed its *possibilities* – so different from her previous dull existence. I well remember her talking about Dunsop Bridge, how there was little to do there, the village possessing nothing beyond a couple of shops, her school, of course, and a church. A few years later, when her personal struggles forced her to retreat home, her opinion had reversed. Throughout our subsequent correspondence, she writing from Lancashire to me at my Surbiton Drive address, she would extol the virtues of the village, its quiet solidity, the constancy of the people. She would often wonder what on earth had made her so eager to leave. I remain hopeful that I shall find Dunsop Bridge a pleasing place to visit. Indeed, I seem to remember Helen once telling me, in one of those letters, that she thought I would love it there.

I shouldn't be surprised, but after years in which I gave her barely a thought, I now find Helen almost constantly on my mind. Things which ordinarily I would hardly notice seem to exist specifically to provoke memories of her. The table at which I sit, for instance. In this coach – and throughout the train, for all I know – alternate tables are decorated with pairs of brightly coloured games boards: chess, and snakes and ladders. Clearly these are designed to entertain children on long journeys, a charming innovation for which I think CrossCountry trains should be congratulated. I can see no evidence of counters or dice, but I imagine one asks a guard. Anyway, the point is, it sets off memories. Helen was always fond of board games. Her favourite was undoubtedly Scrabble, but we also spent many happy evenings one winter, ensconced in the warmth of the lounge at Surbiton Drive, vying with each other across a chess board.

The guard has just been. He entered the coach, swaying nonchalantly with the motion of the train as he walked. As he checked and clipped my ticket, he informed me that I should change at Reading for the 11.27 (which I knew), and told me that my connection would be leaving from platform eight (which I didn't). I simply can't imagine that he comes across too many people making the rather involved journey I am undertaking. I'm mightily impressed at the depth of knowledge which allows such an off-the-cuff command of my itinerary. Furthermore, he has single-handedly dispelled many of my misgivings. If every train on which I am to travel is similarly staffed, I shall encounter no difficulty with my connections whatever. And perhaps my greatest worry – that of being stranded in the middle of nowhere – will come to nothing.

When he'd gone, I tried gazing at the scenery once more, but the view was largely unchanging, field giving on to deserted field, the countryside unremittingly flat. After a minute or two I gave it up and removed my old correspondence file from my briefcase.

This type of file was common enough in the civil service at one time. They may well have a proper name but I have always referred to them as 'string files'. They have two flaps which overlap when closed, and a metal stud, topped with a cardboard disk, through each flap. A length of string is wound around one stud, pulled taut, then wound round the other, keeping the file firmly shut. If extra security is required, the string can be sealed with wax. This file has been languishing in my loft for many years amidst the accumulated junk of a lifetime. I resisted the temptation to open it last night, preferring to postpone the moment until I was finally on my way. After all, were it not for this trip, and the prospect of seeing Helen again, I doubt I would ever have had reason to reread it.

Yet now that the moment is here I feel a definite reluctance, as though there ought to be something better to do with my time. A quick glance across the aisle shows my near neighbour to be huddled in the corner, staring fixedly out of the window. She's a young woman, no more than twenty, with an arc of ear-rings. Below her long blue skirt a pair of muddy boots protrude. Her green jacket clashes quite resoundingly with her short ginger hair and all in all she doesn't look like the sort of person I could share pleasantries with.

The wax cracks and crumbles as I tug at the loose end of the string. Little red lumps scatter over the manila card of the file and I pause to brush them on to the floor. The young woman, perhaps aware of my doing something, looks over. Our eyes meet for an instant, then she returns to her daydreaming. Half a dozen turns and the string is free. The train races on, rocking gently, its wheels beating out their tattoo as they cross the junctions between the rails. I open the flap, revealing the top sheet of paper. I slide it out and start to read.

Telephone: Derwent 8661   DIRECTORATE OF OVERSEAS SURVEYS,
KINGSTON ROAD,
TOLWORTH, SURBITON,
SURREY.

Our Refce.   Your Refce.
GWH/mjd/432/57
19th JUNE 1957

Dear Mr Hopkins,

I am pleased to inform you that, following your satisfactory performance in the Civil Service Entrance Examination and subsequent interview here, you have been allocated the post of Assistant Map Curator.

I should like you to start as soon as possible. Would you be able to make the necessary arrangements by 1st July, say? If this is asking too much then do write to say so, but the Records Section are up to their necks in it and they'll be glad of your help.

Please report to Mr O'Brien who will show you the ropes and fill you in on the sort of work we do here. I shall be away on leave but look forward to meeting you again on my return.

Sincerely

G. W. Henlen
Establishment Officer

J. A. Hopkins Esq.,
27, Cosway Street,
Lisson Grove,
London.

This, I must say, is a complete surprise – not at all what I was expecting. Normal practice would be to arrange things in the opposite order, oldest letters at the *bottom*, most recent at the top. It is many years since I put the file together and I really cannot imagine what I was thinking at the time. If there's one lesson I've learned from my long years of government service, it is never to depart from the routine, never to yield to a whim to do things differently. Organisations only work if everyone sticks to the rules. Still, in this instance I appear to have allowed an aberration and I can only think it was because I knew no one else would ever untie that string. I doubt I thought *I* ever would, so I suppose it didn't make a jot of difference how I chose to file things.

Anyway, reading my letter of appointment again has stirred a strange mix of emotions, not all of which I feel confident of putting a name to. Predominant must be nostalgia, though I'm not sure whether that should be termed an emotion as such. The stationery I hold in my hands is of a size you never see these days, slightly narrower than the ubiquitous A4 and a good inch or two longer. It is also flimsy, crackling to the touch, rather like tracing paper. The letter is typewritten, of course, which makes me realise quite how successfully the word processor has supplanted the manual typewriter. I must have handled such correspondence all the time in the early part of my career and it is a mark of the insidious nature of change that it should look so odd to me now. If one were to receive this letter from a government department today, one would be distinctly nonplussed. It looks insubstantial and gives the impression that the contents aren't worth the paper they are written on. Yet I clearly recall the huge excitement and relief which accompanied its arrival at my parents' house all that time ago.

Re-reading Mr Henlen's diplomatic phrase brought a smile to my lips: *satisfactory performance*. As far as I was concerned, my interview performance had been anything but satisfactory. On passing the general entrance examination, I had been careful not to get carried away. A simple clerical post, deep in the bowels of some ministry or other, was the height of my ambitions –

beavering away on some obscure aspect of British life, standards for road signs, for instance, or dealing with correspondence relating to licensing laws. I didn't want anything earth-shattering, just a career that wouldn't evaporate overnight like my father's had. The civil service offered that. Only in those days a prospective civil servant – at least in the junior grades – had absolutely no choice in where he ended up.

I'd never heard of the Directorate of Overseas Surveys when the interview notice came through. Nevertheless, I went with an open mind. The title of the job, assistant map curator, had a pleasing ring to it, suggestive of hushed museums and musty archives. Geography had been my best subject at school and I had already developed a fondness for maps. I assumed, rightly as it transpired, that it was this aspect of my fledgling curriculum vitae that had resulted in my being considered for this quaint-sounding post.

There was a little confusion when I arrived at Government Buildings, Tolworth. Unbeknownst to me, the Directorate – anticipating Macmillan's 'wind of change' by three years – had recently changed its name from Colonial to Overseas Surveys. Whilst the stationery on which they wrote to me had been replaced, the brass plate on the door had not. For a minute or two I thought I'd come to the wrong place, but a friendly messenger soon put me right and I made it to the interview on time.

The only thing I can remember of the half-hour I spent in that room was the dogged persistence of one of the three men across the table. I lost count of the times he asked me: how would you set about a triangulation of Africa? Of course, I hadn't the faintest idea – my geography A level hadn't prepared me for such a question. So, I kept telling him: I can't answer that. But he wouldn't give it up. The others may have asked me things, I don't know. Afterwards, all I remembered was that the whole interview had been taken up with that one recurring question, a brick wall to me. I was familiar with the theory of triangulation, but how one would put it into practice – that was a matter for other, cleverer people. The sort of people who actually did those things.

And *Africa*. He might as well have asked me how I would set about a triangulation of the moon.

I was bitterly disappointed on the train back to Waterloo. My civil service career appeared to have fallen at the first. All I wanted was to push paper around a desk and receive a regular, modest income for it. Had I been allocated to any other department, such a job would have been mine for the asking, I was sure. In the following days I tried to prepare my parents for the disappointment to come; so much rested on my getting a job. I even went back to the insurance firm where I'd been filling in since the end of my national service, to see whether any permanent vacancies might be coming up.

Naturally, I couldn't have known then that an assistant map curator wouldn't be expected to understand the first thing about a triangulation of Africa; that the interviewer who kept asking me about it was a surveyor and, like many in his profession, thought everyone else should know exactly what surveyors did. Nor, at the time, did I realise that the other two people on the panel tolerated his idiosyncratic contributions for the way they tested candidates under pressure. And I certainly didn't appreciate that my consistent stonewalling, my absolute refusal even to have a stab at answering a question I was completely ignorant of, was just the sort of quality which one of the others on that interview panel would be impressed by, for a role somewhat removed from the curatorship of maps.

My reminiscence was interrupted by our short stop at Winchester. A number of people embarked and two ladies in particular caused quite a commotion. Around my own age, with several bags and cases between them, they became entangled in the manually operated sliding door at the entrance to the carriage. The woman on this side was effectively trapped, the heavily sprung door having shut on her arm. I went to offer assistance and my intervention resulted in a swift and satisfactory conclusion. I helped them stow their things in the racks at the end of the coach, straightened my tie, and we all settled down.

The incident caused something of a thaw in relations. Back at my seat I caught the eye of the young woman across the aisle. She gave me a cautious smile which I returned. She then made a gesture with her bottle of mineral water. I declined with a self-deprecating shake of my head and a repeat of my smile. Neither of us spoke a word but, nevertheless, we seemed to have conducted an entire conversation about the endearing feebleness of our fellow travellers. This young woman is not the sort of person with whom I would normally establish a rapport. But all of a sudden there was unquestionably a feeling of comradeship.

The two ladies in question seated themselves just along the coach. With a certain amount of tugging of jacket sleeves and fixing of hair they restored their composure. The one in the aisle seat, shoulders carpeted with a russet shawl, kept sending me quick looks of gratitude, something which gave me a feeling of quiet satisfaction. Really, I quite surprise myself. I never thought I would feel so at ease, being whisked further and further away from my home, heading into the unknown. I wonder whether Helen will notice any difference. She often castigated me, in the old days, for my refusal to travel, to experience new things. Actually, refusal was her word and I always felt it was too strong: I simply never felt the need, the desire. Anyway, it will be fascinating to see if she thinks I have changed.

I'd left my letter of appointment lying on top of the file. As the passengers around me gradually retreated into their own worlds I picked it up again. *If this is asking too much then do write to say so.* I think Mr Henlen included emollient phrases like that safe in the knowledge that to take him up on the offer would be bad form. It was a tall order, getting accommodation sorted out in the space of a fortnight, but I managed it. The only thing available at short notice was a two-bedroom flat on Surbiton Drive, ten minutes' walk from the Directorate. At the time, I was thoroughly peeved that they should require me to act in such haste. Later, I saw it for what it was: just another example of the way things were done there. The Directorate was at the height of its expansion, producing maps of vast swathes of the empire, staff numbers increasing exponentially. Most of the people working there were driven – there is no other word for it; convinced of the value of their maps to countries struggling to develop. You simply can't build dams, design major irrigation schemes, extend road and rail links, let alone conduct a census of land ownership, or analyse and plan changes in an agricultural economy, without mapping. Nothing was allowed to stand in the way of getting the job done – everyone mucked in. Even the most senior staff would occasionally be found in their shirt-sleeves, wielding screwdrivers, helping to assemble new drawing tables for the next batch of trainee cartographers to arrive at Tolworth.

I put the letter back in the file and stared out of the window. I'm not sure how long I stayed like that. I certainly don't remember much of what I saw: ivy-covered embankments, perhaps; a rail junction, other lines sweeping in to join ours, a Wessex Traincare building like an island in their midst. But most of the scenery, as we sped through Hampshire, on towards Berkshire, was lost to me. The next thing I knew we were stopping at Basingstoke. The platform was crowded and the population of our coach swelled considerably. No one came to sit by me, but a middle-aged couple took the seats opposite the young woman across the aisle. She and I exchanged secret looks: our cosy, spacious set-up was being disturbed. I imagine this is in the nature of travel. Nothing stays the same for long and I shall just have to get used to it.

Shortly after leaving Basingstoke, the guard's voice crackles over the loudspeaker. Twenty minutes to Reading. The time is flying – at this rate I shall be in Lancashire before I know it. I turn my attention back to my file and remove the next letter. There's time to read a little more before I have to make my first connection.

My dear Hopkins,

After two days spent cooped up in various types of aeroplane, my rump getting progressively more sore, I've finally arrived. I'm quite sure the designers of those contraptions are vying for the accolade of Most Refined Human Torture Machine, and good luck to them. I only wish I hadn't had to be part of the experiment. Anyhow, I shan't have to contend with it again for ten months or so, and even then I've a mind to take up the option of a sea passage home and hang the extra travelling time. At least one can get some air on deck and move about as one's fancy dictates.

Africa every bit as awe-inspiring as imagined. Thus far, mostly seen from aircraft windows, but I'm positively itching to get out into it and get my hands dirty. Colossal mountains, vast, sprawling lakes, and every conceivable kind of country from arid plain to thick forest on the way over.

I'm staying here in K— for a few days. The District Officer himself, a nice chap called Hildred, met me at the airport (more of a landing strip with associated random buildings in fact) and brought me into town. Initial impression mainly one of genial confusion – I suppose it would be the same for a first-time visitor to London, trying to make sense of the ebb and flow of life. The streets are chock-full of Africans wearing clothing bright and colourful enough to put one in mind of Ascot. There's roughly the same amount of sitting around on backsides too. Every taxi is a Morris Minor, which looks very odd, I can tell you. I decided on a stroll last night and was the cause of at least one shunt. Hildred tells me – I suspect not entirely frivolously – that your average taxi driver hereabouts is quite certain that any European should be tucked up in the back of his cab rather than be out on the pavement astride Shanks's pony. Spotting a likely fare, he tends to stop on a sixpence. The following traffic attempts to do likewise but doesn't always manage it. The streets are fringed with bits and pieces of car that have become detached in the ensuing mêlées.

I'm quite sure the weather doesn't help safe driving either. Generally it's hot and sunny, then all of a sudden a squadron of clouds buzzes in and deposits what must amount to an inch of rain in the space of an hour or two. Hildred thinks I'm quite mad: these 'showers' are deliciously warm and he caught me standing out in one today, savouring the sensation of fat, tepid raindrops on my face.

I shall write again once I've made the trip up-country to join the field party. By then I shall know an address to which you can write should you be so inclined. In any event, you must let me know if there are bills or repairs to meet on Surbiton Drive. I insist on paying my share even when absent – it's the least I can do towards such a satisfactory arrangement. I'd have to stump up the whole lot if I had my own place, so I shall consider it a bargain.

I hope you're finding life at HQ passably enjoyable. I have to say, I wouldn't swap places with you for the world, but I *can* see what you mean: this lark certainly wouldn't be everyone's cup of tea. Thank God, is all I can say, otherwise it might not have been so easy to land the job. Mind you, the next letter I send will probably find me thoroughly browned off with all things foreign and craving a return to England's green and pleasant. In that case, you shall have the perfect right to say, 'I told you so!'

Yours sincerely,

L. D. Wallace

P.S. Should any post turn up for me, please hang on to it until such time as I've sorted out a forwarding address here. Many thanks.

LETTERS TO THE EDITOR

Sir – Your correspondent's assertion that the political situation has improved enormously in T— is unreliable. What has happened is that the multi-racial United T— Party has collapsed, and the mono-racial T— African Nationalists' Alliance now dominates. Far from being 'reasonable and cooperative', T.A.N.A. has a long history of violence and subversion which in past years has landed many of its prominent activists in gaol.

Your correspondent suggests that African leaders should be congratulated on their moderation. May I remind you that when the African nationalist leaders of Kenya, Uganda, N. Rhodesia and Nyasaland met recently in conference in Mwanza, they declared a policy of 'nationalism virile and unrelenting'. Their aim is 'government of Africans by Africans for Africans'. This is what your readers are being asked to regard as 'moderation'.

Yours faithfully,
S. F. van der Lande,
Editor, *Africa Review*,
2 Great Russell St, WC1
4th MAY 1959

Helen Gardner rounded the corner to be confronted by yet another unfamiliar road. The semi-detached houses were absolutely indistinguishable from the others she had passed. She looked at the sign: Northcote Avenue. The name, like the others – Elgar, Raeburn, Rushton, Sandhurst – rang a distant bell. She *must* be in the right area. She trudged on as far as the shade of the first tree, a coppiced lime, branches sprouting from the bulbous termination of the trunk, then, unable to move another inch, she let her cases drop to the pavement. Clenching and unclenching her fists, the blood creeping tentatively back into her fingers, she scrutinised her surroundings, retracing her steps in her mind, trying once again to remember how she'd got there the month before.

The present situation was, of course, all the fault of her father.

If she'd stuck to her guns and insisted that she be allowed to travel to her interview alone, none of this would have happened. But no, that wasn't how things were done. If a girl went behind her parents' backs and put in for a job hundreds of miles away from home, the only thing the poor parents *could* do was ensure she ended up living somewhere decent, respectable. When Mary McKend had expressed the desire to attend secretarial college, *her* father had gone to meet the principal before even allowing her to apply. And that was only Manchester. If Helen really did intend to up sticks and disappear down to London, she couldn't do so without giving her father the opportunity of seeing her properly settled in. *Think of your mother.* And, indeed, her mother had looked intensely unhappy. Helen – half-way up the stairs, where her father's shouting had finally arrested her – had peered over the bannister at the top of her mother's head, had seen the hands clasped tightly together. But Helen was sure it was as much to do with being left alone with her husband as with the imminent loss of her only daughter.

'All right, then,' Helen had said, voice quiet after her father's angry decibels. '*She* can come with me.'

But he wasn't having that either. So in the end the three of them had travelled down to Tolworth, to the Directorate of Overseas Surveys. Her mother gave Helen's hand a discreet squeeze before she went in to the interview, her father managed a gruff *Good luck.* In consideration of the distance she'd had to travel, she'd been promised a decision within a few hours. Waiting in the canteen afterwards, drinking cup after cup of tea, she was glad her parents had gone off, *to see what the area's like.* She wouldn't have been able to bear it if the establishment officer had come with the news while her father was there. Or at least, she wouldn't have been able to bear it had the news been bad. And when she met up with them later, heady with the excitement of being offered the post, able at last to turn her thoughts to the question of accommodation, Mr Gardner simply nodded, as if he'd known this would happen all along, then told her they'd been to see a very nice boarding house, not ten minutes from the station, and that was where she was going to live.

Stalking along at her mother's side, several yards behind him, glaring at his back, she'd not paid the surroundings much attention. Now, burdened with her portfolio and two heavy suitcases, armed with nothing but the address and the dimmest recollections of the route they'd taken, she was lost. Even allowing for the weight of her luggage, the ten minutes was long since up. She eased the strap of her portfolio from her shoulder and sank down, perching on one of the suitcases, its stout frame creaking a mild protest. Northcote Avenue was deserted in the late afternoon sun. She eased her shoes off, relishing the sensation of fresh, cooling air around her swollen feet. Her shoulders ached and her scalp prickled irritatingly beneath the thick tresses. She felt quite demoralised, failing to cope so soon.

It was all a stark contrast to a couple of hours before, when she'd stepped off the train at Euston. Then, she'd been bubbling with excitement; at the beginning of a great adventure. She'd stood on the concourse amidst the bustling crowds, the air full of strange smells and echoing shouts and hissing steam and shrill whistles and slamming train doors. This was it, she'd arrived in London. Even the Underground to Waterloo – trying to negotiate the long tunnels with her unwieldy baggage, so many people rushing past on either side, inadvertently knocking into her – had failed significantly to deflate her mood. Once or twice, young men had offered assistance, but she'd politely declined, struggling on, half-carrying, half-dragging her cases, trying to look as though she knew exactly where she was going.

The final, twenty-minute leg of the journey had felt like a triumphant procession, the overground train conveying her through the realms of the city that was to be her home. The splendour of Lambeth Palace, Archbishop's Park. The impassive Thames, the snatched views of huge architectural edifices ranged along its north bank – who could say what acts of governance, commerce, culture, went on there? The landscape altered dramatically as they swept through Vauxhall, Queens Road, Clapham

Junction, and she found her sense of wonder giving way to a fascinated horror. But it had been a long day's travelling and she couldn't expect to adjust to the sight of such a cramped, chaotic, urban jumble within minutes of arriving. Wimbledon, Raynes Park, Motspur Park, brought a greener outlook: larger houses with neat gardens; playing fields; tennis courts, white-clad figures knocking balls across the nets, oblivious to their transient spectator. She felt quite cheerful again by the time the train pulled into Tolworth.

And then she'd set off to find Edith Gardens. Her fellow passengers had quickly dispersed, heading to their own homes for the start of the weekend. She hadn't been unduly concerned at first, but as the streets through which she walked grew completely unfamiliar, devoid of any recognisable landmarks, she began to regret not asking for directions when she'd had the chance.

What she should do was knock at a door, she decided, regarding the pebble-dashed façades of Northcote Avenue without much enthusiasm. A map would be better – she could find her own way if she had one – but she hadn't passed any shops for a while, and to retrace her steps to the parades on Tolworth Broadway would be a task of Herculean proportions. Besides which, at well past five, they'd be shut up for the day. She leaned forward, sliding a finger into the heel of one shoe as she returned her foot to its tight confines. She didn't hear the footfalls until the man was almost upon her.

'Can I help you, Miss?'

Helen looked up to find a youth squinting down at her. He was standing beyond the shade of the tree, suit jacket slung over his arm, hat respectfully in hand, his Brylcreemed hair glistening in the sun. With a determined shove, she rammed her other foot home and stood up. The case, unbalanced by her sudden movement, toppled against its fellow and the two bags slumped to the ground like dominoes.

'Yes, I'm looking for a road called Edith Gardens.'

The young man was momentarily distracted by the collapse of

her cases. 'Edith Gardens? That's just around the corner. Here, I'll show you.'

He replaced his jacket and hat, smoothing back a lock of hair that had flopped over his forehead before he did so, then bent down and set about righting her luggage. Words of protest died on her lips – her resolve was gone. After all the travelling, the constant unfamiliarity, the new sights and sounds assailing her in a day-long torrent, all she wanted was to get to the boarding house, be shown to her room, and find some sanctuary in which to take stock. She let him carry both cases, though she kept hold of her portfolio, finding some vindication in his grunt of surprise as he lifted them.

They set off along Northcote Avenue. From time to time she cast sidelong glances, but her companion continued to look straight ahead, as though unaware of her. Eventually, a little perturbed by his apparent indifference, she ventured a comment.

'This is awfully kind of you.'

He glanced over, as if surprised by her words. A single nod. 'Not far now.'

And that was it. Fortunately, what he said was true. At the end of the street they turned left and across the main road she immediately recognised the gates to a park, the sign for Surbiton Lagoon. *This* was the road along which they'd come before; she must have got sidetracked down a parallel. A matter of twenty yards brought them to the corner of Edith Gardens. She felt stupid – so near yet so far.

'Thank you,' she said, coming to a halt, holding out her hands.

The young man hesitated, then set his burden down. 'You're sure you'll be all right from here?'

Helen laughed, grasping the suitcases' handles. 'Perfectly.'

Whether it was the brief rest, or the prospect of an end to her journey, she wasn't sure, but her arms seemed to have regained their strength. She wished the man good day, thanked him again, and started on her way.

'Your accent – you're not from round here, are you?'

The question rang out after she'd taken a couple of paces. She turned, thinking that he looked suddenly rather pathetic, piping up now their encounter was over, his face flushed after his exertions.

'No, Lancashire.'

She'd never had a particularly strong accent, at least not unless she'd wanted. At home, she'd tended to enunciate in an amalgam of her father's southern tones and her mother's Irish lilt, the crispness of the one softened by the musicality of the other. In the playground, of course, it had been a different matter. In her younger years she'd found it prudent to adopt the local inflections to avoid bringing unwanted attention on herself. These still had a tendency to creep into her voice when she was nervous or unsure of herself. She made a mental note to make more of an effort in future.

He nodded, appeared to be on the verge of continuing the conversation, then mumbled, 'Right you are. Well, cheerio, then.'

With that he touched the brim of his hat and wheeled around. Helen watched him as he walked away, rather pleased that her first brush with an authentic Londoner had confounded the predictions of those at home who'd warned her to be on her guard in the faceless, preying city.

Edith Gardens was a stub of a street – a *cul-de-sac*, as the legend at the bottom of the road sign had it. The houses were of an older vintage than the semis of Northcote Avenue, tall, sooty, red brick, with short flights of steps leading up to the front doors. Helen pressed the bell to number five and a few moments later impressionist fragments of colour materialised in the frosted glass panels, coalescing into a figure as the door started to open.

'Miss Gardner? We was wondering what time you'd get here.' Mrs Potter half-turned, bellowing unintelligibly along the hall. A moment later a diminutive man appeared, wiping soap-sudsy hands on his off-white apron as he came.

'Ernie'll take your things.'

Mr Potter grinned a silent greeting then did as his wife had suggested. The three of them trooped up the steep staircase in single file, Mr Potter in the vanguard, puffing like a locomotive, Helen immediately behind him. To avoid the eye-level view of his sagging trouser seat, she studied the fleur-de-lis wallpaper, more dingy than she recalled, edges lifting away from the plaster in places, and the ascending series of English pastoral oils. They were simply framed and all by the same hand, every one composed with an identical lack of inspiration. Trees and bushes crowded the edges of the small canvases, funnelling the eye to the centre, where the absence of vegetation allowed sight of a rock-strewn stream, a flock of sheep, a field in harvest. The landscapes were all flat, undulating at best; even the skies were unvarying, banks of improbably fluffy clouds breaking up an otherwise uniform blue. She doubted any such scenes existed in reality, they so reeked of artifice and idyll. The brushwork was untutored, far from meticulous. Helen looked again at Mr Potter's rear end, wondering whether it might be he or his wife who was responsible.

Her room was off the first-floor landing.

'There we are,' Mrs Potter announced, squeezing past her husband to open the door. Helen stepped inside, finding that she had no recollection of the place from her earlier, fleeting visit. There was a rug alongside the single bed; the boards elsewhere were uncovered. The bed itself was draped with a threadbare turquoise bedspread. There was a chest of drawers, a gas fire, a tall, thin wardrobe, and, in the corner, a washbasin.

'Cold water only in the rooms. Bathroom's upstairs – we try to keep it to one a week, unless the circumstances is exceptional.' Mrs Potter's face was still with concentration. 'Breakfast from seven, supper at half-past six.' She consulted her wristwatch. 'You've got an hour. More than likely you'll be wanting to settle in.'

Helen smiled as warmly as she could. The landlady cleared her throat and directed a pointed look at her husband out on the landing. He shunted forward, deposited the luggage at her feet, wiped his hands on his apron again and, with a wordless nod at Helen, went back downstairs.

Mrs Potter lowered her voice. 'You're more than welcome to entertain in the front parlour, but no visitors in the rooms, please, dear.'

'Of course.'

'And the WC upstairs, that's the one for the ladies.' She gave a little cough. 'Please try to use the bin.'

'Of course.'

With that, Mrs Potter started down the stairs after her husband. Helen waited until the landlady's head had sunk below the level of the landing, then she shut the door and locked it. Turning, she leaned her shoulders against the smooth wood, drawing a deep breath. The back of her blouse was soaked with sweat and the material clung, unpleasantly chill, to her skin. Her eyes ranged more methodically this time, following the line of the unencumbered picture rail round the walls. Here and there a stark, clean patch of wallpaper bore testimony to an absent painting – at least she'd been spared the anonymous artist's efforts in here. The wardrobe, she noticed, stood at a marked slant, tilting towards the window as though attracted by the light. The mirror above the sink was mottled, much of the silvering long since corroded to a dull black. Why was it, dreaming and yearning in the comfort of her childhood home, that the practicalities had never impinged? All she'd ever imagined was the semi-seriousness of work, mitigated by the excitement of new friends, new colleagues, rushing out of an evening to see a play, take in a film, the city around her bright in the day and illuminated by a thousand lights at night. She hadn't even thought of what life in the boarding house would be like, hadn't had any space in her dreams for Mrs Potter's perfunctory welcome, for her husband's sagging trousers, his off-white apron, his soap-sudsy hands. At home she could bathe when she liked, take friends to her room, eat breakfast late if she fancied. And all the mirrors reflected your image back at you cleanly, sharply, brightly. She released her breath in a long, slow sigh. When she let her head flop backwards it banged against a hook screwed into the door.

Jolted out of her trance, she removed her shoes and strode

forward, unbuttoning her blouse as she went. She mustn't allow herself to get into this frame of mind. It had been a long day; she was bound to find the place drab at first. At least it was cheap, would allow her to get started. Once she had some money coming in, she could think of moving on, get herself a nicer room. Perhaps she would hit it off with another trainee, another girl also new to the area. Within a month or two they could be sharing their own little flat. This wouldn't be for long.

She drew the curtains – cutting out half the light and tingeing the rest an eerie green – and slipped her blouse from her shoulders, letting it fall to the floor. A rasp of a zip fastener, a button shelled out of its hole, and her skirt slid round her calves. She unclipped her stockings, rolling each carefully down to her ankles before hooking them off her feet. Pausing for a moment, she gathered to herself the feeling of freedom, of being unbeholden, relishing the prospect of nakedness. Then her underwear joined her other clothes on the floor.

She half-filled the sink. The pipework must have been warmed by the sun – the water was tepid rather than cold. She set about washing herself, first cupping water to her face, then rubbing wet hands over the rest of her body, finishing up with precarious one-legged balancing as she hoisted and dunked each foot in turn. The thought occurred that Mrs Potter's settling in hadn't extended to a welcoming bath, even though the circumstances was exceptional. Refreshed and feeling in slightly better humour, she went to collect her towel from her case. Behind her she left dark impressions of her high-arched feet on the floorboards, marking out that short journey for some time until at last they faded and dried. Long before they did she had flung herself on the bed to sleep.

A knock woke her. She came to abruptly, momentarily confused as to where she was; hot, and a rank taste in her mouth. The knock came again. Suddenly orientated, she threw the bedspread aside and pushed herself upright.

'Hello?'

'Was you wanting supper or not?' Even the wood of the door could not disguise the new note of suspicion in Mrs Potter's voice.

'Yes. I'm sorry –' Helen's wristwatch was buried amongst the pile of clothes by the sink. She had no idea of the time. 'I'll be down in a minute.'

'It's getting cold, you know.'

'Yes, I'm sorry.'

She listened for a moment, but from the silence it was clear Mrs Potter was going nowhere. Suddenly ashamed of her nakedness, Helen hopped out of bed and rummaged in a case until she found her dressing gown. With this wrapped around her, she opened the door to find her landlady standing barely a foot away.

'Settling in all right?' Mrs Potter asked, looking her up and down.

'Thank you, yes.'

Helen could see her eyes darting as she appraised the room. There was the mound of clothes in the far corner; the suitcases open on the floor, lids tipped back, untidy entrails spilling over the sides; the bed in disarray; no progress.

'I must have dropped off.'

'Bound to have.'

Mrs Potter's unsmiling expression belied the sympathy in the words. She sniffed unnecessarily loudly, a noise imbued with the tribulations of one forced to open her home to a succession of feckless youngsters and uncouth salesmen.

'Like I say, it's getting cold. We eat punctual here, and Ernie's done you a lovely bit of gammon.'

Wednesday 5 March, on board the 11.27 CrossCountry train to Edinburgh

The change-over at Reading passed without mishap – thanks to the guard on my earlier train, I was able to make a bee-line for the right platform. Arriving there, I was both surprised and pleased to find, of all things, a telephone box. This sort of convenience for the traveller is a welcome innovation, all the more so as I was experiencing a momentary worry concerning the security of my empty house: I had realised that I might have failed to close the bathroom window before leaving home (I have quite a problem with condensation).

I was able to remove this weight from my mind by means of a call to Mrs Bryant. My housekeeper has kindly agreed to pop in for an hour or so each day and keep an eye on the place. Guessing that she would stick to her usual routine, I tried my own number, and my assumption was proved correct when she answered. She sounded a trifle uncertain at first, and this gave way to a note of alarm when she realised that the caller was me.

'Oh, Mr Hopkins, where are you? Is everything all right?'

I quickly reassured her that I had reached Reading and told her I was having the time of my life. When I explained the reason for my call she said she would go and check the bathroom the minute we put the phone down. The business side of things over and done with, we had a pleasant chat about my journey thus far, and I must say, it was very nice to have someone with whom I could share my experiences. We talked for some time, me feeding the majority of my small change into the coin slot. It was only after I hung up that I remembered the other thing I should have said to her.

I am not making this trip unannounced. I wrote to Helen

nigh-on a fortnight ago, informing her of my plans, and specifically mentioning my intended departure date. There was a little local difficulty with the post last week – a dispute over imposed working patterns – but Royal Mail, when I enquired, assured me that the backlog had been quickly cleared. So I was becoming distinctly apprehensive yesterday when I'd still not heard from her. I contemplated trying to discover her number from directory enquiries and making the arrangements by phone instead. But I swiftly rejected the idea: it had been too long for me to think of ringing her out of the blue. And in any case, there are things one can put in writing that would be difficult to say out loud. So even this morning I was still hoping for a reply. I was in the kitchen, listening to *Today*, when I heard the letter box squeak and clang. I hurried out to retrieve the mail from the mat.

The first item turned out to be a letter from British Telecom's customer benefits team, who wondered if I would be interested in joining their Friends and Family scheme. They gave a list of the ten numbers I dial most frequently, on which I would be eligible for a 10 per cent discount. I studied it for a moment or two, curious to see which I could recognise (Mrs Bryant, work, the rest unknown). My projected annual saving, were I to join the scheme, was quoted as £1.24.

Glancing at the second envelope, I was sure it was from Helen. Only in retrospect did I notice the postmark, and realise that the handwriting was familiar for different reasons. The card inside depicted a still-life: a vase of irises on a table, painted in pastel shades.

To Mr Hopkins,
    Wishing you a Lovely Trip and
hoping things work out for the Best.
    Sincerely yours,
        Florrie and Bill (Bryant)

For some reason, I found this intensely touching, I think because of the careful, childlike way Mr Bryant had written his own name when it would have been far easier to let his wife sign on his behalf. Replacing the receiver in that platform phone box, I realised I'd completely neglected to thank my housekeeper for it. So I called her straight back. The phone rang for some time and, when she answered, Mrs Bryant was quite out of puff. No, I hadn't forgotten to close the bathroom window. She was in the middle of checking the others. I commended her on her speedy action, and went on to say how thoughtful it had been of her and Mr Bryant to send the card. I think she found this somewhat embarrassing and we didn't stay talking for long afterwards. Nevertheless, I have no regrets over raising the subject. As I go on in life I am firmly of the opinion that these little acts of kindness should not pass without comment.

After all the phoning there wasn't that long before my next train was due. This is the longest leg of my journey, taking me as far as Preston, which I should reach shortly after four. This train is more crowded than the last – it started its journey in Brighton – and I have been forced to sit facing the direction of travel. I find it harder on my eyes somehow, the landscape whipping by. We passed an empty football pitch, sentinel goalposts draped in netting; a little later, a deserted fairground, the rides and big wheel motionless in the grey light of the overcast morning. Since then, the line has been embedded, embankments rising up on either side, disrupting the view. Some sort of clearance has recently gone on, countless tree branches and sapling trunks amputated, their splintered ends, stark and white like fractured bones, testimony to the indiscriminate violence wreaked upon them. Naturally, the lines need to be kept free of encroaching vegetation, but all the same it is a strangely brutal sight.

I find I am rather missing the cautious camaraderie of the 09.47 to York. I was the only person from my coach to alight at Reading, leaving the others to carry on their own journeys to who knows where. In time, further influxes of passengers will become assimilated, fresh understanding glances will be swapped, new alliances formed. The solitary man who assisted the ladies caught in the door will be forgotten.

Now, I am an interloper. The other people in this carriage scarcely noticed my arrival. They're chatting amongst themselves, one or two are working on portable computers, many of the others are reading. I wish I had brought a paper, or a book. Something other than my correspondence file, which I had imagined I would be dipping into throughout the trip.

If I'm perfectly honest, Laurance's letter has quite knocked me back. Oh, I knew it was there, that one and many others, but I hadn't anticipated the strength of feeling that would be aroused. I imagine this is what is meant when people talk of reopening old wounds, only I would have thought a more robust weapon than a piece of paper would be required. But then again, it's the words, not the paper they're written on. I always considered him a fine correspondent, relished receiving things from him. His turn of phrase, the easy jocularity, well, it was as if Laurance himself was standing there telling you those things. From the outset I found him to have a particular charm and that, it seems to me, comes through forcibly on the page. Indeed, I know for a fact that Laurance's prose was quite capable of inspiring an affection bordering on the irrational, something it cost me dear to learn.

Yet now, with the benefit of hindsight, I can see through it – I can see through him, if you like. But that's the thing with hindsight: nothing of what happened can ever be changed. I'm still left with the same feelings of regret and impotent anger and pity and sadness. And – why hide it? – lurking fondness for him, a fondness which never quite died from the day we met, in spite of everything.

The Directorate of Overseas Surveys was the sole occupant of the Government Buildings in Tolworth. There are apparently numerous examples of this type of office accommodation dotted around the country, all dating from the immediate post-war period. Each consists of a series of separate single-storey blocks, arranged side by side. A central corridor runs the length of the site, linking each block to its neighbour, so that one can walk from one end of the complex to the other without getting wet – assuming it's raining, which it often is. Government Buildings were designed like this so they could be quickly converted into military hospitals in the event of another full-scale conflict. Some of the rooms even have shallow gutters around the edge of the floor, into which blood can be sluiced should they be needed as operating theatres. To the best of my knowledge, none of them has ever had to assume its alter-ego. Certainly the Directorate never shall; the buildings were demolished a few years ago and the land sold off for a housing development.

All people entering or leaving the Directorate had to do so through the entrance lobby, a dilatation of the central corridor between blocks 3 and 4. When they weren't delivering internal post, or running errands, the messengers would wait around in the lobby, watching out for visitors, or other people unsure of where to go. At nine o'clock on the morning of Monday 1 July 1957, I pushed open the front door – by now bearing its new brass plate, 'Directorate of Overseas Surveys' – and stepped inside. My initial impression stays with me to this day, as does the sensation of suppressed excitement I felt.

A steady stream of people was traversing the lobby. A few of the men were dressed in suits, but most were more casually attired, with V-neck jumpers or sleeveless sweaters. In the case of the women, skirts and blouses were the order of the day. Several people were carrying bundles of files or enormous brown map folders. Even then, before I could possibly have known what was inside, I was intrigued by those outsized packages – a foretaste of the anticipation I would feel time and again before opening one and examining the maps within. Occasional greetings were being called, friends and colleagues were chatting as they went to take their places for the day. There was a purposeful atmosphere, but also good humour to be seen on many faces. I stood for a short time, simultaneously savouring my arrival in the world of work and trying to catch someone's eye, intending to ask where I might find Mr O'Brien, to whom I was due to report. Before I could approach anyone, however, a messenger, whose name I later learned was Albert, cut through the stream of pedestrians, sliding a pencil into the top pocket of his brown overall as he came towards me.

'Starting here today, sir?'

I was taken aback by his prescience. 'Yes, how –'

'Same as the gentleman there, sir,' he explained, indicating a man standing at the far side of the lobby, a framed map sheet hanging on the wall behind him. His hands were thrust deep into his trouser pockets, the linen of his jacket bunched up around his forearms. He was staring up the corridor, head turned in profile. I had an impression of a thoughtful face, eyes shadowed beneath a gently sloping brow, the clean lines offset by a shock of curly dark hair that looked as though it had never succumbed to brush or comb.

Albert took me across. 'Right, if you two gentlemen would like to come with me.' The other newcomer and I fell into step, following the messenger as he headed up the slope of the corridor.

'Laurance Wallace,' my companion introduced himself, hands still pocketed as he walked. 'Your first day too, I understand?'

I confirmed that it was and told him my name.

He glanced at me; his eyes were an impassive brown. 'Hopkins? Don't remember you from Newbury. Have you been doing something before this?'

I wasn't at all sure what he meant but I made a guess from the context. 'Just a bit of insurance work, covering absences, that sort of thing.'

'Ah, private, eh?' He surprised me by giving me a wink. 'Well, I wouldn't let on about it round here if I were you. Very bad form.'

I was beginning to feel quite at sea and decided that the best way to avoid showing myself up was to turn the spotlight. 'And how about yourself?'

'Me?' Laurance laughed. 'Never done a day's work in my life. Giggleswick, Cambridge, Newbury, now here, all without so much as shooting a single angle in earnest. Quite surprised they took me on, in fact, but apparently they can't fill the vacancies. The life's too hard for most, so the story goes.'

We walked on in silence, it dawning on me that whatever job Laurance Wallace was starting, it was far removed from my humble assistant map curatorship. I knew very few people who had gone to university, let alone Cambridge, and although higher education was something my teachers had talked of as being within my capabilities, our family's financial circumstances were never going to allow it. Everything about Laurance, his crisp speech, his self-possession, smacked of a class several notches above my own. The loose linen suit, beige in colour, crumpled in appearance, was a distinct contrast to my own navy Burton's two-piece with its sharp leg creases. And I had spent a considerable time the previous evening polishing my shoes. Beneath Laurance's flapping trouser ends he was wearing rough suede desert boots.

'Bit grim, isn't it?'

I gathered from his nod that he was referring to the generality rather than to any specific feature. The corridor, stretching for hundreds of yards ahead of us, was indeed fairly dingy and windowless. The bituminous floor was breaking up in places, leaving scooped-out depressions in the surface. The walls were coated in creamy yellow paint but the pattern of the brickwork showing through rather undermined the attempt at decoration. Here and there heavy radiators were mounted on brackets and sets of double doors marked the entrances to successive blocks of offices and drawing rooms. Some effort had been made to brighten the place up: at regular intervals, framed map sheets had been hung on the walls, an ad hoc gallery of the Directorate's achievements. Abstracted portions of the Gold Coast, Basutoland, Dominica, Antarctica, Zanzibar, the bright colours of a soil map of central Trinidad contrasting with the monochrome functionality of a preliminary plot of a small corner of Tanganyika. My head turned as we passed each one, eyes taking in the lines, the shading, the contours, the symbolic code by which reality is represented.

'I know what you mean,' I told him. 'But I have to say, I rather like the maps.'

The minute the words were past my lips I regretted them: Laurance's air of studied indifference served to render them gushing, gauche. I braced myself for his reply, expecting some sort of comment along the lines of: it would take more than a few pretty pictures to impress me. But it never came. At that moment a high-pitched horn tooted behind us. I was vaguely aware of the sound of an engine, approaching fast, then a motor scooter buzzed past, filling the air with pungent exhaust, its rider crouched over the handlebars.

Albert grinned, his teeth smoke-stained. 'Mr Wainwright,' he explained. 'He'll get a rocket one of these days.'

We had come to a halt by a set of doors and, while I was still trying to assimilate the bizarre sight of a moped tearing along the corridor, Albert showed us through to the offices beyond. He knocked on another door then left us, saying, 'There you go, gents. He'll be with you shortly.'

I heard a voice shout, 'Come!' Laurance reached for the handle and I followed him into the room where I imagined we would find Mr O'Brien waiting.

The white-haired man behind the desk had an austere face and protuberant chin. He looked at us through black-framed glasses and introduced himself as Lt Colonel Humphries, one of the deputy directors. I listened, with something akin to disbelief, as Laurance announced that we were the new surveyors. Even as it dawned on me that there had been a dreadful misunderstanding, Humphries got to his feet and went to stand beside a huge map of Africa spread across the wall behind him, the continent annotated with black ink tramlines marking out the planned progress of work.

'Which of you is Wallace? Right, you'll be joining the T— field party, here.' His finger came to rest on a cluster of white paper rectangles pinned to the central-eastern part of the map, each bearing a handwritten name. 'You'll be helping them run a chain of triangulation across to connect with the Arc of the Thirtieth, here.'

What I should have done was to pipe up immediately, say I had thought I was being taken to meet a Mr O'Brien and that I had evidently come to the wrong place. But before I had a chance to do so, Humphries launched into a description of the type of country Laurance would be working in and recounted a few anecdotes concerning run-ins Directorate surveyors had had with elephant and lion in the region. Laurance listened to it all without a flicker of emotion disturbing his face, although I certainly experienced a moment of alarm on his behalf when Humphries talked about a porter who'd been mauled to death in a night-time attack on a camp.

'You, Pickering,' he continued, shifting his attention to me, 'will be . . .'

I shall spare myself the embarrassment of dwelling too long on the ensuing five minutes or so. I recall Laurance repeating, in a loud voice, 'Pickering?' The sudden change in his insouciant manner was sufficiently startling to cut Humphries off in mid-flow. I embarked on a stammering attempt at explaining myself, but I don't think I'd got very far before a knock heralded the arrival of a rather red-faced and out-of-breath man, who – amidst profuse apologies for being late – introduced himself as the missing Pickering. Humphries was very decent about the whole thing, even stepped into the corridor with me to point the way to the Records Section. Throughout the confused process of clearing up my identity, I managed to avoid catching Laurance's eye, sure that he would be fuming at the way I had made a fool of him. Not that I'd really *done* anything, I'd simply been swept up in a misunderstanding, an unwitting impostor.

When I eventually tracked Tony O'Brien down and explained how it was I appeared to be late, he thought the whole episode highly amusing. It helped get us off on a good foot. He even suggested I write a piece on it for the house magazine, the *DOS Gazette*, along the lines of 'My Brief Career as a Surveyor'. The incident receded to the back of my mind as he took me on a tour of the survey data and map libraries, and my head was soon swimming with the intricacies of the different filing systems. I remember being overawed by the sheer scale of the operation. Drawers and drawers full of maps, all produced by the Directorate. Dozens of yards of shelving housing the aerial photography catalogue. File upon file of data for each map sheet: base-line measurements, descriptions of every trig point ever surveyed, astronomical observations, triangulation results, height control and computations, tide and gravity and magnetic readings, railway profiles – so much information. Yet amidst my bewilderment, I also felt the beginnings of pride: Tony O'Brien made it clear that the Records Section was at the very heart of things. At every stage of production – initial planning, aerial photography, field work, computation, cartography, field completion, round again to the planning of revision mapping – if the huge quantities of data could not be accessed and evaluated, the whole process would founder.

Later in the morning he went to a meeting and left me to browse in the library, opening drawers at random, pulling out map sheets of different countries around the world. I spent a happy couple of hours poring over depictions of alien terrains: soaring escarpments, endless swamps, deep rift valleys, creeks snaking inshore from broken coasts. I amused myself trying out tongue-twisting and exotic names: Nkasala, Zomba, Chingali, Mirale. From time to time, a seemingly insignificant detail would stop me in my tracks – wondering at the labour that lay behind the single arrow-straight line, inches (miles) long, marked with the simple words, Water Pipeline, for instance. And most of all, I recall being stung by the sheer scale of humanity implied by the sight of so many ordinary things – Cathedral, Power Stn, Race Course, Sch, Stadium, Hosp, Mkt, Cem – scattered across every city in every corner of the globe. Getting to know my new territory, so to speak, I soon forgot about Laurance Wallace. He was destined to spend most of his time abroad, while I would be ensconced within these four walls. I didn't imagine our paths would ever cross again.

He was waiting outside the library when I emerged at

lunchtime, leaning against the wall of the corridor, the sole of one
foot flat on the bricks behind him.

'Hi! Hopkins!' he called, spotting me. I went over to join him,
feeling a trifle apprehensive. 'Look,' he said, 'I'm terribly sorry
about this morning. Dreadful mistake.'

I told him it really didn't matter. All the same, I was relieved –
and flattered – that the reason he'd sought me out was to
apologise.

'That old fellow – the messenger? – told me there were two of
us expected. Must've been frightfully embarrassing for you.'

I assured him it hadn't. He asked me a few things about the
Records Section, none of which I could answer at that stage.
When the conversation petered out, I fully expected him to say his
farewells and that would be the end of the matter. He could hardly
be interested in me and my mundane life. But he said he'd been
told of a good pub called the Toby Jug, just up the road. Would I
care to join him for a spot of lunch?

Something that has interested me throughout my long association
with maps is the question of scale. Obviously, to be useful, a map
must be of manageable proportions, certainly not much bigger
than a broadsheet newspaper when unfolded. The larger the
ground area one wishes to represent, the less detail one is able to
include. The map-maker makes decisions, based on what he
thinks the users will want to know, as to which features to include,
and which to minimise or leave out. Take my destination, Dunsop
Bridge. My Travelmaster of northern England has to cover a lot of
ground, and villages the size of Dunsop Bridge are very much
bottom of the pile when it comes to representation. Hence there is
just a grey blob and a ℂ to indicate a public telephone. Certainly,
as far as I could see, studying the Travelmaster in my lounge late
last night, there is no sign of a PH – which raises a question as to
where I might be able to stay. I had hoped that Helen would have
provided me with this sort of information, or even invited me to
use a spare bedroom. In the absence of any communication from
her, I assume I shall have to make my own arrangements. I will

address this problem when I am nearer the locality, but all the same it is a nagging concern.

Anyway, the point is, the Travelmaster may be useful to someone planning a route across the north of the country. But for someone intending to visit one specific small place, it is less than helpful. What I should have done was obtain the relevant Pathfinder which, with its larger scale, would have given me much more idea about the local facilities. For all I know, there may very well be an inn, its presence considered inconsequential to the overall aims of the Travelmaster. Indeed, I distinctly recall that Helen went to Sch in the village, yet, unless it's been closed down in the intervening years, that isn't marked either.

It seems to me that scale and hindsight have much in common. Consulting a Travelmaster, the first-time visitor to Dunsop Bridge might be forgiven for thinking that a grey blob and a Ⓒ are all that there is to know about the place. When one is wholly ignorant of somewhere, one is entirely in the hands of the map-maker for one's view of it. The frequent visitor, however, someone who is utterly familiar with Dunsop Bridge – someone in possession of hindsight – would doubtless find its Travelmaster representation distinctly unsatisfactory. They would be able to see by their absence all the things which the map-maker had chosen to omit.

Anyway, rereading Laurance's letter put me in mind of this very question. It would certainly have been Laurance who suggested that he retain the second room in the flat on Surbiton Drive – I felt myself to be very much his inferior in those days, and even if the idea had occurred to me, I would never have dreamed of proposing it. I cannot recall when exactly the subject was raised, though it may have been on that first trip to the Toby Jug. Whenever it was, I'm sure I swiftly agreed: it suited us both. He needed somewhere to stay between tours abroad; he disliked the lodgings he was in and had no reason to suspect that others would be any better. From my point of view, Laurance's retainer meant extra money to spare for my parents, yet I would still have the flat to myself for ten months a year.

So, we pat ourselves on the back for coming to such a

satisfactory arrangement – *an absolute bargain* – and the question never arises as to why a man such as Laurance would be bothered with the likes of me. Why he wouldn't want, in his spells of home leave, to return to wherever it was he came from.

And in the warm haze of mutual interests served, no one notices the innocuous postscript to his first letter, the casual afterthought about what to do with his mail. So that when letters arrive – not many, perhaps as few as two or three a month – each addressed in the same hand, written in the same royal blue ink, all bearing the Cambridge postmark, no one gives it a second thought, putting them together in the hall until such time as they can be forwarded to their rightful owner, who by that time is busy running a chain of triangulation somewhere in Africa.

Sir – The Prime Minister's visit to Africa is a tribute to the gravity of the issue he goes there to study. Africa represents one of the most morally challenging situations ever posed by the colonial empire. The greatest difficulty lies in determining the strength of African nationalism.

With so many nationalist leaders in detention, untried, cut off from each other and their British friends and advisors, how will Mr. Macmillan be able to assess the depth of their indignation? The Africans' principal problem is in communicating the powerful conflict of hope and fear which inflames them. All too often their sense of despair at ever conveying their point of view, which they feel is outweighed in any event by the powerful European voices ranged against them, tempts them to violence as the only means of demonstrating the strength of their opinions.

How often in our historical experience, and at what cost, both financial and human, have we failed to gauge the force of young nationalisms? Our temperamental distaste for emotion in politics blinds us. It is to be hoped that Mr. Macmillan travels to Africa with widely open eyes and that he will cast his gaze as far about him as is possible.

Yours faithfully,
Margery Cooke,
St Peter's College,
Oxford.

11th MAY 1959

'So, a two-dimensional map cannot accurately represent the surface of the earth in all its spheroidal glory. How do we get round this?'

Mr Gaselee tapped the umbrella he was using as a pointer against the easel-mounted blackboard. Helen glanced along the makeshift table at the line of her fellow trainees, five faces staring forward, each wearing an expression somewhere between extreme concentration and blind panic. She saw the Adam's apple of the man at the far end bob up and down.

'Projections?'

'*Projections.* Very good, Dearlove.' Mr Gaselee paused to allow the obligatory giggling to subside. Seeing the flush rise yet again over her contemporary's cheeks, Helen concluded for the umpteenth time that if *she* was a man, and that was *her* surname, you wouldn't catch her answering questions, whether she knew the answers or not.

Mr Gaselee tapped the board again. 'In other words, you have to *project* the earth's features on to a flat surface. At its most basic this is a plane, but it can also be a cylinder, or a cone, depending on which bit of the globe you want to depict. However, *none of them is a sphere*, so they all involve distortions of area, distance or direction.'

The superintendent of training fished a piece of chalk out of his blazer pocket and started to sketch yet another diagram on the board. In the lull, Helen's gaze drifted round the F Section drawing room to where other cartographers, more advanced in their training, were at their desks. Some were crouched over map plates, drawing instruments in hand; others were deep in discussion with supervisors, taking advantage of the interruption to have a quick smoke, grey-blue plumes hazing the air above their heads as they talked. On their first day, the new intake had been shown around and Helen had looked over shoulders, admiring the work being produced. It struck her as just like etching, the sharp points of the drawing pens scoring fine lines in the reddish Astroscribe film that coated the plates. There was nothing spontaneous or free-hand about it, however: the cartographers were following detailed plans, plotted from aerial photographs and field-survey data by the photogrammetry department. Yet, despite the constraint of these frameworks, she'd seen glimpses of the way the cross-hatching, the shading, the shoals of rippling contours, could liberate hills and crags and river valleys from the strictures of two dimensions; could turn abstract plots into something visually appealing, visually *useful*. The canvas may have been marked out by scientific processes she didn't yet understand, but here was where artistry came into play; the two disciplines hand in hand, each dependent on the other for the clarity and success of the final product. She'd felt impatient to be allowed at a drawing table, to start to get to grips with her chosen craft. But since then there'd been nothing but lectures, punctuated only by lunch and tea-breaks. Oh, and one mind-numbing session spent practising drawing perfectly straight lines of absolutely consistent gauge with which it seemed fault could *always* be found by the hawk-like supervisors, no matter how hard one tried.

Mr Gaselee finished his diagram and started to lecture again, attempting to demonstrate why lines of latitude, which are regularly spaced on the globe, become progressively closer together towards the poles when projected on to a cylinder wrapped like a huge cummerbund around the equator. Helen blinked hard and tried to concentrate, struggling again to ignore the sense of despondency that had been assailing her throughout her first week. She'd had some ridiculous notion that she'd be set to drawing almost from the outset, had no idea that there'd be so much theory to come to terms with first. Neither, she now suspected, had Mr Andrews, who in many ways was responsible for her being there at all. A memory: the two of them, alone in the classroom after double art, the teacher shaking his head slowly, his face unusually serious as he contemplated her question. In the end, his advice had been oblique. *D'you know, Helen, in the past year alone I've lost four periods a week from my timetable. There's only so many hours in the day, and if there's one thing I'm sick to the back teeth of hearing, it's that there's never owt new to teach in art. The writing's on the wall: science and technology are centre stage now, or at least moving that way fast. And what's true in school is true out there. If you want my advice – if you want a decent career, something to stand you on your own two feet – you'll find a way of working with them.* So far as Mr Andrews could see, the choice came down either to illustrating textbooks – *drawing cut-up dead bodies, that sort of thing* – or to making maps.

As she stared unseeingly at Mr Gaselee's blackboard, Helen felt suddenly wistful. She'd been in London one week and already her life in Lancashire belonged to another world. A wave of yearning threatened to break over her and she forced herself to fight it off.

There was no going back, no returning to the certainties of a life eighteen years in the moulding. She'd made the leap, come to this city packed full of strangers, to the bottom of the pile, ignorant of the first thing to do with cartography. If she allowed herself even to wonder – well, there was no telling where it would end. The very thought of returning to Dunsop Bridge . . . the image of her father's mocking, told-you-so eyes.

'*So!*' Mr Gaselee's voice startled her. She found him looking directly at her. 'You can see that cylindrical projections are accurate for the equatorial regions – Africa and the like – but they greatly distort the higher latitudes, making things in these temperate parts look smaller and less significant than they actually are. With a bit of mathematical jiggery-pokery, which I *don't* think we need concern you with –' he flashed the group a smile but mainly it seemed intended for her – 'you can correct this by modifying a cylindrical projection into a Mercator, a name with which you will soon become *very* familiar.'

As if sensing a convenient moment to interrupt, the bell, ringing throughout the Directorate to signal the end of the working day, all but drowned out his last words. The F Section drawing room erupted into noise, people starting to chat and to pack away their things.

'Any questions?' Mr Gaselee raised his voice against the din. 'Good, we'll leave it there for today. Simple and poly-conics on Monday.' He grinned again, pocketing his chalk and tucking his umbrella beneath an arm. 'No, there is no escape.'

Helen closed her notebook, the virgin page unsullied by any jottings, and sat watching while the superintendent cleaned the blackboard with a rag, his double chins wobbling with the effort. She felt utterly lost. Two of the others – Dearlove, and the other female in the group, an older woman by the name of Joyce – approached the tutor, the three of them huddling together, evidently discussing the lecture. She should go and stand a respectful distance away, wait until the group broke up, then approach Mr Gaselee and tell him: I'm terribly sorry but I haven't followed a single thing you've said all week, is there a book I might read or something? Instead, she slid her things into her bag, swapped a grimace with one of the other trainees who was also making a sharp exit, and left for Edith Gardens and her second weekend in London.

'I'm sure it'll get better, love. You're bound to feel homesick at first.'

Helen bit her lip and gripped the handset more tightly. The fingers of her other hand were twisting the delicate chain round her neck, from which dangled the little St Christopher medal given as a good-luck present just a fortnight before. She wished she hadn't called now. Letters only, at least for the first month, till she found her feet. It was lovely to hear her mother's voice, but the price was too high.

'No, it's not that – I'm missing you, of course, but it's not homesickness. I don't know – it's just not what I was expecting.'

She listened to the faint crackle and hiss of the trunk line for a full five seconds.

'*What?*'

'Well, what were you expecting?'

Helen drew a deep breath, let it all out in a rush. 'I don't know, something more *adult*, I suppose. Not him standing up there, tapping the blackboard, the sarcastic comments, the questions. Oh, and the bell – start of day, lunchtime, end of lunch, home. Honestly, Mum, it's as though we're all still at *school.*'

A lorry rumbled past the phone box, rendering her mother's reply inaudible.

'Sorry, what did you say?'

'I don't know, Helen. I don't know what *to* say.'

They waited in silence, mother and daughter hundreds of miles apart, connected only by a series of thin wires. She really shouldn't have called, it was weak, stupid. What did she expect? She'd made her bed. No one had *forced* her to come away, leave Dunsop Bridge behind, try to carve out a different life for herself. She felt herself flush, imagining what her mother might say later about their conversation.

'Mum? Is he there?'

'No. It's the fête this afternoon, he's up at the school.'

'Don't tell him I called, will you?'

She heard her sigh. 'No, love, if you'd rather me not.' Another pause. 'He'd love to hear from you, though.'

'No, Mum. Look, I'd better go.'

'Helen?'

'Mm?'

'Helen . . . When I first moved up here – when *we* first moved up here – well, I was quite unhappy. I was used to the London life, your father was too. He had his work, of course, so I don't think it bothered him so very much. But I was here on my own all the day with only a screaming baby for company.'

The words succeeded in raising Helen's first smile. 'I know, I know. You forced yourself to get out and meet people, invited yourself to things if no one was going to ask. But people are *different* here. Not unfriendly, just not *friendly*.'

'Well, you've to make them friendly.'

'It's not that easy.'

'Don't I know it, though. I thought I was banging my head against a brick wall. You know what the village is like.'

Helen stood there, glumly remembering. The village was close-knit; people couldn't do enough for you. As long as you were one of them. Outsiders – and even after seventeen years, the Gardners were still thought by some to be outsiders – had an altogether tougher time.

She heard her mother laugh. 'D'you know what I did? I made a list of all the things that were making me unhappy, then I set to and changed them, one by one. Started with Mrs Bacon and her wretched flower rota and worked my way from there.'

It was an oft-told story, no doubt embellished over the years. How her mother had forced her way on to the church rota by the simple tactic of taking bouquets from the White House garden every week and placing them beside those already there until enough of the ladies of the parish grew tired of the duplication and persuaded the recalcitrant Mrs Bacon to give her her own slot. But far from inspiring her, the recollection renewed Helen's sense of misery. Her boats were burned. She could never return to the pettiness of village life, the good Christian folk behaving so childishly. The thought of her mother's list depressed her further.

'You never got to the bottom, though, did you?'

'Sorry?'

'Your list. You never got to the bottom.'

Another long pause. Her mother's voice was more terse when it came.

'No, Helen, I didn't. There are some things you just have to learn to live with.'

*

1 Mrs Potter snooping on me.
2 Mr Potter brushing against me when he serves breakfast.
3 My room.
4 Don't know anyone – no one wants to *do* anything.
5 Haven't drawn for months.
6 Hate Mr Gaselee's lectures.
7 Hate not knowing anything.
8 Hate the time bell.

Helen laid her pen on the bed and studied the list. Eight things. The more she looked at it, the more she realised she'd written it in the wrong order. Start from the top and work your way down, that's what you do with lists. That's what *most* people do with lists. Just as most people live where they've always lived, marry the man they were always going to marry, stay with him when he proves to be a bastard (sorry), mostly because they've got a child and there's nowhere else to go.

She would be different. This list she would tackle in any order she liked. Mrs Potter's nosiness she couldn't think how to stop anyway, but as soon as she could move out it wouldn't matter. As for her husband, if she ceased going to breakfast – he only *ever* does it when his wife isn't around – that would probably make his wife's suspiciousness worse. Number five wasn't a bad one to start with, and it could solve number three at the same time. If she did some drawing, some painting, she could brighten up her room. But if she could do something about numbers six and seven, then three, two and one might become redundant at a stroke. She hadn't enjoyed her first week as a trainee carto one little bit. So she ran away at the end of the day. If she could tackle six and seven, then maybe she'd sort out number four, get to know some folk and perhaps find someone to move out with. No more Potters, no more poky little dingy little room.

She put the sheet of paper to one side, suddenly overwhelmed. Everything was connected, entwined. Life couldn't be defined in terms of a list, a logical sequence. Everything flowed from everything else. Her mother might have succeeded in getting on the church rota, won the right to serve Our Lord in the way she'd been used to doing in Kilburn. She might have stopped the shopkeeper from palming off the worst of the fruit and veg on her, might even have shoe-horned her way into a circle of friends of sorts. But happiness didn't necessarily come from it. Not if you could never sort out the most important part of your list.

Demoralised, she crumpled the paper, squashing it into a tight ball between her palms. She threw it across the room, where it hit the wall and rebounded, coming to rest at the edge of the narrow rug. For a while she sat still, listening to the sounds of the Potters' Saturday afternoon pottering below. A few blobs appeared on her skirt as tears rolled off her cheeks. Eventually she got up, went to the bathroom at the top of the stairs and blew her nose into a wad of tissues. Back in her room, she tried to summon some of her resolve, telling herself over again: you won't get anywhere if you give up. She knelt on the floor, in a parody of prayer, and smoothed out the paper. Wiping the moisture from her eyes, she resolved to take them one at a time, in any order she could. She would start with number eight, the only unconnected thing on the whole list. Nothing like success to breed success. First of all she would sort out the time bell.

The thought of time made her leap to her feet. Five and twenty

c/o Overseas Surveys,
P.O. Box 47,
K—
4th November 1957

My dear Hopkins,

Well, by now you will almost certainly have given me up for dead. I should like to excuse the unconscionable delay in writing on grounds of work, although I'm afraid to say that wouldn't be the whole story by any means. Anyhow, a fine crop of blisters on both feet and a slight temperature – damn silly business and altogether my own fault – leave me stranded at base camp for a few days with nothing to prevent me catching up on correspondence neglected thus far.

Where to begin? It hardly seems possible that as little as two months ago I was freshly arrived from Blighty with as much idea of what I was about as a Methodist in a brewery. I distinctly recall writing to you from K— in bullish frame of mind, thinking what a lark this all was. That lasted precisely until the moment Hildred (local D.O.) shut me, my kit, and his driver in a 2½ tonner in order to bring me out to join the D.O.S. field party.

The journey up-country started off well enough. The first 120 miles were to be on the main road, which has the distinction of being the only one in the entire country with more surface than pothole. This is T—'s backbone, running from coast to deepest interior. Everything, and I do mean everything, that wishes to traverse the country by road has to use this route. Elsewhere it would be called the A1, but given that there's really no plausible candidate for the title of A2, I imagine no one's thought to name it.

I digress. We set out early, but evidently late enough to join half the population on their travels west (the other half seemed to be going east, and not always on their own side of the road). Roughly every fifth vehicle was a thundering lorry, known locally as a Mammy-wagon (Mammy is a street trader who deals in practically everything). I've simply no idea which variety of truck these started out as, and I am quite sure that even the manufacturers would be similarly baffled. It seems to be a matter of some pride to paint the lorries' wooden sides in the most virulently clashing colours possible – green, orange, blue and pink being a fairly typical combination. Against this backdrop are daubed all manner of slogans, and I amused myself for some time noting different examples: *Get in*; *Stay out*; *Mind your own business*; and, most disconcertingly, *God help us*. Umbi, my chauffeur, informed me that these are meant either to entice customers in, or to ward off bad spirits, traffic police and transmission problems respectively. Actually, he didn't present it anything like so neatly, and any semblance of logic to the above is entirely of my own making and quite probably incorrect. The Mammy-wagon cab doors have mostly been cut in half, rather in the manner of a stable door, and flap about like elephants' ears when the vehicle is in motion. In some cases they've been removed altogether. These modifications serve to keep the drivers cool, or so Hildred's chap informed me.

Anyhow, these Mammy-wagons are invariably in a tearing hurry, and it seems to be the responsibility of pedestrians (*always* four or five abreast), cyclists, cows, goats, and the ubiquitous Morris Minors to get out of their way. Potholes and heaps of dirt in the fairway add to the general sense of excitement. I was greatly relieved still to be in one piece when, after 120 hair-raising miles, we came to turn off on to a deeply rutted rural track. 'Track' is more or less right, though some might consider it overly generous – maximum speed consistent with continuing integrity of vehicle: 10 m.p.h. I was able to bear the constant bone-shaking only because the landscape was so enchanting – absolutely *miles* of deserted bush (head-high grass, stunted trees, the occasional glimpse of zebra) then all of a sudden we'd see a collection of mud huts and a smattering of people, who seemed at least as surprised by our abrupt appearance as I was by theirs. On a couple of occasions there was relief from the relentless jolting when we had to halt for a line of elephant crossing our path up ahead. But these periods of respite were short-lived, and it was a considerably rattled skeleton I hauled down to blessed Mother Earth some eight hours later, when finally we arrived at base.

So much for the trip out. Camp was deserted, bar one African cook and some relief porters, the entire survey contingent being out in the field. No, bwana, it was not known when they would return, and given that it was perfectly dark by then, I didn't imagine I'd see a friendly face at least until the morrow. Umbi disappeared off for 'home-brewed' beer and a sing-song with some of the porters round the fire. Somehow I managed to pitch my tent, retrieve my camp bed, and stack the rest of my kit in a pile beneath another canvas in case of rain. Then, following Umbi's exemplary lead, I settled down in my tent with a bottle of duty-free. Cook rustled up a rice dish of some description, and within the hour I was feeling considerably more content with my situation.

What with the arduous journey, and the warm glow from the whisky, I soon slipped into insensible sleep. I woke some time around 3 a.m., stone-cold sober, no doubt because my poor addled brain had finally perceived the most chilling nocturnal chorus from the bush around us: all manner of drawn-out screeches, hoots and cackles, strange, strangulated barking, and even the occasional no-mistaking-it roar. Well, I was pretty much frozen to my bed, and only the passage of time – in which no marauding creatures appeared through the tent flaps, and no screams came from a luckless porter – served to quieten my racing heart. Sleep was impossible to recapture, though, and I lay the rest of that night, ears scrutinizing every nuance, constantly trying to gauge whether the originators of some of the more gruesome noises might be getting closer, all the while feeling pretty small and insignificant within my thin canvas walls. Come morning, when neither Umbi, nor cook, nor porters showed any sign of having been perturbed by it, I had to conclude that this was fairly typical for a night in the bush.

We unloaded the stores from the lorry and I waved Umbi goodbye. Funny feeling that. Hardly knew the fellow, yet he seemed like my last link with civilization. Realized I'd grown quite fond of his gapped-tooth grin and his particular African treatment of the English tongue, which has the effect of highlighting the words, rendering them unfamiliar, reawakening one to the beauty of the language. (Umbi, for example, describes himself as my 'dreva'.) Anyhow, my 'dreva' drove off, and I spent the following three days generally kicking my heels – still no sign of the others. I used the time to have a good nose around camp and get my own little 'house' better set up. A surveyor's tent is high enough to stand upright in, and at 10' by 12' probably not that much smaller than my room at Surbiton Drive. When everything is installed it feels really rather homely. Kit includes field desk, complete with capacious pigeonholes in which one stows various manuals telling one how to be a field surveyor, which I doubt one ever gets round to reading. Each man has a set of ingenious collapsible chairs constructed from wood and canvas but reasonably comfortable all the same. Thought I'd been given an extra, deformed one, but this turns out to be a portable canvas wash-basin. Found what I took to be a particularly voluminous specimen of women's underskirt, which actually proved to be my mosquito net. The kitchen equipment comprises not only the usual cutlery and crockery but also a set of whisky tumblers and a soda siphon!

Each subsequent night was more or less the same as the first and I surprised myself at the rapidity with which I became able to sleep through the animal din. I was feeling positively blasé about it by the time the first of the survey parties returned, something which has rather strengthened my hand with them. I don't think they expect newcomers to be so apparently well-adjusted, and I haven't let on about the sheer terror of my first night to anyone. The other thing that impressed them was the stock of duty-free I saw fit to bring out. That evening we launched a concerted assault and managed to make quite a dent in it. I was roused at 5 a.m., head as thick as you like, and told there was time for a quick breakfast before we set off. None of the others looked remotely the worse for the previous evening's 'sun-downers' and, at the time, I had them down as coming from robust stock indeed. Two months later, I realize it is simply a question of acclimatization, and I am somewhat chastened to admit that therein lies much of the explanation for my lack of correspondence.

And so to work. The party leader, a first-class chap named Colling-wood, ex-Royal Engineers, has taken me under his wing. As you might recall, we're running a primary chain across to the Great Lakes and the Arc of the Thirtieth. It's ideal triangulating country: sweeping expanses of high-veldt savannah, here and there mountains rising like icebergs from the plains. Essentially, the task is to occupy one of these peaks, while half a dozen surrounding summits fore and aft are scaled by the local labour, who comprise the light parties. The theory goes something like this: when everyone's on station, the light parties focus their beams on the trig point, helios by day, electric lamps by night. Collingwood or I shoot the various angles with the theodolite, then we all push off home for tea. Next day we move one station along and do it over again. As with all theories, this is a complete nonsense.

To start with, the stations can be as much as sixty miles apart, nearing the limit of direct sight, and the only communication is by means of Morse on the lamps. It can be absolute hell trying to get the various lights focused, not least because at that distance the beams are vulnerable to attenuation from the most inconsequential haze. Then, when you think you've got everything set, almost invariably one or more lights subsequently fails to show, and no amount of signalling raises a response. It's then a matter of fine judgement whether to sit tight for a day or two in the expectation that whatever problems are being experienced by the light party will quickly get ironed out, or whether to go to all the bother of descending, trekking across, climbing up the other side, only to find that the light-keepers have – for any of a number of entirely understandable reasons – deserted back home.

Even when all's running smoothly vis-à-vis the human side of things, the elements usually have a few tricks up their sleeves. Conditions might be the clearest imaginable down on the ground, but on top of one's mountain one can be struggling to see five yards in front of one's face – let alone a light source three score miles distant. The hills act as precipitants, generating clouds in much the same way as Marilyn generates male hangers-on where e'er she goes. One is left snatching at brief moments of visibility and the whole business drags on and on, increasing the chance of one of the light-keepers – stuck on top of a hill in the middle of nowhere with little but the local lions for company – deciding that we've all pushed off without him and that it's high time he made himself scarce also. Collingwood and I camped on the summit of T63 for five weeks before we finally completed what could, in perfect conditions, have been one afternoon's work.

All that said, when things are going well, the job can be sublime. I find it difficult to convey the sheer brilliance of the views one sometimes has from four or five thousand feet, the greens and yellows and browns of God's country stretching away as far as the eye can see, the pale blue ribbon of a river trailing across, in the distance chameleon hills forever changing from black to green to a rich purple depending on the light and the atmosphere. On occasion, one is right above the cloud base, and huge banks of cumulus hover over the land like great Zeppelins, casting shadows that race over the bush though the clouds themselves seem to be still. Far below, a tiny dust plume thrown up by some vehicle might be the only discernible trace of other human existence. And at night, the moment when you look round at a ring of faint but constant lights twinkling at you from the tops of hills across a hundred miles of moonlit Africa, while thousands of feet below, the toils and troubles of life lie still, the nation slumbering, completely oblivious to the fact that high above their heads their land is being properly defined for the first time. Well, at such moments, one truly feels like a king.

Anyway, Hopkins, such sentimental tosh aside, there's basically a lot of hard slog involved, and the correct footwear is essential. Collingwood has a hunting licence from the local D.O. and after our T63 marathon, we set off to see what we could bag by way of reward for the boys, who'd been subsisting on beans and mealie-meal for the best part of a month. We'd had a fair amount of rain, and thinking – with so much game to be heard round and about – it would be a short safari, I went in my waders. We ended up walking for miles before Collingwood downed a duiker doe. The boys got spit-roasted deer and I got this splendid collection of blisters, which has at least ensured I can bore you with the contents of this letter. It's an ill wind, &c.

Hope all is well in Tolworth. Letters will reach me if sent to the above address – Umbi comes out fortnightly with a lorry-load of supplies and the post. I should dearly love news of home, and to hear how you're faring – it can make one feel quite alone, everyone else sitting around of an evening reading letters – but I shall fully understand if you can't find the time to put pen to paper.

I remain, &c,

L. D. Wallace

DIRECTORATE OF OVERSEAS SURVEYS
INTERNAL MEMORANDUM

4th January 1958

Dear Hopkins,

Would you call into my office on Thursday lunchtime, around twelve? There is something I wish to discuss with you.

<u>M. Hotine</u>
<u>Director</u>

J. A. Hopkins Esq.,
Assistant Map Curator,
Records Section.

Wednesday 5 March, on board the 11.27 CrossCountry train to Edinburgh, just outside Oxford

The director, Brigadier Martin Hotine – most often referred to as the brigadier – was a legendary figure by the time I started at Tolworth. The Directorate was his child, conceived during the war, an extraordinary example of the confidence of those charged with steering the country through those years. As early as 1941 – while I was an evacuee in Colwyn Bay, far from my parents and their London home – discussions were underway in various rooms in the Colonial Office, with the Committee on Post-War Problems considering how Britain should restore her fortunes and the strength of her empire when victory was won. Hotine, at that time head of Military Survey, had himself been abroad in the thirties, triangulating large sections of southern and central Africa. He understood the central role mapping would play in colonial development, and he also knew how little of the empire had been properly surveyed. Largely as a result of his arguments, 1946 saw the foundation of the Directorate, with Hotine – forsaking the army and elevation to the rank of general – at its helm.

This much was a matter of folklore around Tolworth and new recruits were quickly apprised of the legends surrounding their director. These lent him an aura of immense stature and we would fall silent, or at least hush our voices, should we pass him in the corridor. His annual staff talk, habitually delivered on the occasion of the Christmas party, would be faithfully attended. His vision of the Directorate's work was inspirational. But he was an enigmatic figure. Contradictory rumours circulated: about his wry humour; his towering intellect; his common touch; his refusal to suffer fools gladly or otherwise; his affable interest in the personal lives of his subordinates; his implacable opposition to the increasingly common practice of surveyors taking their wives with them on tours overseas. For a humble assistant map curator – six months into his time at the Directorate – a memorandum summoning him to the brigadier's office the next Thursday was a matter of considerable concern. I showed the memo to Tony O'Brien, who tried to be reassuring. But I could sense his unease, and he could certainly shed no light on what I might have done that would have brought me to the director's attention.

I had little sleep on the Wednesday night, spending most of the early hours listening to a fearsome west wind buffeting my bedroom windows. Over the months, I had become really rather fond of my job. There was a lot of routine work: cataloguing the thousands of aerial photographs received each week, filing surveyors' monthly field diaries, supplying batches of survey data to the cartographers. But there were also more interesting tasks. In particular, I had begun to relish my involvement with the evaluation of new mapping projects, assembling comprehensive briefings covering every aspect of any new proposal. Nothing, it seemed to me, could be more satisfying than the moment when one finally finished compiling, grouping and indexing a hitherto random collection of field reports, old maps, government minutes, press cuttings, economic papers. Order was wrought out of chaos – by reference to my index an item could be swiftly extracted, where previously a frustrating hour might have been spent sifting through the shapeless mound of documentation. And the whole file, newly created, would have a quiet beauty all of its own: a smooth, logical, dispassionate assessment of the case for new mapping.

I was constantly surprised at the diverse sources from which I would find useful information. The Directorate might receive an urgent request from a colonial government for medium-scale maps of their northern territories to assist with the execution of a new policy of land redistribution. Initially, one might find there was existing coverage of the area, and that the maps, though decades old, were of passable quality – one's instinct was that the request would be given low priority. But further ferreting would reveal newspaper cuttings covering the construction of a huge dam there a few years previously, which had resulted in vast tracts of land disappearing beneath a great lake. Shaking one's head in disbelief that the submission from the country's own government should have entirely failed to mention this man-made mutation of geography, one would realise that the whole project suddenly looked far more compelling. I took great pride in trying to assemble the most comprehensive briefing files possible and I would await with interest the directing staff's adjudications as to which projects would get the go-ahead. More often than not I found I could successfully anticipate their decisions.

Anyway, the point I am trying to make is: I had become immensely content with my role in the Records Section. That Wednesday night, the thing that kept me awake was the fear that I would lose it. There seemed no other explanation for my summons to the director's office, though the precise nature of my misdemeanour remained obscure. I think by the time sleep finally claimed me I had thought through every possibility. An administrative cock-up in the wake of my interview seemed the likely front runner, resulting in my being taken on by mistake. But I had other, more fanciful notions. I'd recently been put up for the committee of the local branch of the Institute of Professional Civil Servants. I suppose one would term this our trade union, though I wouldn't want you to think that in my younger days I was some sort of tub-thumping radical. The IPCS was a gentlemanly body, concerned with civil servants' working conditions but carrying out its representations in a civilised and cooperative manner. It strove to improve things but did so in a behind-the-scenes fashion. To some, whose style was more confrontational, this might have been a source of annoyance – the IPCS was sometimes accused of being ineffectual – but that was just the way it was. Anyway, the DOS branch was keen to attract new blood and shortly before Christmas I had been persuaded to join the committee. I suppose I had been rather flattered by the interest shown in me, and my father's enthusiasm when I talked it over with him only egged me on, but lying awake in the dark of that January night I saw it for what it was: a hopelessly ill-considered move. No doubt such precocious interest in trade union activities had rung alarm bells at the highest levels in the Directorate. What sleep I did manage that night was fitful and troubled, my mind a mess of regret and self-recrimination.

My colleagues, in deference to what, I imagine, was assumed to be my imminent demise, gave me a wide berth in the morning. I was left to my own devices, tucked away in a corner, half-heartedly sliding typed-up index cards into one of the heavy black Kalamazoo files. Eventually, after a seemingly interminable time, during which the hands of my watch gradually closed together like the proverbial hare and tortoise, the hour of my appointment arrived.

The brigadier's office was one of the only rooms at Tolworth to be carpeted. That much I managed to notice as I opened the door, in what could only be described as a state of extreme trepidation, at midday. Hotine looked up at me from behind his desk, his face blank for a moment before he realised who I was.

'Hopkins? Come in, take a pew. And don't look so worried, man – I shan't eat you!'

I clearly recall his expression. His eyes were sparkling in a way that made me think of sunlight on water, his lips tight together, corners slightly down-turned at either end of his greying moustache, as though trying to keep a lid on his mirth. I seated myself across the desk from him, perched on the edge of the chair, and allowed myself the first faint hope that all might not be as bad as I had feared.

He didn't beat around the bush. 'Hopkins, tell me: how would you set about a triangulation of Africa?'

I floundered for a second or two. Slowly it dawned on me what he might be alluding to.

'I'm terribly sorry, sir,' I managed, my voice coming out in a croak, 'but I haven't the faintest idea.'

'Excellent! Good man.' He got to his feet, looking surprisingly tall at such close range, and came round from behind his desk, collecting a scroll of map sheets on the way. 'Mr Henlen told me about your interview.' He motioned for me to rise. 'Let's adjourn to the bar.'

It was a strange experience, out in the central corridor, walking briskly along at Hotine's side. He was making small talk and I'm fairly sure I observed the formalities, interjecting yes and no at appropriate places. But in the main, I was fascinated by the reaction of the people we passed, the way they would stare without staring, break off their conversations, perhaps venture a cautious nod if they were of sufficient seniority. I would have liked to have been seen by one of the others from the Records Section, would have liked to witness their confusion at the sight of me, so evidently at ease in the director's presence. But throughout the walk to the conference room we met none of my colleagues.

I had, naturally, heard about the Sub-Tense Bar, but in common with almost all HQ staff, I had never been there. Tucked away at one end of the conference room, the bar – exactly like any you would find in a public house – was strictly out of bounds to the likes of me. Established by the directing staff a few years before my arrival, it was the preserve of the senior echelons, a place where returned surveyors could be informally debriefed on their experiences abroad, and visiting VIPs could be entertained. Entering the conference room with Hotine, I was surprised to find that what I had always considered to be an apocryphal tale was in fact true. Above the bar hung a painted mock-up of a pub sign – a watercolour of a piece of apparatus which, despite my ignorance of such matters, could safely be assumed to be a faithful depiction of the item of surveying equipment which had given the place its name.

I recognised the barman as one of the canteen staff, presumably seconded for a spell of drinks dispensing. I made some noises about a simple tonic being sufficient, a suggestion which Hotine denounced as nonsense, and I ended up joining him in a pink gin. The place was practically deserted, the only other drinkers two heavily bearded men, who, by virtue of that aspect of their appearance, were easily marked out as surveyors just back from a tour with the Falkland Islands' Dependencies Survey. Hotine exchanged greetings with them, then led me to a table on the far side of the room. He spent a minute or two enquiring as to how I'd settled in, what I thought of the Directorate, before lighting himself a cigarette.

'Now then, I expect you're wondering what all this is about?'

Despite the cautious optimism that his friendly manner had engendered, I experienced a wave of apprehension now that the moment of truth was at hand.

'What I'm after, Hopkins, is someone in Records to act as my TA. Your predecessor did the job admirably and, from what I hear, you'd make an eminently good replacement.'

Although it seems remarkably blinkered now, all I could think at that time was: what a relief. It didn't occur to me to wonder why the director himself should have wanted to approach me about taking on additional duties. To be honest, my immediate concerns were nothing more than how on earth I was going to find the time. Flattering though it undoubtedly was to have been earmarked by the brigadier as a likely technical assistant, my days were already full to overflowing. The Directorate's activities were generating work for us from every point of the compass. A lengthy list of future projects awaited evaluation. Nevertheless, I clearly had no choice in the matter, so I confined myself to a cautious nod and a sip of my pink gin, waiting for Hotine to explain further what it would entail.

He reached instead for the furled map sheets he'd brought with him from his office.

'Tell me, what do you make of that?'

As he spoke, he unrolled the scroll, holding either end down against the table. The legend across the head of the sheet stated that it was a Directorate map of part of Kenya, dating from 1952, a region of low hills and coffee plantations from the look of the contouring and vegetation symbols. Hotine nodded silently as I voiced these observations, then let go of one end, the paper springing back into its original shape, revealing another sheet beneath.

'And that?'

It was the same map. Yet there was a difference. Superimposed on the identical topography was a series of irregular boundaries, printed in faint green, each enclosing an area of many square miles. At the centre of each, in green lettering, was a surname. Charnock, MacPherson, Innes, Dalgleish. I looked up at Hotine.

'What else?' he asked, as if able to read my mind.

I studied the map for a while longer, but, apart from those green markings – which I realised must be delimiting the various settler farms in the region – I could make out nothing at variance with my impression of the first sheet.

'I'm sorry, sir, but I'm not sure what you mean. This one is a cadastral version of the other – that's the only difference I can see.'

Hotine transferred an elbow to the task of keeping the map flat on the table and tapped a finger on the legend at the top of the chart. It identified the map area by the same series number but in place of the Directorate's name were the letters GSGS.

'It's what I call a Mau Mau map,' he said. 'GSGS is General Staff, Geographical Section.' The corners of his mouth turned down slightly again: more mirth to be suppressed. 'Not an entirely satisfactory term, I'm afraid, but we have to play along with it. They're terribly keen on their euphemisms over at the War Office.'

I often derive a certain amount of entertainment from the attempts of all manner of businesses, great and small, to describe themselves in terms of corporate slogans. These are everywhere one looks nowadays. I was delivered to South-ampton Central this morning by A2B Taxis, slogan: *Getting you where you want to go.* As it happened, the car arrived some thirty minutes before arranged, so I passed the time at the station by drinking a cup of tea in the QuickSnack cafeteria on platform one, slogan: *Eat and stay, Fresh takeaway.* The latter example I am particularly fond of, conveying, in a few short words, both homely welcome and a sense of efficient nutrition for the traveller-in-a-hurry.

It is tempting to dismiss this sloganeering as a modern phenomenon, arising out of current obsessions with image, public relations, the sound-bite. But it is not such a new thing. The Directorate adopted its own corporate motto as far back as 1960. At the time, our direct government funding had been largely withdrawn and we were finding ourselves increasingly vulnerable to competition from rival mapping agencies. In response, a drive towards greater efficiency and improved presentation was undertaken. I myself played a not insignificant part in the process. And, if it is not immodest to say so, I was the one to hit on the slogan which would eventually come to define our business. I can remember sitting long hours at my desk, doodling on scraps of paper, wrestling with unwieldy and wordy submissions from various staff members, each an attempt at a statement which would succinctly encapsulate the core reason for using our services. None of them seemed quite right – Directorate of Overseas Surveys: *Pointing you in the right direction*; *Charting your future development*; *Mapping for prosperity*. The inspiration, when it came to me, was ridiculously simple: *First a plan*. The idea was taken up with alacrity by the others on the Efficiency Committee. Beside this neat trio of words every other contender paled. No other motto seemed to express, with such commendable economy, the notion that in order to develop and control the natural world, one had first to tame, define, understand it. Throughout the years I was to spend at the Directorate, I would experience periodic flushes of pride at the sight of my words bannered beneath our logo, a schematic representation of the globe, criss-crossed with lines of latitude and longitude, suspended like a circular spider's web within the triangular frame of a trig-point symbol.

I had no such input when, many decades later, my subsequent employer, Ordnance Survey, adopted its own slogan: *Linking you to the real world*. This was greeted with a certain amount of ambivalence by the members of my own small department, the ragged remnants of the Directorate staff who had been swallowed up to form OS International. Many of them had friends whose jobs vanished when the Directorate was closed and whose lives had never been the same. 'Kicking you into the real world, more like,' I recall one cartographer remarking, when the new corporate slogan was circulated.

I, however, never had a moment's doubt about the suitability of the phrase to describe the map-maker's project. Reading the words, I was put in mind of the day, so very early in my career, when I met with the brigadier to discuss becoming his technical assistant. The meeting went on for perhaps an hour. I wouldn't want to sound melodramatic, but it was the point at which my view of maps started to change for ever. Before, I had thought of them simply as delightful documents, constructed in their own, secret code. Documents which set me fantasising about parts of the world I would never see. I remain attracted by this sense of the exotic. Since retiring, I have often found myself at my desk of an evening, sifting through my collection of Directorate maps, my mind alive with random thoughts thrown up by the charts from my past. What goes on at Katchikally Sacred Pond, a few miles north of the Bakua Kunku Hotel Staff Training School? How did anyone construct the impossible concertina of road leading to the summit of Long Mountain, from which one can presumably cast one's eye across the expanse of the city of Kingston? Who were the National Heroes to whom the park is dedicated, and what did they do to deserve the accolade? What is, or was, the purpose of the steel bollards jutting inexplicably from the water in the middle of Famagusta harbour?

No, maps still intrigue and excite me, but my appointment to act as the brigadier's TA altered irrevocably the nature and the slant of that intrigue. Initially, gaining the additional title of technical assistant made little difference to me, beyond an extra sixty pounds per annum. Certainly for a month or two my work in Records was unchanged, and it began to seem that anyone could make a good TA to the director by virtue of the fact that there was absolutely nothing to it. But eventually, requests for assistance started to filter through.

Not all of these were from GSGS. Some were from outside agencies or private companies who wanted access to information or expertise within the Directorate. These liaisons I was free to discuss with all and sundry, and they rapidly became the most interesting part of my job, the beginning of my long association with so-called Special Projects. But from time to time, confidential memoranda would arrive from GSGS. They always came via the director's office, except when he was away on tour, in which case one of the deputy directors would vet them. Whoever had done so would scrawl in pencil at the top of the paper messages like, 'TA(D) – please oblige,' or, 'TA(D) – please expedite.' I would make a discreet trip round the library, gathering the map sheets as requested. And often, while I waited for the courier, I would spend the time studying the charts, trying to imagine what might be happening on the ground depicted in front of me. My mind would be filled with no doubt fanciful visions of khaki-clad white soldiers stalking line abreast through dense bush, rifles at the ready, eyes probing the thickets ahead, fingers tense on triggers, the only sounds the rasping of their breath and the scrunching of leaves and twigs underfoot. Then a sudden, single, echoing report, chips of bark flying from a tree trunk a foot from a startled private's head, twenty soldiers dropping to their knees, twenty rifles jerking to the shoulder and unleashing a ragged, deafening volley in reply.

Eventually, aware of the march of time, I would seal the package, and sooner or later the War Office courier would appear. I would send the maps away. They would return, weeks or months later, absolutely unchanged, except perhaps for an inadvertent crease here, a smudged, anonymous finger-mark there, and I would replace them in their respective drawers in the library. And if, as happened on a number of occasions, a colleague in Records – or anyone else for that matter – were to ask me what the map sheets had been wanted for, I would reply, 'I'm terribly sorry, but I really haven't the faintest idea.'

*

It strikes me, sitting here on this train, leaving behind the sky-probing spires of Oxford as we head further north, what a funny thing memory is. In my hands I hold the brigadier's memo. His note is characteristically concise and those two simple sentences provoked a whole tumble of different thoughts and recollections. Yet reading Laurance's second letter, page after page after page of it, I could think of only one evening.

I'm not sure when exactly it arrived, whether before or after Christmas '57 – the post was so slow in those days. But I do recall where I was when I read it. I resisted the temptation to skim through it at breakfast, left it at home when I went to work so as not to find myself reading it in my lunch hour. Instead I waited until the evening in the lounge at Surbiton Drive, the airmail pages illuminated by a pool of light from the standard lamp, the only sound the ticking of the mantelpiece clock while I read of nights filled with drawn-out screeches, hoots and cackles, strange, strangulated barking, and even the occasional no-mistaking-it roar.

I was delighted to have got word from him. Apart from that earlier, brief letter, I'd heard nothing. At some point, his first monthly diary had been delivered to the library and I read it avidly before filing it away, even trying – in vain – to locate his position on a wildly inaccurate turn-of-the-century map. As the weeks turned into months and no second letter arrived, I resigned myself to the fact that he wasn't going to write again. We'd spent just a short time together in the flat before his departure for Africa. I convinced myself that he had forgotten our acquaintance the minute he'd become immersed in the life of the overseas surveyor.

Yet for me, Laurance had lingered on in Surbiton Drive. It took some time to adjust to the emptiness of the place once he'd gone. I'd become used to returning from the Directorate to find him slumped in an easy chair, a technical document relating to the Wilde T-2 Theodolite, or some other surveyors' manual, open on his lap, his breathing heavy and regular and his eyes closed. The banging of a door, the whistling of the kettle, the flushing of the cistern – sooner or later something would rouse him. He would promptly shove the manual in the magazine rack by the side of his chair, leap smartly to his feet and arch his back in a languid stretch. Then a proposal for the evening would be made, as though he'd had nothing else to think about and plan all day. I was rarely permitted to plead tiredness. We would go for supper at the Toby Jug; play a game or two of chess once the meal was eaten, or draughts if I was really all in. Other evenings we'd sit in instead, listening to the Home Service news, then a discussion of some issue or other would start up – developments in newly independent Ghana, the state of emergency in Northern Ireland, Britain's first test of a hydrogen bomb, the decimation of the rabbit population caused by the introduction of myxomatosis. I soon learned that Laurance had a love of playing devil's advocate. To begin with he had no difficulty in hooking me on some outrageous opinion. He would then sit back and enjoy the spectacle of me thrashing about at the end of his metaphorical line. After a while, though, I grew wise to him – but I could never effect the same trick in reverse. If ever I were to spot his gambit and parry with an ironic or preposterous viewpoint of my own, he would simply laugh, slap his leg, and cry, 'Well *done*, Hopkins!' or, 'Oh, I say!' For all that I struggled to keep up with him, they were stimulating and companionable times.

So aside from everything it told me of his new life, that second letter also told me that I hadn't been forgotten. It gladdened me. Naturally, I found the content fascinating. In those days travel was the preserve of the few, and even if one owned a television, I doubt there were many programmes bringing images from the far-flung corners of the globe such as we seen in modern times. The life Laurance described both intrigued and horrified me. For several days after receiving the letter I looked anew at the world around me, finding succour in its certainties. I tried to imagine him out there in the bush, wondering if he was craving the orderliness of London life: the comfort of a sprung mattress, a home made of bricks and mortar, milk delivered daily, *The Times* dropping on to the door mat, double-decker buses trundling along the road beyond the gate, heat available at the twist of a knob on the side of the gas fire. He never said as much – one wouldn't have expected him to – but in the final paragraph of that second letter, with its plaintive appeal for news, I thought I could detect a yearning for the world he knew. I could almost picture him, marooned in the vast continent of Africa, surrounded by colleagues reading correspondence from loved ones, his own hands empty, save for a tumbler of whisky, wishing he could return home.

When I'd finished reading the letter for the second or third time, I folded it and got to my feet. I hadn't yet bought myself a desk, so for safe-keeping I tucked the wad of airmail paper behind one of the pair of silver-plated candlesticks with which our landlord had decorated the mantelpiece. Alongside these ornaments were a number of my own things: a framed photograph of my parents, one of me with the members of my national-service squadron, a wooden-cased carriage clock, that sort of thing. I experienced a moment of sadness, slotting Laurance's letter away and noticing this mantelpiece clutter. He'd never seen fit to put any of his own things there, not even photographs of family members. It seemed to me, at the time, to be an indication that he viewed the flat as temporary, not somewhere to think of as home.

Nevertheless, he had written, so I would do my bit in return. As soon as I had his address, I forwarded the collection of letters which had arrived for him at the flat, imagining his face lighting up the day the driver from K— brought such an impressive bundle of mail out to him. And I myself wrote back within a fortnight, conscious of my duty to keep him in touch with his homeland, to prevent him from sinking in moments of despair. I couldn't but think that he had made a dreadful mistake, going out there, though I never expressed the opinion in quite those terms on the page. It was perfectly understandable to me that the Directorate should have such difficulty recruiting surveyors. Why would anyone want to spend the best years of their life far away

200 AFRICAN WOMEN IN COURT
Canning Factory Strike
From Our Correspondent
T—, 24ᵗʰ May 1959

Two hundred African women and 87 African men working in a T— canning factory chanted 'Not Guilty' when charged in the basement of a magistrate's court to-day with striking. The workers, almost the entire labour force, were alleged to have refused to implement a shift system to accommodate the seasonal fluctuation in fruit supply. The reasons given were difficulties with transportation at night, and the threat of assault and robbery in the native areas after dark.

The firm decided to institute the shift system regardless, and enjoined the native commissioner to address the workers to this effect. The following morning found the factory idle and the workers sitting down outside. They refused the order to work.

Emerging from his crowded court basement, beleaguered presiding magistrate Mr. Justice Rose said he expected the cases would take more than a week to process. The hand of local nationalist leaders could be detected, he added.

After the airy brightness of the F Section drawing room, its high windows admitting streams of sunlight, the survey data library struck Helen as distinctly gloomy. She hesitated just inside the door. A steady background patter was coming from different points of the room: murmuring voices, a drawer bumping shut, the occasional cough. But no one could be seen for the shadowy maze of towering shelving and metal cupboards that filled the entire library. She grimaced. Presumably one could spend hours in here, buried in the alleys and aisles between the rows of shelves, without coming across another soul. She hovered indecisively at the entrance, half-hoping that one of the originators of those noises would appear and find her waiting. On the other hand, she felt distinctly apprehensive at what she had come to do, and every moment that her arrival went unnoticed was another moment in which she retained the option to turn around and leave. In the end, with a brief exhalation at her own ridiculousness – imagining what her mother would say were she here – she ventured a shout.

'Hello?'

She waited. The mumble of conversation continued unabated. She was on the verge of calling out again when a man's voice, seemingly coming from nowhere, startled her.

'Can I help you?'

She looked round.

'Can I help you?'

Suddenly she saw him, a good ten feet above the ground, peering round the shelves right at the end of the alley ahead of her.

'Yes, I'm looking for a Mr Hopkins.' She spoke loudly to be sure her words would carry. 'I was told I'd find him here.'

The man disappeared. There was the scraping of feet and some loud wheezy breathing – audible even at that distance – then he stepped into view, looking surprisingly small now he was standing on the ground. He grasped a length of string dangling from the ceiling and gave it a sharp tug. Helen squinted against the sudden light issuing from the bare bulbs hanging at intervals along the aisle. She noted the man's portly belly, his rolled-up shirt sleeves, quite certain that this would prove to be the Mr Hopkins she was seeking, so exactly did he match the figure she'd imagined.

'He's back here.' The man jerked his head.

She walked the length of the narrow alley, into the heart of the library, glancing at the numerous brown box files ranged on the shelves either side as she went. Now and then she could make out the writing on the labels: jumbles of letters and numbers, presumably some form of class mark, followed by intriguing names: Huntings Air Surveys; Spartan Air Services; 82 Squadron RAF. When she reached the end of the aisle the man pointed past his step-ladder towards a door in the far corner.

'In there, love.'

'There' transpired to be a small office which was as dimly lit as the main body of the library, a single narrow pane of frosted glass set high in the wall. Helen paused in the doorway. The only occupant was a young man, probably no more than a few years older than her. He was sitting at a desk strewn with papers and illuminated by an Anglepoise lamp, seemingly absorbed in his reading. His shoulders were thin and bony, jutting against the cotton of his shirt like a coat-hanger. She went to speak but hesitated. She'd been expecting someone much older.

'Mr Hopkins?'

He looked up.

She stepped further into the room. 'My name's Helen Gardner. I'm a trainee carto, in F Section.'

As she introduced herself, she felt her face flush. It still surprised her to hear herself say those words, the first time in her life she'd been able to describe herself as anything other than plain Helen Gardner, the first time she was defined as anything other than the local headmaster's daughter.

'Mrs Penrose is dealing with issues this week.'

'I'm sorry?'

'If you wish to draw material from the library, Mrs Penrose will arrange it for you.' He nodded at the door through which she'd just come. 'She's out there somewhere.'

Her blush renewed itself. 'No, it's not that. I've come about the bell.'

'The bell?'

She hadn't intended to raise the subject so abruptly. 'Yes, I was hoping you could get something done about it, through the union. It makes me feel as though I'm still at school.'

Schoool. She bit her lip. Traces of Lancashire came through in unguarded moments.

Mr Hopkins sat upright and seemed to examine her more closely. 'Are you referring to the time bell?'

Helen nodded. She was starting to feel a little uncomfortable, standing there like this. There was a pair of vacant chairs and she had to resist the urge to go ahead and sit herself down – *not* good manners. Ordinarily that wouldn't concern her with someone so close in age, but she did want to stay on the right side of this fellow. Still, if he gave *any* indication that he might be about to invite her to take a seat . . . But instead, he was staring at her in a thoroughly disconcerting way, his eyes narrowed, brow creased in a frown, as though utterly perplexed that she should be here. Yet she'd specifically been given his name as the IPCS representative to whom trainees could take any matters they wanted to raise. Eventually, after a pained silence which she couldn't for the life of her think how to interrupt, he spoke again.

'I'm sorry, but have we met?'

It was Helen's turn to stare. She scrutinised his features: neither handsome nor otherwise, nose a little on the large size, almost aquiline; sincere-looking eyes. Nice enough, in an unassuming way, but certainly not familiar. She'd been introduced to so many new faces in the few weeks since she joined the Directorate. 'I don't think so, no.'

With a barely perceptible shake of his head, the librarian returned to the subject of the time bell. Helen stood where she was, shifting her weight from foot to foot, as he started to explain the issues. It seemed, from what he was saying, that the matter had been raised in meetings with the directing side in the past.

'Of course, what *they* say is that we can't not have it – people coming in when they like, sloping off early – the place would fall apart. In a way it's true: there are always a few individuals who would take advantage of a lack of central control over their timekeeping.' He leaned back in his chair, bringing his hands together, his gaze drifting off into the middle distance. 'Then there's the expense of putting clocks in all the rooms, the difficulty of synchronising them. You can see their point: imagine the uproar if the clock in one section was a few minutes fast and other staff saw their colleagues leaving ahead of time.'

She listened as carefully as she could, struck by the expansive air that had come over him as he warmed to his theme. But he did seem to have rather a lot to say. She'd had no idea there would be so many facets to the problem; he kept quoting sub-paragraphs from civil service regulations and citing certain precedents at the Treasury and the Colonial Office. As he continued to speak, she began to realise that there *was* something vaguely familiar about him. Her concentration wavered as she thought back over the past few weeks, to when she'd been shown around, the people she'd been introduced to in the canteen, men who'd caught her eye in the central corridor.

'. . . we've put in on the agenda again – September's Whitley is the earliest we could manage, I'm afraid – but I can't say I hold out much hope. For all its good points, this place is still run along rather military lines. Not that it's anything *like* as bad as at Ordnance Survey, from what I understand. There, the section superintendents score a red line across the register at nine o'clock sharp. Anyone who hasn't signed in above the line has the devil's own job explaining it.'

A few moments passed in which he seemed to be waiting for her to make some response. But by then she'd completely lost the thread of what he'd been saying. Her only thought was how embarrassing it was that she should have failed to recognise him. For a second she flirted with the idea of glossing over it – after all, he hadn't been too sure himself, and he'd probably already put the thought to the back of his mind, dismissed it as a mistake. But to do so would be rather rude, considering the kindness he'd shown her.

'I'm awfully sorry,' she said, eventually, 'but we *have* met. You helped me with my cases, didn't you? When I was trying to find Edith Gardens?'

She paused, watching his face. There was the same earnest, somehow distant expression that he'd worn during their previous encounter. But gradually, as if her words were slowly sinking in, a smile edged across his features, making her think of the tentativeness of a kitten venturing outside for the first time.

'I did wonder –' The fingers of one hand gathered a wayward lock that had flopped across his forehead, smoothing it into place. 'It was your accent. Your hair's quite different.'

Helen returned his smile, self-consciously touching the back of her head, where the stylist had cut it shortest. 'You're absolutely right, of course, I . . .'

She left the sentence unfinished, not sure how to explain. She still wasn't used to it, still had to take a second look whenever she glanced in a mirror or window. At the time it had seemed the perfect thing to do. Watching the loops and sweeping commas of brown falling on the salon floor, she'd been struck by the symbolism: the shedding of her old life. Here at work she wore it tucked behind her ears, neat, tidy, unremarkable. But in the evening, or at weekends, she removed the grips and let it fall as the stylist had intended, soft curtains framing her face. Mrs Potter had acknowledged its arrival with a curt statement as to how short it was. But already it had made a difference. Every breakfast-time since, Mr Potter, fetching through the bacon and eggs, or replenishing the toast rack, kept his distance. She'd noticed the faint sheen on his forehead, his upper lip. Time and again he would hover hesitantly behind her, as though trying to muster the courage to take that one step forward. The first couple of occasions she'd held her breath, braced for the contact between the front of his trousers and the side of her arm, yet it had never happened again. Her confidence quickly grew. Now she had to battle not against revulsion but against the urge to laugh at him. All of a sudden he had become powerless, pathetic, intimidated by a simple hairstyle! The turning of the tables, once started, had been swift – these days she would breeze into the dining room, call a cheerfully mocking 'Good morning!' through to the kitchen and take her seat.

'Well, it suits you, anyway.' Mr Hopkins's comment brought her out of her reflections.

'Thank you.' She smiled gently again, as much at the reticence that had re-entered his voice as anything, now he had stopped talking about Whitley committees and synchronised clocks and the advantages of central timekeeping. They stayed like that, the pause becoming strained, until Helen realised, with an acute sense of awkwardness, that she was still standing.

'Might I sit down?'

'Please. Please do.' He half-rose, sinking back once she was settled on one of the chairs.

'You'll have to excuse me –' she crossed her legs and straightened her dress – 'I'm afraid I rather lost track of what you were saying about the time bell.'

A frown flitted across his features but he merely shrugged and embarked on his monologue once again. As she listened, taking in more of what he said this time, she found to her relief that the union seemed to have the matter in hand. She'd procrastinated about coming to see him for the best part of a fortnight, reluctant to stick her head above the parapet so soon after starting the job. Still, this was ideal. She'd finally plucked up the courage to go along to the representative and there he was, already planning to do something about it.

At last, he got to the end of his piece. She thanked him for taking the time to go over things with her. He flustered a bit, saying she shouldn't mention it, but he looked rather pleased with himself. They exchanged a few pleasantries about Directorate life – which she *was*, she decided, there and then, beginning to find more agreeable. When the conversation finally faltered, she got to her feet.

'Are you settling in all right? You were down from Lancashire, you said.'

She looked at him, remembering his tacked-on question at the corner of Edith Gardens those weeks before. She felt a sudden warmth, something about the shyness of his manner – a far cry from the attitude of the youths at dances at home, who seemed to think it was enough that they should have bothered to come across to talk to you, while their friends huddled together, laughing, at the far side of the hall.

'You've a very good ear for the accent,' she said. 'Have you ever lived there?'

He touched his chest lightly with one hand. 'Goodness, no. Londoner all my life, war excepted.'

She nodded. 'Well, as I say, a very good ear.'

They looked at one another for a moment, then his eyes flicked down to the desk, as though he was suddenly mindful of the work he still had to do.

'Well, goodbye, Mr Hopkins.'

He looked up. 'Goodbye. And by the way, it's John.'

This time he stood fully, reaching out across the desk.

'Helen.' She shook his hand.

'Helen,' he repeated, his voice quizzical, letting go of her fingers. She smiled uncertainly, waiting for him to go on, expecting the usual sort of rot, something along the lines of what a lovely name it was.

'I don't suppose you know many people around here, do you?'

She laughed in spite of herself. Everything he said was couched so cautiously! His alarmed expression made the urge to giggle even worse, but she forced herself to be serious.

'Not a soul, no.'

He nodded, looked at his watch, patted his pockets. 'It's just that there's this rather good pub, just up the road, the Toby Jug. Lots of people go there for lunch. I could show you if you like. It's such a lovely day.'

She wasn't at all sure how he could tell what the weather was like. The window was so narrow and grubby that, although she knew it to be brilliant sunshine outside, from in here one would think it was dull and overcast. She watched him, standing behind his desk, completely ignoring her, more interested in straightening the edges of a pile of documents.

'Why not?' she said, her voice causing him to look up and meet her eyes. 'That would be lovely.'

'No, not at all, actually. I was born in London, Kilburn way, so it's more or less like coming home.'

John nodded at her comment, turning his attention to his plate once more. Helen watched his knife and fork working away at the crust of his steak and kidney pie. Her own lunch was largely untouched. She was talking complete tosh, of course, had no memories of London whatsoever – six months old when the scandal broke and a few weeks past her first birthday when they'd finally left, the way her mother told it. She had no idea what it might be like to come home, had no idea of where home might be. London was as good a place as any.

She watched John deliver a loaded fork to his mouth. The utter ordinariness of the action sparked a peculiar sadness in her. How easy it was to create an illusion. Even as she'd been painting the picture, coming out with just the sort of phrases and opinions one might expect of the carefree young girl-about-town, she'd been aware of the nagging sensation in the pit of her stomach that had dogged her off and on since her arrival. *Why* couldn't she just come out and admit it: she was lonely, lost, a little scared; she wasn't at all sure that she'd done the right thing. *He* wouldn't care, wouldn't think any the less of her. And if he did, well, she need never see him again. But every instinct told her not to appear weak. It was the same feeling she used to get at school whenever she cheeked a teacher. Walking out of the room, holding her head high, twenty pairs of her classmates' eyes burning into her back; the door banging closed, the corridor so awfully quiet. Making her way to the headmaster's office, legs increasingly wobbly the closer she got. Opening the door, waiting, staring at the rule being brandished in his hands, not daring to meet his eyes. You had to keep your nerve. You'd done it now. The only thing was to keep your dignity, keep up the pretence that it really didn't matter, that you didn't care. You had to maintain the hint of a smile, the aura of insolence, even as the sharp edge of the wooden rule cracked down again and again on the backs of your outstretched fingers.

She reached for her drink, raising the glass to her lips, the aroma of juniper from the gin acting like smelling salts, rescuing her from the memory.

John had just said something, she was sure. She held his gaze – frank, questioning – for a moment, trying desperately to retrieve his words from the air. Nothing but the drone of other customers' conversations, the clinking of glasses, reached her ears.

'I'm awfully sorry – I was a million miles away.'

He smiled. 'I said: so you've got family down here?'

'Oh, no.' She returned his smile, forcing herself to make it a bright one. 'No, there's an elderly aunt in Crouch End, but I haven't see her in donkey's years. My mother's side are in Ireland. We don't see much of my father's.'

'Well,' he said, easing himself back in his chair, laying his knife and fork neatly together on his plate. 'I'm full of admiration for you, I really am. I'd hate to be away from mine.' He glanced at her plaice and chips. 'No good?'

'Oh, it's lovely – I'm just not hungry.'

He nodded then twisted to look at the clock above the bar. 'Well, I expect we'd better be getting back.'

She took a few more sips of gin and tonic while he drained the rest of his half pint. She felt decidedly tipsy: it was only the third or fourth time she'd been in a pub in her life. Christmas excepted, alcohol was banned at home. She rested the glass down, hoping John wouldn't notice it was still half-full. If he did, he voiced no comment and she made her way gratefully after him, smiling politely at the barman when he called them a farewell.

The walk back to the Directorate was a struggle. She really shouldn't have agreed to his suggestion of a G&T. A numbness cloaked her. Even the thought of trying to put a sentence together filled her with fatigue. Fortunately the beer seemed to have loosened his tongue somewhat and for most of the journey back John kept up a steady chatter. He seemed completely fixed on the subject of families. She endured his description of his wartime evacuation to Colwyn Bay, of how dreadfully unhappy he had been, thinking all the while of his father out amongst the bombs with the volunteer firefighters, his mother crouched in the Underground as the sirens wailed. She tried to be attentive as he told her of his national service, two years spent administering stores on a windy RAF base in East Anglia, and of how he had looked forward to returning home in his periods of leave. The nearer they got to the Directorate, the more anxious she became. She could feel her innards churning. *Please! Can't we talk about something else?* When at last, perhaps dimly perceiving his garrulousness, he half-turned to her, making some concluding comment as to how much he admired her pluck, it was all she could do to keep her composure. A deep breath helped, the swelling of her lungs seeming to squash the turmoil firmly down inside. With an immense effort, she produced her brightest, most incongruent smile. She laid her hand on her forehead, dropped it to her wrist, fingers reaching for a pulse she knew to be racing.

'There!' she told him, coming to a halt which he mirrored, a surprised smile on his face. 'Not a trace of homesickness. And that's the last word I'll say on the matter.'

The following Saturday, after a couple of hours spent trapped in her room, the blank page of her sketch pad mocking her absolute lack of inspiration, Helen caught the train to Waterloo. She wasn't sure where she should go from there, she knew only that she had to stop moping around. Her indecision at the bus terminus outside the station was evident enough for another girl, who introduced herself as Bridget, to recommend a route and destination. It was a small gesture but Helen felt grateful – only the second time anyone had even *noticed* her here, let alone offered her any help.

Half an hour later she was trying to keep her balance, the crush of people on the crowded square platform lurching as one when the bus braked. She still found the proximity of so many others disorientating and, gripping the pole and launching herself from the platform into the swell of Oxford Street, she had a moment of panic. But once amongst the jostling humanity on the pavement, she felt calmer somehow, anonymous, cocooned in the busyness all around. Here, no one would notice that she was on her own. She set about exploring the shops of London, bewilderment rapidly giving way to a sense of awe at so many *miles* of window displays, so many things from which to choose.

The first store she actually went into was called Bourne and Hollingsworth and she did so because it had a sale on. But even with the end of season reductions, she blanched at the prices. She'd never had control of her own money before. Besides which, she didn't *have* any of her own money: it would be another week before she received her first month's pay. Her father had opened her account with fifty pounds, an impossibly large sum which she'd fondly imagined she would hardly need to touch. She'd had visions of sending it back almost immediately, a clear statement that things were going along just fine, that she was no longer dependent on him. But the balance had been severely depleted by the train fare down and the advance payment to the Potters – and a visit to a hair salon that charged more for a single cut than she would spend in six months at Marguerite's in Clitheroe. At this rate she'd have very little left by the time she got her first wages and it would take an age to pay him back.

Nevertheless, she tried numerous things on, collecting together a huge pile of possibles, though in the end she bought only a couple of blouses and a dress in bright yellow cotton patterned with small white flowers. If she had a moment of regret at spending so much in her first port of call, nothing of what followed reinforced it. She wandered in and out of boutiques and department stores, often going no further than the first rail of clothes, turning around at the sight of the price tickets. After a while she came across a shop called Evans. She noticed nothing amiss at first, yet as she started to traipse the displays she became puzzled: the smallest size was a sixteen. A discreet survey of her fellow customers solved the mystery – a whole shop devoted to the needs of the larger lady! She thought of Miller and Sons, of Camilla's, of their small but eclectic clothes stocks which catered for every age and size of womankind. Suddenly acutely conscious of her own lithe figure, she beat a hasty retreat, imagining a dozen pairs of accusing eyes on her as she headed for the door.

Eventually, growing tired, she caught the bus and train back to Tolworth, satisfied that at the very least she had started to live a little. Mrs Potter was coming down the stairs as she opened the front door and her purchases were subjected to scrutiny. She braced herself for the expected barbs, the terse criticism of quality, colours, styles. But at worst the landlady was neutral, regarding the blouses with nothing more than a grunt, the dress actually winning grudging words of admiration. Mrs Potter, Helen observed, with a new perspective and an unaccustomed sense of vindictiveness, would be much more Evans than Bourne and Hollingsworth. She wondered whether such segregation would be a relief or a humiliation.

Alone in her room, almost without realising what she was doing, she took up the abandoned drawing pad and a stick of charcoal. She started to sketch out different scenes, inspiration emerging from the mêlée of memories of Oxford Street. Botticelli women, nude or almost so, rolls of fat tumbling chaotically, postured in front of changing-room mirrors – in one version laughing, a head thrown back in a frozen moment of exquisite pleasure, a dress clasped joyously to a voluptuous bosom, relaxed and content in each other's company. In another version their expressions – reflected back at the observer by the mirrors – were dull, resentful; their new clothes were held crumpled in hands, arms dangling limply at their sides, all pleasure in the act of shopping destroyed by the confrontation with what lay beneath the cloth.

That night, Edith Gardens quiet save for the distant snoring of Mr Potter, Helen lay awake, the uncomfortable scoop of the ancient boarding-house mattress far from the only reason for her sleeplessness. Suddenly in possession of a startling yet oddly exhilarating perception, she couldn't stop thinking about Mrs Potter. The landlady had rarely treated her with anything other than suspicion, at times bordering on contempt. Yet what if it wasn't *her* that Mrs Potter disliked; what if it wasn't Helen Gardner to whom she was hostile? What if it was what she *represented*? How many other young, slim, single girls had made this room their home over the years? At what stage in their lives had Mr Potter started his breakfast-time indecencies? Helen had always thought Mrs Potter to be the dominant one, her husband to be a weakling, ineffectual. Yet what things might she have had to put up with over the years? Perhaps her absence from the dining room at the start of the day had less to do with a habit of lying late in bed and all to do with being unable to bear the humiliation of watching while her husband . . .

Helen was filled with an awful guilt, her previous, uncharitable thoughts towards her landlady glaringly unjust, misdirected. In an effort to salve her disquiet, she slid from her bed, knelt on the thin rug, the floorboards beneath pressing painfully against her knees, and recited her prayers – the first time she had done so since her arrival in London. *Our Father, who art in heaven . . . Hail Mary, full of grace.* It was no help. She got back in bed, pulling sheet and blanket around her, and tried to think of something else. But she couldn't. And lurking behind it all, at the back of her mind, was the pained face of her mother, looking silently on.

She forced her thoughts round to the lunch the other day with the young man from Records. John had been solicitous, almost too eager to ask her about herself. She wasn't used to it. The few boys she'd dated at home were terminally interested in themselves, going on and on, as though the more they told her about their lives the more she would desire them. John had seemed fascinated by *her*. He'd had no amusing stories to tell, no entertaining anecdotes. In fact, she couldn't remember laughing once during the entire lunch.

She sighed, staring at the ceiling silvered with moonshine. It had crossed her mind, on the walk to the Toby Jug, that John might prove to be what the girls at home called a 'possibility'. But he'd simply been dull. His interest in her, which had at first seemed such a flattering thing, had eventually seared a raw nerve. Her theatrical gesture on the way back had succeeded in curtailing his interminable eulogising of the family. After that, he'd fallen silent until they reached the entrance lobby. There they parted, he returning to the library, she to the drawing room for an afternoon practising scribing perfect right angles. Before he left her, he'd made some remark about how nice it had been and how he hoped they would do it again. She'd smiled politely. But at some point between arriving at the pub and returning to work, she'd come back down from her brief excursion from the earth.

c/o Overseas Surveys,
P.O. Box 47,
K—
23rd March 1958

My dear Hopkins,

Very many thanks for yours of 14th January, which took six weeks to reach me and which I then devoured in about as many minutes. I was thrilled to get news of home – you've no idea how far away it can all seem out here. Glad to hear that you're getting along so very well – promotion so soon. What is Hotine like to work for, I wonder? He's something of a legend around these parts. Indeed, I met two genteel old spinsters in K— who remember him (with unmistakable fondness in eye and sighing of voice) from the days before the war when they were living in Abercorn and he was surveying out of Kate base.

I am very much one of the troops now. My probationary period under the eagle eye of Collingwood was pleasingly short-lived and I have my own gang of boys with whom I survey my own sections of the chain. To take your specific questions in turn.

i) There are four of us: myself, Collingwood, Urquhart, and a Polish surveyor the phonetics of whose name approximate to 'Bar Fly' and whose behaviour approximates to the same.

ii) We have close to sixty native boys between us who act as light-keepers, cooks, drivers, tea-makers, porters and jobbing builders when it comes to erecting trig points.

iii) I'm afraid you will only be able to follow our progress very broadly from any existing maps for the good and sufficient reason that these are all wrong. Nevertheless, as I write, we are camped at a new base two hundred and sixty miles more or less due west of

K—, at the southern-most extent of a mountain range known locally as the Mfubo Hills.

iv) You are, of course, quite correct: the life is exceptionally prone to uncertainty, but that is its main charm.

v) My Gray Nicholls is in a case in my room and you're more than welcome to borrow it for the coming season should you so desire.

vi) The shrub by the back door is, I think, *Euphorbia griffii*, and I rather suspect you'll be too late to cut it back this year by the time this letter arrives.

Thank you also for your concern for my health. The blisters on my feet soon healed and I have been as fit as a performing flea since last I wrote. The smoke of London seems very far away and the exercise and fresh air suit me well enough. One can usually get reasonably close to each hill by Land Rover but even so there are many miles of bush to hack across thereafter, plus of course some fairly arduous hill-walking to get to the summit once one finally reaches the base of the mountain. The bush is pretty inhospitable: thick, sharp elephant grass as high as your head and forests of bamboo. I tend to take the lead, the boys following on with the camping kit, surveying equipment and provisions hoisted up 'on heads'. Consequently, I take the brunt of it. I don't know why it is but a loose bamboo always seems to manage to hit one in the face.

Sometimes things have been made considerably easier for us by our animal brethren. Just the other day we had a twelve-mile trek across country and found to our delight that we were following on the heels of some beasts who had thoughtfully broken the trail for us. I'm no expert but I'm fairly sure they were elephant: no other animal could possibly have such an intestinal capacity. Many of the dung heaps were still smoking. We never caught sight of the elephant themselves, but there was plenty of sobering evidence of their playfulness with large trees.

I do have a guide, a young lad by the name of Saidi, and by rights he should probably be in the vanguard, but in all honesty he's little more use than a regular porter. Despite extravagant claims to the contrary, he's never been up whichever mountain we're aiming to occupy – hills are something which your average African quite sensibly goes round, not over – and I've swiftly learned that it's down to me to spot the best route up if I don't want the whole party to come to a grinding halt at the foot of some sheer rock face which Hillary or Sherpa Tenzing would balk at. Still, these minor obstacles aside, I'm thriving and thoroughly enjoying myself.

My little gang is fast becoming a very jolly crew indeed. Most of the boys come from families which have been converted (to a greater or lesser extent) at some point and they have accordingly picked up 'Christian' names. These are quite peerless. The cook is known as Prosper and my head light-keeper as Medicine (his mother had a difficult labour, apparently). Medicine has been working for the Directorate since the late 'forties and is consequently vastly experienced. He has a passion for surveying and has picked up an enormous wealth of knowledge as well as becoming fluent in English. He's seen numerous surveyors come and go and seems to be profoundly proud of his role in the mapping and development of his country. He has a particular love of signalling and experiences a sort of schoolboy glee if ever his great chum Baya – who is Collingwood's head light-man – can be raised on a distant peak. They are capable of conducting an entire argument in pidgin Morse over who owes whom fifty cents and it is always a matter of great regret when I have to butt in and insist that we use what limited sun there is to shoot some angles instead.

If Collingwood saw to it that I got to grips with the applied art of triangulation, Medicine has ensured my education in practical aspects of life in the bush. It's more difficult than you might think, organizing a safari of some twenty souls, provisioning it, deciding on schedules of work which will get the light parties in position at more or less the same time. Even setting up camp has its own problems. Early in my first solo sortie I thought I'd found the ideal spot – nice flat, clear ground, not thirty yards from fresh water. Medicine pointed out that I had chosen a site bang in the middle of a major nocturnal thorough-fare for thirsty animals. We tramped off some way and cleared an area of grassland instead, and sure enough, all night I could hear the comings and goings of various creatures – including the muted trumpeting and geyser-blowing of elephants at bath time – every one of whom, it seemed, had plodded through the spot where I would have had us sleeping.

Even if one picks one's ground carefully, one is not assured of an intruderless night. We were hunkered down at the foot of a hill one evening, having arrived too late to carry the kit up the same day, when a hell of an uproar broke out among the boys. I woke to conflicting shouts of 'nyama', meaning game in general, 'mbogo', meaning buffalo, and 'simba', meaning of course lion, ringing out. Thirty pounds had sorted me out with a rifle on our last trip into K—. I hastily gathered this and rushed to see what all the fuss was about, bitterly regretting that I hadn't done more in the way of practice shooting.

Outside my tent there was general confusion, the countryside alive with the flitting outlines of fleeing porters, each of them trying to find a suitable tree up which to scramble. Medicine – who was the only one who didn't seem to have gone completely mad – filled me in on events: it appeared that a wild pig had suddenly run through the circle of light around the fire, snorting and squealing, the cause of its alarm becoming clear the next moment as a lion came through a close second. Said lion, evidently distracted from its chase, then gave up the pig and ranged around the camp for a bit before disappearing behind my tent. Medicine and I were peering somewhat ineffectually into the bush in that direction when Prosper pitched up with a torch. Sure enough, there was a pair of bright green eyes in the grass, moving this way and that, trying to get out of the light but never ceasing to look at it. Well, I shoved over the safety catch pretty smartly, but from somewhere amidst the general panic, advice from Collingwood came back to me along the lines of: a wounded lion is far more dangerous than an unhurt one. Not being what one might term a sharp shooter – and with the rest of the party scattered God knows where in the bush – I took careful aim at a particularly bright constellation of stars and let drive so as to scare the beast off and put some heart into the boys. This had the desired effect; the green eyes disappeared pronto. I was pretty dazed by the recoil and when the ringing in my ears subsided somewhat I could hear another cry going up of 'mtu moja anakufa', or one man is dying. Had a bit of moment: images of landing up in gaol for murder of native porter. But it turned out to be one of the boys who had fallen out of his tree in the excitement and who was suffering nothing more deadly than a profusely bleeding nose and a goose egg on his forehead. The rest of the gang eventually traipsed back in and a head-count showed us to be undiminished, if rather spooked. The boys stoked up an enormous fire and raised hell around it till first light.

I have to say, lest you should be imagining me some sort of incorrigible old hand at this sort of thing, that Collingwood subsequently tells me that the 'lion' was more than likely a variety of hyena. The boys will apparently identify any four-legged creature as a lion given a fleeting glimpse in sufficiently dubious light and Collingwood tells me that a true big cat wouldn't have behaved in such a fashion. Nevertheless, whether or not our lives were actually in jeopardy, the incident did result in the development of a very definite sense of camaraderie in the party. Although I pushed off to bed shortly afterwards, sleep eluded me, what with the excitement and the general din. So after a while I emerged and went and sat at the fire with them all. That caused something of a stir – there's usually a decorous distance between us surveyors and our boys – but within minutes I was being made to feel very much part of the crowd. I couldn't join in the singing, nor was I prepared to abandon my whisky in favour of their chibuti, but all the same it was a fine night.

Medicine, our top English speaker, took it upon himself to act as my mentor, explaining the words of the songs, some of which were surprisingly risqué! In between, he and I swapped stories about our lives. He's a splendid chap, very solid, with a placid sort of philosophy on things. He's a great craftsman, always whittling away at some bit of wood or other, making little toys for his young children, and the most splendid carvings which he stockpiles and takes to sell at market on periods of leave. His wife and family are many miles away, not far from K— in fact, and he sees them only infrequently. He maintains a cheerful front but any fool can see that he misses them dreadfully, being away so very much of the time. He's on the top (A) scale and he sends them the majority of his 160/- each month. I fancy, despite his love of the job, he would much rather be close to home, but he tells me there are few ways he could earn that sort of money otherwise, and he wants a decent education for as many of his children as he can afford. His eldest son is nearing the end of law school and another is training to be a doctor. It seems that is the way of things out here: there's no such thing as a pension, even for a government employee like Medicine, so one looks to one's children for security in later life. Not that I think that's the whole story with him. I suspect that as a father-figure he's not supposed to express any sentimental notions about his children having a better lot in life than he, and he prefers to dress it all up in practical economic considerations as befits the man-of-the-house.

Anyway, I'm full of admiration for him. At least I had a choice in coming so far away from home, and if I were missing England, I could pack my bags, get on the next flight back and hand in my resignation in person. He's compelled by necessity yet bears the separation from his loved ones with equanimity. I find him quite an example, and never more so than for the exceptionally cool head he displayed when all around were losing theirs.

Speaking of which, until the night of the lion/hyena, I had come to suspect that most of the boys had developed a rather poor impression of me, mainly because I had singularly failed to bag them any game (why else does bwana bring a rifle on safari?). The notion that I had dispatched a lion with a single bullet in the pitch black soon gained wide credence round that camp fire. The absence of any yellow furred corpse in the morning did nothing to dent the story. Consequently I am enjoying elevation to the dizzying heights of most-favoured surveyor and there has been a certain amount of jockeying among the boys back at base, with those from the other parties trying to get on to mine. My position has been further strengthened by Medicine, who has maintained a helpful silence about the elevated angle of my shot. The only price exacted has been our tacit understanding that he be allowed half an hour's uninterrupted signalling to Baya whenever conditions are favourable.

We had a few days' leave in K— last month. Umbi (my 'dreva') swapped his supplies for four weary surveyors and I retraced my journey out – though this time, in deference to Collingwood's seniority, I made the trip bouncing about with Urquhart and 'Bar Fly' in the back of the truck.

A strange experience, returning to civilization: roofs over our heads, running water, clean linen, sprung beds, other folk to talk to. K— is a far cry from London, but compared with where I'd been for the previous five months, it seemed a veritable metropolis. We put on quite a show, doing the rounds of the bars, practically living on Gordon's 'Old Tom' and tonic. There is no doubt about it, bush surveyors have a certain cachet in the towns, something I have only begun to appreciate having seen my Polish colleague – the aforementioned 'Bar Fly' – in action. He omits to shave for a day or two, carefully selects his most tattered and torn bush clothes, slips tennis shoes on his bare feet, and generally looks like the proverbial dog's dinner. The ladies love it. Into a club he strolls, leans himself against the bar, and within minutes he's surrounded by a whole clutch of fawning and fluttering females. His accent, I'm reliably informed, adds to the charm – he certainly plays it up on these occasions. It drives poor Urquhart – a very personable Scot whom I've no doubt will make someone a perfectly serviceable husband given half a chance – absolutely mad. And you can imagine the effect it has on the administrative types who otherwise comprise the male contingent of K—'s white population. Poor sops have the undivided attention of the womenfolk almost the whole time and probably think they're getting on very nicely thank you very much, what with their nine-to-five jobs and their polo matches and so forth. Then in walks this rugged apparition from the deepest interior, tanned as a piece of old leather, lisping in an alluring East European fashion, and suddenly the girls drop everything and dance attendance on him, leaving their chaps nursing their drinks in a sullen huddle in the corner.

Naturally, I've no sympathy for them, but I have to say I'm less than enamoured with 'Bar Fly'. From what he tells us, bragging about his exploits, he has no honourable intentions whatsoever. In my opinion, he simply adores the fuss. Collingwood (briefing me in the strictest confidence, so not a word at H.Q.) tells me there was an awful rumpus last year involving the wife of a major who was up-country at the time. Seems Mrs Major fell rather heavily for 'Bar Fly', who proceeded to capitalize on it, compromising her in no uncertain fashion. Gossip spreads no more slowly here than in any other place on earth and it took less than a week after his return for the cuckolded major to catch wind of what had gone on. Said wife was packed off home sharpish, divorce proceedings are in the offing, and it took one hell of an effort on Collingwood's part to contain the matter locally. Doubtless 'Bar Fly' would have been shipped elsewhere, if not demobbed entirely, had word of the affair reached London.

First-rate chap that Collingwood is, I can't but wonder why he went to the bother of hushing it up – the difficulty of finding a replacement, I suppose. I have little affection for our Polish colleague, who has put my back up on any number of occasions. He treats his boys in an appalling manner and consequently has the highest desertion rate of any of us. It doesn't take much to move him to apply his boot to a black backside and Collingwood has on several occasions had to reprimand him. He seems to derive a malicious amusement from poking fun at the natives' beliefs, but with half a second's thought one can quite clearly see the justification for a lot of them. Moving into a new area, for instance, we often encounter grave suspicion, if not downright hostility, from the local chiefs, who fear we are sizing up the land in preparation for another war. Plain daft. Until you consider that the last time a party of white men arrived bearing strange metallic instruments, that's *precisely* what happened next – and it wasn't just the warring soldiers who got mangled in the crossfire either.

'Bar Fly' also displays a complete inability to accommodate local superstitions. I'm happy to admit that at first glance these do appear rather odd: your average African – even a supposedly converted one – lives in perpetual terror of that most omnipresent of complaints, the 'Evil Eye'. All manner of trees and hills are said to be inhabited by spirits. Playing along with it can result in significant delays to the work – having to re-route a safari to avoid a 'juju' site, or finding the whole line of one's boys straggling further and further behind as they ascend a hill – until it appears that they might actually have begun to walk backwards – all for fear of the awful retribution that awaits those who disturb the particular spirit who is reputed to dwell on the summit. But as with many of our own superstitions – the conjunction of walking under a ladder and colliding with a bit of falling masonry being a good example – one can often work out how they came into being. There was an occasion atop one hill when I went to dismantle a cairn which was protecting an old trig point from a pre-war survey. A rather nervous porter advised me that on no account should it be touched as cairns are apparently irresistible to dislocated spirits in search of a home. Of course, I paid absolutely no attention whatever and was busy demolishing said pile of stones when all of a sudden a black blighter with a hood – some sort of mamba – slithered out a foot away from my hand. I didn't think to measure my jump but it must have been somewhere near the record from standing. We carry antivenene, and lancets and permanganate, but I don't long to use them. Clearly, if one adheres to the prescriptions of the native superstitions, one's chances of living a long and healthful life out here are greatly enhanced.

Anyway, Hopkins, I realize I will have tried your patience for too long, and I can well imagine your despairing of my inability to keep to the point (whatever that might originally have been). I shall sign and seal this – Umbi is here tonight and if I deliver this into his hands before too much chibuti is imbibed, it stands a good chance of getting into the postal system on his return to K— tomorrow.

Yours, as ever,

L. D. Wallace

Wednesday 5 March, on board the 11.27 CrossCountry train to Edinburgh, Leamington Spa station

After finishing the next long letter from Laurance, which for one reason or another took me a good while to get through, I broke in order to get myself some lunch. I dithered for several minutes in the buffet car – the entire selection consisted of different types of fast food – before settling on a cheeseburger. Back at my seat, I admit to being pleasantly surprised. The combination of condiments imparted a tangy flavour that quite ambushed my palate. Below the list of exotic ingredients printed on the polystyrene box (American-style mustard, Chinese leaf, sun-dried tomatoes) I happened across another corporate slogan: *CrossCountry – providing InterCity® train services.* This, I have to say, struck me as distinctly uninspired, a flat, unambitious statement of function somewhat at odds with the more dynamic *We're getting there* of the old British Rail.

Anyway, I munched my way through the burger, gazing out of the window as I did so, and I'm pleased to say the day started to look up. The cloud, which had formed a dismal, smothering blanket ever since I left Southampton, began to fray, allowing weak sunshine access to the earth below and cheering my mood to boot. The Warwickshire landscape became increasingly interesting too – more hilly, the russets and browns of the working farms a refreshing change from the unbroken, idle green of Oxfordshire. New-born lambs – surprisingly early I would say – were suckling in a frosty field.

As we entered the outskirts of Leamington Spa I had something of a bird's-eye view of the place, the railway line running in on a raised embankment. It looked to be a charming town, what I could see of it from my window. The narrow side-streets were lined with neat red-brick Victorian terraces which delighted the eye. One sees very little of this sort of housing in Southampton. I imagine it was once there, but much of the city was bombed to rubble in the war. Wednesday is evidently bin-day in this part of Leamington, ranks of grey wheelie bins standing to attention, sentry-like, on the pavements.

As we approached the station we gradually slowed and I was able to peer innocently into the back gardens abutting the embankment. It being winter, there was little activity to be seen but I imagine in summer the view could be quite interesting. Presumably, living in such close proximity to the railway, the residents would be inured to the passing trains, and one would catch a candid glimpse of people relaxing in their own private plots of land: gardening, playing, canoodling, reading, snoozing, sunning themselves.

The Government Buildings at Tolworth were also overlooked, the line from Waterloo to Chessington passing the rear of the Directorate on a similarly elevated embankment. In fact, as I think about it, my supposition that interesting views might only be afforded to the train traveller in summer is quite wrong. The day that caused the problems back then was in deepest winter, on the occasion of the 1960 Christmas party, when by rights one would have thought it too cold for people to be getting up to high jinks out of doors.

The Christmas party was a tradition dating back to the early days, when the HQ staff numbered dozens and when everyone knew everybody else. By the time I joined the Directorate in '57 several hundred people worked there. Nevertheless the style and atmosphere of the end-of-year festivities had been preserved, even if the scale had increased dramatically. In the run up, the whole of the Government Buildings would gradually become unrecognisable, each section undertaking to transform its drawing room or offices along the lines of the chosen theme. I can't remember what this was in 1960, quite possibly the Japanese Garden, or it may have been the Fairground. Actually, I'm certain that the theme that year was Venice. Anyway, the point is, the whole place would be decorated with paintings and hangings and so forth. With so many of the cartographic staff coming from artistic backgrounds, there seemed no limit to the creative ingenuity on display. On the day of the party itself every room would be vibrant with colour. Strips of plain lining paper across which various panoramas had been painted would be tacked and taped over the habitually bland walls. In the Venice year, I strolled quite happily past gondolas floating motionlessly on canals, admired the square of St Mark's stretching, by a trick of perspective, for hundreds of yards, marvelled at our very own Renaissance frescos, ate my Christmas lunch in a canteen transformed into what I was assured was a quintessentially Italian café. Nothing was left undecorated. Helen had a good deal of fun, I remember, disguising the entrance to her photogrammetry room as a large wine rack. Sets of unremarkable swing doors became huge, medieval oak portals. Even desks and filing cabinets were festooned with flags and bric-à-brac which were more or less pertinent to the theme.

To begin with, the party that year ran its usual course. Come noon, all serious work stopped. The HQ staff, together with any surveyors who happened to be home between tours abroad, crammed into the canteen to partake of turkey with all the trimmings. Even though it was Christmas, Laurance was around – there was a considerable amount of unrest in T— late in '60 and his survey party had been pulled out pending better conditions. I had a very enjoyable lunch with him and I clearly recall his admiration for the decorations. In his undergraduate days he had been on a trip to Italy, though I think his destination had been Florence rather than Venice. Nevertheless, he was struck by the authenticity of the scenes, something which rather tickled Helen, sitting on my other side. It was her second Christmas at Tolworth and she had played a significant part in the painting, throwing herself into the business of what she termed *real art*. In fact, her involvement with the decorations had put something of a strain on our relationship. For over a year we had been seeing each other regularly outside of work, but in the months leading up to the party there was so much for her to do. I lost count of the number of evenings she stayed late, calling off a game of chess or a walk in the park in favour of a few hours' painting with the others on the decorating committee.

Anyway, however burdensome the preparations had been to her, now that the end result was at hand, it must all have seemed worth it. And there was Laurance telling us how very lifelike it all appeared. With his first-hand experience of Italy, it was a ringing endorsement of her efforts.

'I'm terribly glad,' I remember her telling him, peering round me as I attempted to stab a particularly mobile Brussels sprout with my fork. 'None of us on the decorating committee has ever been, you know.'

The revelation caused Laurance some difficulty. Out of the corner of my eye I could see him frown. 'How on earth did you know what it *looks* like, then?'

'Oh, there's all sorts of ways of finding out.' Despite her airy tone I could tell Helen was pleased by his incredulity. 'Photographs are useful, of course, but one can even get a fairly good idea from reading a well-written guide book.'

I recall being somewhat smug, listening to their exchange. From our discussions over the years I knew Laurance to be almost absurdly proud of his travelling. In this respect he was no different from the other surveyors, who held themselves to be a species apart because of it. He always took something of a dim view of my contention that I was, in a sense, in possession of a broader view of the world than he, by virtue of the diverse projects I had been involved with in every corner of the globe. Even though he had intimate knowledge of just one small part of the vast continent of Africa, he would dismiss my assertion, arguing that one couldn't really know about a place unless one had actually been. As Laurance fell silent, turning his attention back to his Christmas lunch, I consigned Helen's words to memory, lest he should at some future point need reminding of the day his theory received a telling setback. I gave Helen an approving look, but something about her expression made me fear for a moment that she might be about to expand on her comments. I needn't have worried. Had she been about to mention Laurance's own letters, the temptation quickly passed.

In the afternoon, the lunch things cleared away, the atmosphere became progressively more merry. Best behaviour was maintained until the brigadier had delivered his annual talk, but thereafter bottles were emptied in ever increasing numbers and the mood of many of the staff became frankly buoyant. DOSCAR, the Committee for Activities and Recreation, had arranged for the hire of a radiogram and the latest records were playing. A few of the more adventurous and with-it souls commandeered a section of the hall as a dance floor, but most of us remained chatting to colleagues, giving ourselves a well-deserved break from the routine.

Of course, as in any group of people, there were invariably those who let their hair down too far, so to speak. For someone such as myself, the Christmas party was always an entirely innocent affair, a chance to relax, pull a cracker or two, don a paper hat, and celebrate the approaching season of goodwill. For others, it was an occasion on which the normal rules of behaviour were in some mysterious way suspended, an opportunity to act in a fashion completely out of keeping with their characters. There would usually be a good deal of high-spirited running around, the odd fire extinguisher discharged. And every year, for days afterwards, the Directorate would be awash with rumour as to who had disappeared with whom. It was well known that the photogrammetry rooms – tiny, blacked-out cupboards in which plots were made from stereoscopic projections of aerial photographs – were the sites of illicit liaisons. In 1960, perhaps as a presage of the decade to come, it seemed that there weren't enough photogrammetry rooms to go round. The result was a spillage out to the back of the building, away from the prying eyes of colleagues, but unfortunately into the direct line of sight of railway commuters returning from London to the upright Surrey suburbs. The spectacle of several entwined couples up against the wall at the back of F Section clearly caused a stir and in the ensuing week or so the director received a string of complaints. As I recall it, one was quite explicit, but the majority were restrained, in keeping with the times, no more than hinting at what had been observed from the window of the 04.15, simply posing the question as to whether civil servants had nothing better to do with their time.

I was by then working closely with Hotine and I witnessed his reaction at first hand. I can honestly say he wasn't angry – even with the responsibilities of his position, he remained admirably tolerant of the various ways people chose to let off steam. But he was embarrassed and disappointed. The episode was particularly ill-timed – for a number of reasons the senior staff were becoming concerned that the Directorate should sharpen up its image and this unfortunate incident was yet another straw to the camel's back. Hotine himself asked me to make enquiries, but after a couple of days I was forced to go back to him and say that I was terribly sorry, sir, I really hadn't the faintest idea. Further attempts were made to discover the identities of the culprits, but these met with a perhaps predictable wall of silence.

Even so, I don't think the intemperate behaviour of a few staff would have had quite the consequence it did but for the clutch of other problems arising from the party that year. Hotine received a strongly worded letter from the parents of one of the junior typists, expressing their horror at the inebriated state in which their daughter had returned home that evening. And a small, easily contained fire in the computing section had led the safety officer to put on record the hazard that the decorations posed. Hotine had no choice but to act. The Efficiency Committee was the result, headed by the chief cartographer, with myself co-opted in my capacity as IPCS representative to put forward staff views.

I don't blame Helen for the way she conducted herself around that time. It was only her second Christmas party and I imagine the novelty hadn't worn off. Plus, of course, she'd so enjoyed helping to organise and produce the decorations.

All that said, I do remember being a little taken aback by the strength of her reaction when she came to see me the following

February, in 1961, the day the Efficiency Committee's deliberations were published. I had been Hotine's TA for several years by then and the Special Projects side of the job had expanded unrecognisably. Accordingly I had been allocated an office just along from his; I hardly went to the Records Section at all. I recall being over at the window, contemplating – as I often did in my lunch break – the activity in the local bird population. I heard my door open, no knock at all, and the next thing I knew Helen was speaking to me.

'John, this is so unfair.'

I turned to face her. In her hand she held a copy of our memorandum to all staff.

'Would you like to close the door?'

I realise that in the heat of the moment she was perhaps a little angry, so I shall spare her the reproduction of her next remark, which had the effect of conveying her complete disinterest in whether the door remained open or closed. Nevertheless, at the time I was rather shocked and I turned back to the window.

'You can't let them do this.'

'I don't see that there's anything I can do about it.'

'Oh, come on, John. You haven't even *tried*, have you? You know how important the party is to the staff. It's a tradition.'

I thought for a moment as to how best to phrase my reply. 'I think the days of tradition are behind us now.'

I should explain that the gradual change from empire to Commonwealth was bringing many changes to the Directorate's way of working. For the newly independent territories the era of paternalistic aid from the Colonial Office had gone. They had control of their own affairs and as a consequence were expected to commission and pay for any mapping they required. The Directorate had also been removed from Colonial Office control and no longer received an annual budget. Our new masters in the Department of Technical Cooperation expected us to earn our keep. We were experiencing increasing competition from emergent mapping agencies in France and Germany, as well as from private companies at home, all of whose abilities in salesmanship seemed far in excess of our own. It was clear that we could no longer take anything for granted. Our monopoly was over. Several contracts had been lost in the months before – although Directorate maps were still second to none, the appearance of the place was frankly shoddy and there was no hiding it from potential customers who came to discuss their requirements. The Efficiency Committee had decided that in order to stand the best chance of continuing to win work, we had to present a more professional image to visiting officials from overseas. The Christmas party in its traditional form was to be one of several inevitable casualties.

All of this Helen knew from reading our memorandum. Nevertheless, I went through it again for her, in some detail too, though I thought it had already been spelled out clearly enough.

I heard her take a deep breath behind me. 'I can understand the need to tidy up the drawing rooms.'

She was right about this. In the course of our inspections, we had noted the innumerable extraneous items cluttering the desks: flag day emblems, ashtrays, newspapers, coffee percolators, aspidistras, even remembrance poppies left over from the previous November. The drawing tables themselves looked rather down-at-heel, ink and Astroscribe blots tarnishing the surfaces.

'But I don't see why you have to . . .'

Before she could continue, we were interrupted by my secretary, who, not unreasonably given the fact that the door was open, walked straight into the room.

'Not now, please, Margaret,' I told her and she left without a word. Though brief, the interruption seemed to derail Helen's line of argument. I turned back to the window, waiting for her to continue, curious as to what she would have to say, yet at the same time distracted by the sight of one of the pair of kestrels, which each year nested near the building, soaring into the sky.

'Look, I know you're angry, John, but I'm not even going to *be* here next Christmas. Banning the party is only going to hurt everyone else – I don't see why you should take it out on them.

You're supposed to be representing their interests, not siding with the directors.'

Perhaps I hadn't been paying sufficient attention – I can't imagine any other reason why I should have been so perplexed by her final comments. I was about to say as much when the kestrel I had been keeping an eye on suddenly folded in its wings and dropped, talons extended, fifty feet or so, swooping on an unsuspecting sparrow. I must have let out an exclamation of some sort at the abruptness of the kill.

'Please! Will you leave your precious sparrowhawks for one minute.'

This was an inflammatory remark. The year before, in happier times, Helen had spent many of her lunch hours with me in that office watching our very own birds of prey in action. She knew, from my repeated explanations, that they were kestrels. Granted, it was unusual to see them feeding on sparrows, but then I suspect the urban environment precluded their usual diet of small mammals. In any case, it was abundantly clear from their behaviour that they were members of the falcon family. Sparrowhawks hedge-hop, flushing out smaller birds and outflying them in the open. Only kestrels hover like that, searching for prey from a high vantage point, dropping like a stone when the moment is right, taking the unfortunate creature completely by surprise.

'John? Please?'

I turned to face her, realising that I had perhaps been a trifle rude.

'It's all in the memo. I don't think there's anything else I can do.'

After a lengthy wait at the station we are at last on the move again. As we gather speed the houses, shops, Belisha beacons, cars, pedestrians of Leamington blur into a kaleidoscope of ordinary life. Eventually it becomes too confusing for my eyes, the details subsumed by the general whirl, nothing remaining still long enough to be focused on. Turning from the window, I remove my correspondence file from my briefcase. I stowed it there when I returned with my lunch, a precaution that the drips of relish escaping from the cheeseburger subsequently vindicated.

Opening the manila flaps, I experience a moment of alarm: Laurance's letter is out of place at the top of the file. Its pages are disordered too, jumbled into a more or less random sequence. A quick survey of my fellow passengers reveals the same heads buried in the same books. Those who were communing with their laptops continue to stare at the screens. No one seems the slightest bit interested in me. In such a crowded carriage, would anyone dare steal across and interfere with my file while I was buying lunch? I can't conceive of it, yet it seems the only explanation. A feeling of disquiet comes over me and I make a more careful assessment of the situation.

Though they've been shuffled about, all the pages of Laurance's letter are still there. I spend a while rearranging them into their correct sequence, a task made more difficult by his failure to number the individual sheets. Try as I might, I cannot remember exactly how I left things when I went to the buffet car. I've absolutely no recollection of putting the letter back in the file; yet, if I had, the habits of a lifetime should have ensured it was returned to the correct slot. I do recall, as I reached the final lines, experiencing a wave of physical discomfort. I had been sitting still for far too long, my behind was numb, my legs desperately needed a stretch, and, unnoticed, a nauseating hunger had stolen up on me. Could it be, in my haste to get out of my seat, I had left the letter out on the table? Laurance's neatly looping writing, redolent of an era of copperplate script, the ancient airmail paper – could these have pricked the interest of a passing passenger, proved an irresistible temptation?

Not that there is anything terribly confidential about that particular item, unlike some of the documents later in the file. Rather as with maps, it strikes me that letters have distinct phases to their existence. For a time, they are contemporary, detailing events in the lives of people in the real world. In that phase they should be guarded, lest the information, thoughts, opinions contained within fall into unintended hands, causing embarrassment or damage either to writer or recipient.

But as with maps – when borders change, countries are renamed, buildings or whole villages are destroyed, land is developed or falls into disuse – as with maps, letters eventually become historical, records of how things once were. Their information ceases to have much relevance to the living. It is of concern only to the dead – if, that is, the dead can be said to be concerned about anything.

As my career progressed, I came to see how the twists and turns of knowledge and politics and environmental history are embodied in the maps of the past, each chart a snapshot of the world as it then was. Indeed, in my final years in OS International this came to be an important part of my work. I handled countless requests from researchers in different parts of the world, all of them wanting access to the Directorate's maps and aerial photographs of certain regions. From these, a stroboscopic vision of man's progress, and the marks he leaves on the world in which he lives, can be discerned. Cities expand, populations shift, land is reclaimed to grow food, food is replaced by cash crops, rivers dry, land is submerged to provide reserves of water. And where once there was one name, another suddenly appears: Northern Rhodesia, Zambia; Gold Coast, Ghana; Basutoland, Lesotho; Bechuanaland, Botswana; Nyasaland, Malawi; Tanganyika, Tanzania.

Letters, it seems to me, eventually take on a similar guise: frozen records of thoughts and experiences at given points in time. If one is lucky enough, or diligent enough, to have kept a whole series of correspondence from one person, one can perhaps glean a similarly jerky view of the progress of their life, the way their thinking changed, the battles won and lost with themselves.

I realise this is simplistic, that the boundary between the contemporary and the historical is rarely as clear cut as I am making out. A thoroughly out-of-date map, for instance, fit only as a baseline for the study of rural to urban drift, might still prove perfectly serviceable if all one wanted was to see where the

mountains are. And maps have other functions: as legal documents, for example, the means to record ownership of a plot of
land. Mind you, letters, too, may sometimes have a legal function.
Indeed, that very letter of Laurance's was once an exhibit in a
courtroom. At that time, the information therein arguably
assumed a greater importance than at any point in the letter's
existence before or since. But any such significance has long since
evaporated, and there can have been no harm should someone
have taken advantage of my absence to leaf hurriedly through its
pages.

Even so, my failure to recall whether or not I left it lying on the
table for everyone to see is a source of some concern. I find myself
increasingly forgetful nowadays. Not about the past – the details
of that are, by and large, crystal clear, more vivid than ever in fact.
But many little things in the here and now seem to pass me by.
These days I am better able to recall the view from my Directorate
office window in 1960 than something as important as whether I
shut my bathroom window before leaving on a trip which may
well take me away from home for several days.

Not that my recollections of my youth are entirely flawless. One
thing in particular troubled me throughout my lunch – my failure
to recall the surname of Laurance's head light-keeper, the man
called Medicine. Though I never properly met him, I would have
thought his full name would have been branded on my mind for
all time. Quite apart from everything else, I still have the wood
carving, depicting a long, thin, mournful African face, which he
fashioned by hand from a lump of ebony, and which Laurance
presented to me in 1958 on his return home for the first full
summer we spent together at Surbiton Drive.

No, much as I hate to admit it, the years are clearly taking their
toll on my mental powers. I slide Laurance's reordered letter into
its chronologically correct position in the file, resigning myself to
the fact that I will probably never get to the bottom of the
incident. The one thing I can be sure of is that *I* would never have
shoved the letter back out of place, and in such a chaotic and
disarrayed state.

Fresh Disturbances in T—

From Our Correspondent
5th September 1959

Security forces opened fire yesterday on a violent crowd outside a Native Authority court in Mpande, where two T.A.N.A. officials are charged with taking part in a recent illegal procession. A patrol in the area came across a crowd of 200 demonstrators outside the court, some armed with sticks and iron bars. They were ordered to disperse. They refused to move and demanded the release of the two prisoners. Stones were thrown, hitting a police vehicle and your Correspondent's car.

The police then used tear gas and the crowd were again ordered to disperse. When they failed to do so, a riot proclamation was read, but the crowd remained violent and the security forces opened fire. Four rounds were discharged and two people in the crowd were injured. One has since died, the other is in hospital. The trial continues.

Helen collected her bicycle from alongside the boarding-house steps, wheeled it backwards towards the low railings which bounded the small front garden, and pushed it, rear wheel first, out of the gate. She checked that her bag was safely lodged at the bottom of the basket, then eased herself astride the saddle – still a little high – and set off. An immediate telltale draught caused her to gather a fold of skirt and wedge it between saddle and thigh.

Turning out of Edith Gardens, she started down the gentle incline of Surbiton Drive. Gradually she gathered momentum, freewheeling from time to time as she levered the gears up another ratio. The unusually hot summer was finally fading and the mornings had recently become noticeably cooler. Even so, the air was crisp rather than cold and the sun, suspended above a cloudless horizon, was casting a clear light through an atmosphere unsullied by winter smog. The local bird population, as yet undiminished by the irresistible urge for migration, was in full voice as she cycled along. In short, it was a wonderful morning, and by rights she should have been rejoicing in it. Instead, as she sailed past the newsagent's, a paperboy collecting his sack from the proprietor outside, she attempted to marshal the unruly emotions squabbling inside her.

At some point during the night she had come to a decision. She wasn't quite sure *what* she'd decided – just that when she'd gone to bed she'd been a trainee carto, turning in in preparation for the next day at work. Yet when she'd woken – early, the flimsy curtains at least partly to blame – that was no longer the case. She'd been at the Directorate nearly four months and, once the initial novelty had worn off, every day had proved as dreary as the last. For the past few weeks they'd been full time at the tables and even that breakthrough had failed to fulfil its promise. She had to face it: the drawing of maps was not for her. Sitting in the canteen at lunch, listening to her fellow trainees' conversations – their caricaturing of the supervisors, their swapping tales of progress, their impatience to finish training so they could start to produce *real* maps to help *real* people, their blind, unquestioning determination to become good at the craft – she found herself increasingly estranged. How could they be so interested in something she found so *dull*? It wasn't as though there was nothing in common – on the face of it she shared interests with several of them. Joyce was a keen painter, spending her holidays on spinster-solitary sojourns to the Cornish coast, just her and her easel, alone with the stark rocks and crashing waves and circling gulls. Dearlove, she'd discovered, had come to the Directorate after completing a foundation year and had even had an exhibition at a minor gallery in Pimlico. He'd brought some of his work in to show them: vibrant gouaches, surprisingly modern and disturbing, quite at odds with the impression she'd formed of their creator.

Approaching the junction with Deedes Hill, she slowed a little, the brakes squealing. A snatched glance behind showed the road to be clear and she left the company of the kerbside, veering into the centre of the street to take a right turn.

It wasn't just the social side of things, though it had been galling to have her few approaches politely rebuffed with transparent falsehoods. Dearlove in particular was a great disappointment. From the subject matter of his paintings, and occasional unguarded comments, she suspected that he had something of a Bohemian existence away from the Directorate, quite at odds with the clean-cut, conscientious persona he presented at work. She was pretty sure he was a homosexual and that only added to the fascination. It was the kind of life she would love to glimpse – Mr Andrews used to tantalise her with stories of his own days at art school – yet Dearlove, beyond showing her some of his work, had resolutely barred her from closer contact. She thought she knew why. How could you give someone a true impression of yourself in such conservative, austere surroundings? If he could appear the regular nine-to-fiver, then what must she look like? A fresh-from-school country lass, apparently believing, with extraordinary naïvety, that the drawing of maps was the last word in artistic aspiration. And there was no way to dispel such impressions, not when everyone's conversation was couched in such cautious, correct terms. How could you hint to someone that you yearned for something different when every reservation you expressed about the work on which you were all engaged was greeted with perplexed smiles and awkward subject changing? Yet some of them *must* feel it too – Dearlove at the very least. But no one was going to admit it, not to other people, not to themselves.

At the junction at the bottom of Deedes Hill she paused to allow a beige Beetle to buzz past, its exhaust tinkling loudly in the morning stillness, before she turned into Kingston Road. The Directorate was a few hundred yards further along and she glided through the pegged-back gates. It was very early; she wasn't even sure that the doors would be unlocked at such a time. Parking the bike in the deserted racks along the front wall, she checked the time, found it to be a little before seven: the bike was certainly good for that, chopping the journey time to a few minutes, though the hills made the return leg longer. It pleased her, the feeling of speed and freedom. The bicycle had been her reward to herself, a bargain at just under five pounds and the perfect congratulation for paying off the last of the money she owed her father. The day she sent the final cheque she'd settled down with a *Kingston Advertiser*, ringing in blue ink the notices advising of bicycles for sale, just as many months before she had circled an advertisement in *The Times* seeking applications from those interested in a career in cartography. What she was doing at work so very early she wasn't at all sure, but neither could she think of anywhere else to pass the intervening hours before the bell rang out for the start of the day.

A surprised cleaner let her in. The central corridor was deserted and her footsteps echoed around, racing ahead of her in the unaccustomed silence. Reaching F Section, she turned off the thoroughfare, the double doors swooshing closed behind her, and regarded the carto room. The ranks of drawing tables, which later in the day would be alive with human activity, stood silent and still as sleeping horses. Anglepoise lamps were frozen in squatting, craning, twisting postures. Above her head, strip lights and electric plugs dangled from the ceiling, their cables trailing like the exotic aerial roots she remembered from a photograph of a Borneo jungle in her father's *National Geographic*.

She sank down at the table to which she had graduated at the end of basic training, spending a few minutes aimlessly tidying, trying to restore some order to the mess of pencils, paperclips, notes in front of her. Her life was spinning out of control, that much she knew. Nothing here was as she'd expected. Nothing had captured – no, sustained – the enthusiasm with which she'd arrived. Cartography had rapidly proved to be dry, airless; the people likewise. No, that wasn't quite fair. But she couldn't get through the aridity, to the moist, breathing, pulsing lives she knew must lie beyond.

She propped her elbows on the edge of the drawing table, resting her chin on her palms. A noise in the corridor startled her out of her thoughts and she sat up, staring at the doors, expecting any minute to see them swing open. But the footfalls passed, steadily receding: the cleaner again, or an early bird from another section perhaps. She picked up a pencil and started to doodle on the reverse of a Bander sheet of notes – drawing nothing, endlessly connecting line after line after line in a desultory satire of her cartographic exercises, the confusion of grey lead rapidly amassing on the paper in front of her.

Eventually, with hardly any white space left to fill, with nowhere else for her pencil to go, she laid it down, looked at the web she'd drawn. She'd give the Directorate a little more time, to the end of her six months' probation. Now she'd settled her debt, she could start to save. If it got no better, then she'd take a leaf from Mary McKend's book, sign up for an evening class in secretarial skills, set off on another tack. Do it in London? Perhaps. She wasn't sure where else. Not back home, that was for sure. Either way, she'd live as frugally as possible, put by what she could. She no longer cared about Mr Andrews' pessimism, no longer believed in her teacher's defeated view of art in the world. So what if it led her nowhere? She would save until she had enough to try for a foundation course. Which was what she should have done from the word go.

Letting out a wry exhalation, she got to her feet, started to wander the drawing room, gazing at work in progress, the monochromatic red of the Astroscribe quickly defeating her eye. Another couple of months, then she would decide. In a few days' time the group was to break up and she was due a placement in photogrammetry. If nothing else, it would be a chance to escape the strictures of F Section.

Eventually, time dragging, she settled back down and started to doodle again, more constructively this time. She sketched the carto room around her, the ranks of tables, the forest of lamps. But in place of the electric cables dangling from the ceiling she drew tangled vines, aerial roots, trails of vegetation, reaching down, encroaching on the geometric lines of the desks below, winding and insinuating themselves round the sharp angles of the lamp stands. By the time she'd finished, the first few cartographers were drifting in to start the day, nodding to her or murmuring greetings. None of them knew she'd been there for hours, wouldn't have known what to make of it if they had. Quite out of the normal routine. The secret knowledge gave her a quiet pleasure and she smiled to herself, putting the pencil sketch away in a drawer in her desk.

The working day, when it finally came, seemed that much more bearable now that she'd practically decided to leave, to branch out on her own again. Sooner or later she'd find what was hers. Her mood was brighter than it had been for weeks. So much so that, after the three o'clock tea-break, when the diffident young man from Records, whom she hadn't seen for ages, came to find her at her desk specifically to tell her that the directing side had agreed at last week's Whitley council meeting to scrap the Directorate's time bell, she acceded with little more than a moment's hesitation to his tacked on suggestion that they repeat their lunchtime excursion to the Toby Jug later that week.

'It's made by a company called Zeiss. Can't beat the Swiss when it comes to precision.'

Helen looked doubtfully at the mess of hydraulic pipes, wheels, handles, columns, drums, all finished in gun-metal grey, which together comprised the c-5 plotter. It was far bigger than she'd expected and looked impossibly technical, disjointed, mysterious, like something one might find in a boiler room, or a factory, or deep in the bowels of a battleship. It would be quite beyond her, she was sure. All the while she contemplated, a quiet whirr, more of a hum, emanated from the machine. The photogrammetry trainer, a senior cartographer named Stevens, took a pair of black and white photos from a table and loaded them into the twin drums on top of the machine. The utter simplicity of the pictures, the fragility of the paper on which they were printed, these things struck her as completely incongruous with the mass of metalwork in which they were placed.

'Go on, I'll show you how it works.'

She sat down, stood again while he adjusted the chair – pumping it up with his foot, twisting a handle to alter the angle of the back – then seated herself once more. Directly at eye level was what appeared to be a pair of binoculars, slanted downwards, the twin barrels disappearing into the grey box at the heart of the machine.

'You shouldn't get a crick in your neck,' Stevens said as she leaned forward slightly, the Bakelite of the eyepieces cool against her forehead and cheeks.

For a moment all she could see was a fuzzy jumble of shapes and outlines. She grasped the side of the binoculars, as though there might be some way of adjusting them.

'Just let your eyes go. Lose your focus.'

She tried to do as she was bid but nothing seemed to happen. There was nothing recognisable in the blur. She was on the point of sitting back again, already resigned to her failure, when for the briefest of moments the lines before her sharpened. She pressed herself harder against the eyepieces, tried to recapture the fleeting clarity.

'Not too hard, that's the common mistake.'

Swiftly learning from trial and error, she found that by telling her eyes to look into the far distance rather than directly at the fuzzy outlines, she could focus the picture at will. Once accomplished, no further effort was required to keep it there. What she beheld was extraordinary. She couldn't reconcile it with the brace of flat photographs she'd seen loaded into the machine. She was looking directly down on a long row of buildings, trees clustered around their perimeter, throwing sharp shadows across the ground. But it wasn't a picture. This was no artist's trick of perspective, clever shading and foreshortening tricking the eye into perceiving three dimensions. This was *real*. The buildings, the trees, were absolutely solid, actually rose towards her out of the plane of the ground. She could even follow the subtle undulations of the grassy banks. It was as though she was looking down on a perfect scale model, an architect's mock-up, a toy village. The land, and the man-made structures upon it, were so lifelike, yet so *tiny*, it made her want to laugh. She could surely reach inside the Zeiss, feel the corners of the buildings, allow her hand to rove around, brush the grass, touch the little trees, pick one up, examine it from all sides before placing it down elsewhere. To one side of the buildings, little dark rectangular blocks were arranged in neat ranks and rows – cars; it was a car park. And over to the right of the scene snaked a pair of railway tracks, like infinitely long ladders laid flat, raised up on an embankment. Even the mottled texture of the stony bed on which the sleepers lay was startlingly clear, looked as though it would be rough to the touch of a fingertip.

'Good,' Stevens murmured. 'Know what it is?'

Helen briefly wondered what it was about her posture, her attitude, that had let him know she had finally seen the picture.

'It's here!' The photogrammetrist laughed, as though aware of the impact the revelation would have. 'You're looking down on yourself!'

Helen spent a minute or two drinking in the view, more detail becoming clear, her startled surprise gradually subsiding. He was absolutely right. There was the apron of ground in front of the Directorate's entrance, the bike racks. Even the bicycles were perfectly represented and she searched in vain for her own machine with its wicker basket – probably the aeroplane had overflown the site, taking its photographs, long before she had come. Here and there thin lines jutted out from the walls at various angles. Open windows. The picture must have been taken at the height of a summer.

Suddenly there was a click and she was aware of the lights in the room going off. A bright speck appeared in the middle of the scene.

'That's the cursor,' Stevens explained.

She felt him touch her hand, prise it free from the barrel of the binoculars, lift it and guide it through darkened space. Her fingers touched something cold and hard – metal, the rim of a wheel. Stevens's hand was hot and damp in comparison.

'Turn it.'

She did as instructed, the wheel somewhat stiff and resistant. But as it rotated, the bright speck moved through the grounds of the Directorate. She sensed rather than heard Stevens shuffle behind her, felt him take her other hand and place it on a similar though smaller wheel. She experimented with that also, finding that the cursor rose in the air, came up towards her, then dived straight down, plummeting towards the ground. Her forehead creased beneath the Bakelite. How could that be? The tiny blob of light actually appeared to be – actually *was* – below the surface of the earth.

'The secret is what we call hand-eye coordination. Once you can keep the cursor on the ground you're half-way there.'

She tried a few manoeuvres, running the spot of light towards the railway lines, then coaxing it up the sheer sides of the embankment. She was amazed at the subtlety: the minutest turn of her left hand and the bright speck was clearly hovering above the grass; a twist the other way and it sank below the sod. She wasn't at all sure how it worked – what was actually going on inside the machine to produce this extraordinary visual effect? Yet work it did.

'Anyway, when we're doing a proper plot –' the click and again the room was flooded with light – 'we fix the cursor on a ground control point of known height, then move it to all other points of the same elevation.'

She sat back from the eyepieces, blinking to get him into focus.

'The plotter,' he indicated an assembly to her right, a drawing pen held perpendicular to a square of paper by a system of levered arms, 'marks them on a scaled grid corresponding to the area in the photographs.'

He grabbed the wheel beneath her hand, giving it a sharp turn, and the pen, hovering a fraction of an inch above the paper, jerked to one side. Balancing himself carefully, he eased a foot just in front of her legs, tucked beneath the Zeiss, and pressed on a pedal. The pen dipped down, leaving a tiny mark on the paper.

'Join up the dots and, hey presto, contours! Anyway –' he

flashed her a grin, withdrawing his leg again – 'that's all for this morning.'

He held out a hand, helping her up from her seat. 'Can I buy you lunch?'

Helen returned his smile. 'No, thank you. I'm meeting someone already.'

Arriving at the survey data library, she was in buoyant frame of mind. That had been *fun*. She had often wondered how the photogrammetrists produced the plots from which the cartographers drew the maps. She'd assumed, she supposed, that it would be a similarly sterile process – if the final artwork was dull and restrictive, then she couldn't imagine any preparatory stage being any better. Yet the morning had been a revelation. Strolling through the library, between the towering shelves, she gently chided herself for her reticence when first faced with the plotter. She'd never get anywhere if she was going to allow herself to be put off by outward appearances. The machine had looked utterly unworkable, yet a short period of training and she was already getting the hang of it.

Passing the foot of a step-ladder, she called a cheery greeting to Maureen Penrose, balanced on the top rung, a pile of files cradled in her arms.

'Oh, hello, Helen, love.' The librarian wobbled precariously, her downwards glance sufficient to unsettle her balance. Helen stopped for a moment, steadying the ladder until she was sure that the older woman was stable again.

And what a wonderful thing the plotter was! Walking on, Helen relived, for the umpteenth time, the moment when the scene had leapt into three dimensions for her. And to be confronted with a bird's-eye view of the very buildings in which she worked! She wondered how often Stevens had pulled this stunt on young trainees. His patter was certainly slick, the words spoken with the air of a performer, a conjuror perhaps, laced with the mild amusement of someone who knows he's about to spring a dazzling trick on an unsuspecting public.

As she headed towards John's office, she glanced at the boxes which lined the shelves on either side. She felt a shimmer of excitement, wondering at the thousands of aerial photos contained within, little fragments of time and space, sequestered moments of history – startling, vivid visions of foreign lands lying dormant, awaiting stereoscopic liberation by those in the know. Gazing down on the Directorate, moving the pinpoint cursor, she'd allowed her imagination to run away with her, pretending that the dot of light was in some way representative of herself, that it was she who was running over the grassy slopes, up towards the railway embankment, hopping nimbly over the fence, scrambling up to the tracks overhead. She was still smiling at the thought when she arrived at the office door. Walking in, she was surprised to find Geoff Price, one of the other map curators, sitting at John's desk.

'He's moved up in the world,' he said, fixing her with a steady, enquiring look when she asked for him.

'How do you mean?' She hoped her blush wasn't as noticeable as it felt.

'Too good for the likes of us.' Geoff softened his words with a hint of a smile. 'Got an office right next to the brigadier.' He tapped the side of his nose. 'Hush, hush. Special Projects.'

'He's in a meeting.'

'Do you know when he'll be free?'

The other woman tutted, looked up again from her typing, her elongated beehive exaggerating the movements of her head. 'They never tell *me* that sort of thing.' She reached for her phone. 'Can I say what it's concerning?'

'Oh, nothing – it's personal.'

The secretary rested the receiver back in its cradle.

Helen glanced pointedly at the row of chairs against the far wall. 'Well, do you mind if I wait?'

This elicited a deep sigh. 'If you've nothing else to do. I shall have to get on, though.' She flipped a page over on her ring-bound pad.

'Fine.' Helen gave her a long look then went to sit herself down. Crossing her legs, watching the woman's fingers flying over the typewriter keys, listening to the click-clack-clack, she felt a flush of annoyance. John hadn't mentioned anything about a move from the library. Mind you, she hadn't seen him for some months, perhaps it wasn't such a recent thing – that might explain his forgetting to mention it. And when she thought about it, they hadn't in fact arranged to meet in any specific place. She scrutinized the secretary's face. What if she was lying? They had to do that, secretaries, didn't they? Protect their superiors. Even with her fruitless trip to the library, she was still a little early. Mr Stevens, perhaps in his eagerness to issue his own lunch invitation, had curtailed the session well before half-past twelve. What if John had sneaked away early and the secretary was covering up for him? He might be in F Section even as she sat there, wondering where on earth *she'd* got to. She hadn't thought to tell him that she'd be over in photogrammetry either.

It was an awful bind. The secretary had been far from friendly, would hardly take kindly to Helen asking whether she was sure John was in his office. She could go off, try to find him in F Section, but what if she missed him? Yet if she sat there while he was traipsing round the Directorate looking for her, how long would it be before he gave up, returned here? It was a mild shock to realise that she was actually looking forward to seeing him. If nothing else, assuming he retained his previous interest in her life, it would give her the opportunity to tell someone about the startling vision she'd been presented with when peering into the plotter. She resolved to give it five minutes then decide on a plan of action.

The secretary gave a loud tut, ceased her flurried typing and reached for a rubber. Helen watched with dull curiosity as she scratched at the error, blew sharply, chalked the paper, and typed over it. She could never be a secretary, sitting there all day long banging away on a typewriter, answering the telephone, making cups of tea. It would turn her sour. She clung to the faint hope that had arisen that morning. Perhaps there *was* something she would find passably bearable, something to allow her to continue here long enough to save the money she'd need for a foundation course. Her first taste of photogrammetry had intrigued her; she couldn't wait to get back to the plotter to sample more.

Mind you, she'd need to acquit herself in cartography if she was to go on to work in that section. Over the preceding weeks she'd been restless, unenthusiastic. Her work had suffered, of course, and Mr Gaselee had made several barbed comments about unfinished projects: practice maps abandoned without label stencilling, shoddy line drawing, insufficient attention to detail. At the time she really couldn't have cared less. She wasn't going to be a cartographer, that much was certain. The superintendent had taken her aside not one week before: a long pep talk about *discipline, pride in one's work, application to the task in hand.* She'd let it wash over her, daydreaming as he droned on. Now, waiting for John in the anteroom to the director's office suite, she had an unnerving feeling of regret. Perhaps she'd been a little precipitate.

She fidgeted on her chair. She desperately wanted to discuss it with someone and there seemed no one better than John. There was no one *other* than him. She hardly knew him, but he'd been the only person here to take any proper interest in her. She felt a twinge of guilt. After their first lunch date she'd written him off, resolved not to encourage further contact. Whenever she'd had to draw material from the library, she'd made sure it was Maureen, or any of the other curators, that she went to. After several visits, in which she'd seen neither hide nor hair of him, she'd learned that her caution had in fact been unnecessary. Geoff Price it was who – struggling to find the file she needed amongst the pile awaiting shelving – had complained about the amount of *routine work* they were all having to shoulder, now that *one of our number* spends his time in the library dealing exclusively with Special Projects. She smiled at the memory. Geoff had used that same nose-tap-hush-hush gesture then too.

The secretary coughed loudly and artificially. Helen stared at her but the other woman kept her eyes fixed on her typing. This was such a nuisance, being trapped here like this. The clock on the wall told her it was just before half-past twelve. Surely, if he were here, he would free himself soon.

At that moment, the bell started to ring, shrilling its news of an hour of liberty. The sudden noise, louder here than in the drawing room, caused Helen to start. The next instant, one of the doors giving on to the anteroom opened sharply. She looked over to see John burst in, one arm in his jacket, the other flailing behind as it tried to locate its sleeve. In his haste, he half-stumbled, his fringe flopping untidily, but rather attractively, over his forehead.

'No, I was just sitting there doing paperwork. Got quite a shock – I hadn't noticed the time at all.' He met her gaze, smiling self-consciously. 'I, for one, shall miss the time bell when it goes.'

Helen returned his smile, rather puzzled all the same. 'I'm sure she said you were in a meeting.'

'Who, Margaret?'

She nodded – presumably that was the frosty secretary's name.

'Funny fish is Margaret.' He frowned. 'No idea what she was thinking of. Anyway,' his tone brightened and he picked up his beer, raising the glass in her direction. 'Here we are!'

He had steak and kidney pie again, she went for the toad-in-the-hole and this time she ate with gusto. His discomfiture at her having witnessed his whirlwind exit from the office had amused her. His embarrassment when discussing it now they'd reached the pub gave rise to an affectionate feeling. She could quite imagine that, had she been at her drawing table in F Section, he would have contrived to compose himself before arriving, sauntering calmly in and collecting her for lunch with an indifferent air, as though he wasn't especially bothered but it was a pleasant enough way to spend the spare hour. As it was she'd been privy to a glimpse of the human heart beneath the aridity and she felt tremendously well disposed towards him. Flattered, too, by his evident disarray as he'd shot out of his room, which could only have been due to the thought that he might be late in meeting her. And starting the date on such unguarded terms seemed to have broken invisible ice. John proved much more interesting, still intent on what she had to say, yet willing to talk more about himself, his work. It seemed he coordinated all sorts of projects only indirectly related to the production of maps, aspects of Directorate life that never filtered through to the cartographers. There was the Forestry and Land Use Section, tucked away in separate accommodation on the eighth floor of Tolworth Tower, advising foreign governments on optimal ways to use their land according to geology and climate. And the research and development of machines called 'electronic computers' being carried out in conjunction with Military Survey – John thought it likely that these would, at some future point, put many of the computers out of their jobs. At one point her concentration drifted elsewhere, trying to put a finger on the difference between this and their first lunch together. She could come up with nothing better – half-listening to him telling her about the Whitley meeting at which the time bell had met its nemesis – than that this time their conversation felt *natural*. This decided, she leaned forward again, resting her chin on her hands, gazing at him as he talked, further amused at the way her sudden attention caused him to avert his eyes, looking at his plate, his glass, the table, anything but her.

'. . . I have to say, I thought the brigadier was going to throw the whole idea out on its ear. Eight hundred pounds – that's what we'd costed the electric clocks at. Anyway, there was this long silence, everyone studying their laps, waiting for the eruption, then he laughs this little laugh and says, "Well, that's less than I and my deputies manage to get through in the way of pink gin in a year!" Motion carried unanimously. Quite extraordinary.'

'Thank you for sorting it out, anyway.'

'Don't mention it.'

They fell silent, concentrating on their meals. As she ate, Helen tried to think of a new topic of conversation. She'd told him about her morning in photogrammetry on the way there and, although she wasn't sure that he'd fully appreciated the extraordinariness of the phenomenon she had witnessed, he'd seemed genuinely delighted at her excitement. Try as she might, she could think of nothing else to say. Chewing on a mouthful of sausage and batter, her mood deflated slightly. Not much of a life, if that was the only thing of remark in it. There were other things, of course: her art for one, though she had always felt that to be intensely private. Not even Mr Andrews had seen her more personal work. Even so, she was trying to frame a suitable sentence with which to hint at the topic when John downed his cutlery as if struck by a thought.

'Are you by any chance a chess player?'

She exhaled involuntarily at the incongruity of the question. 'Well, I much prefer Scrabble, but I do play a little, yes.'

She waited for a rejoinder. The seconds passed; John contemplated the remainder of his pie. In the end they both spoke at once.

'Go on,' she got in first.

'Well, I was wondering – I mean, do you have anyone to play against down here?'

'Which?'

'Sorry?'

'Chess or Scrabble?'

'Well – either, I mean –'

'John?' she interrupted, her lips pressing together in a smile. Finally, he looked at her directly. 'Yes, I'd love a game some time.'

c/o Overseas Surveys,
P.O. Box 47,
K—
14th October 1958

My dear John,

I should start this missive by saying what I ought to have said before leaving London, namely, what a splendid summer I had. Somehow these things are easier to write than to say out aloud, don't you agree? In any case, a splendid summer it was.

I'll admit to a degree of melancholy on the flight back out. It's a strange thing; I hardly missed England for the entirety of my first tour – was quite reluctant to take my home leave, in fact – yet two months in the bosom of Britannia and I never wanted to go again. Gazing stolidly out of the aeroplane window as we overflew this wretched continent (how I love her, how I hate her!) I was consumed with envy at the congenial life you lead: creature comforts, regular hours, a pleasant bunch of fellows, cricket and beer every Sunday. (I've still not forgiven you that catch!)

Before your cock starts to crow too loud, however, I should point out that these sentiments lasted precisely two hours after landing in K—, so all bets are still on, I'm afraid. When I got to Hildred's, who should I find waiting for me but Medicine. He'd been back for a spot of time with his family and, in the way people do here, he'd got wind of the fact that I was due to be flying in. One look at his beaming countenance, hearing his, 'Welcome back, Massa Laurents,' and my misgivings melted away.

Umbi was not due to make the trip up-country until the weekend, so I had a few days to while away. When he learned this, Medicine invited me to visit his home, in a small village some forty miles north-west of K—. Hildred was discreetly against the idea – offered to find me some jobs to do, by way of a tactful get-out clause – but I thought, why not? Never been so pleased with any decision before or since.

Medicine not being a car owner, we took the daily bus. This in itself was a revelation. It's more or less unheard of for a European to travel by this mode of transport and to start with I felt rather awkward with all the looks being sent my way. The bus station I can only describe as chaos incarnate: people everywhere, hanging round in groups, folk camping out under makeshift shelters such is the wait for some of the more infrequent services. Vendors wove in and out, offering every variety of food from bananas to parcels of these little dried fish which one eats, skeleton and all (this one didn't, I should say). There were no discernible bus stops but people seemed to have some sort of sixth sense as to where to wait. From time to time a dust-covered coach would grumble in, coming to a halt in front of the very hoard wishing to board. When the bus was full, on to the roof they went. I must confess that around this time I was thinking I should have paid a little more attention to Hildred, but Medicine kept up a humorous line in chit-chat, gossiping about the different members of our survey party, and I didn't really have the chance to worry unduly.

Our bus eventually turned up (that's the other thing, there's no such thing as a timetable: your average African seems perfectly content to wait around, for days if necessary, secure in the knowledge that sooner or later the expected service will appear). Anyway, ours pitched up and we got on board – thankfully we managed to squeeze into a pair of vacant seats – and I started my first African bus journey. As I've intimated, I was initially the object of intense curiosity. Medicine kept chuckling and muttering to me that our fellow passengers had no idea what to make of me. Couldn't see how he could tell, myself: to all intents and purposes it was just like any other trip on the Clapham omnibus. But after twenty minutes or so, when the novelty of a white man on board had worn off somewhat, the atmosphere underwent a transformation.

A group of nuns started it; must have been a dozen of them all told, clad from head to foot in brilliant white, spread in twos and threes throughout the coach. It sort of crept up on me, but at some point I became aware of the softest singing beneath the general road noise and chatter. The volume soon swelled until all twelve Sisters were singing lustily – African hymns, so Medicine informed me. Now, you wouldn't get this on the number 72; neither would you get the majority of the fellow passengers gradually joining in, till in the end the whole bus (so it seemed) was chorusing these haunting, wonderful songs. I was quite overwhelmed, if truth be told. Even now I have blurred impressions of looking around, seeing smiling, laughing faces everywhere, my ears filled with the richest, most resonant harmonizing. Quite magical. And on and on it went – they were still in full swing when we came to disembark. As I walked up the aisle, following Medicine's lead, any number of folk were grinning at me – not at all mockingly, with touching warmth and generosity. I stepped out on to dusty earth quite light of spirit, a feeling of real inspiration. I think I must have arrived at the assumption that it was all for my benefit, for when Medicine explained that this was more or less the norm, I had the briefest moment of deflation. But it lasted not the blink of an eye. Am I making any sense? The idea of these buses trundling all over the country, full to overflowing, most of the people as poor as people can be, but so *happy* that they would want to burst into spontaneous, musical praise. I don't know, I'm sure I'm making no sense whatever. I can only say it was an extraordinary experience.

Matched and surpassed – not in decibels but in profundity – by my stay chez Medicine. I was a little taken aback to start with. Having worked with him, doing all these surveyor-type things, I think I expected that he'd have some sort of house. And in a way he does. His home is basically a collection of mud huts, all contained within a fenced-off compound. Each hut is round-walled, topped with a thick toupee of elephant grass. The floors are fashioned from compacted mud, repeatedly wetted and pounded until the surface has the same smooth, shiny hardness of ceramic. The different huts have their specific functions: kitchen, dining room, men's quarters, ladies' quarters, grain store, &c. The compound itself is dust, but his wife rakes it at least twice daily such that the dirt is as neatly groomed as an Axminster. When we arrived the entire family was hurriedly assembled outside, the children grinning at their feet and shuffling about a lot, and I was to go along the line, solemnly shaking hands with each and every one as though I were royalty. This I found intensely embarrassing but I suspect that not to do so would have been considered disrespectful. They're such a formal people here. Chance meetings between acquaintances at the roadside can last interminably: there's a strict protocol of questions each asks the other about the health of the members of every stratum of their highly extended families, winding up with enquiries as to the general well-being of their respective animals.

Anyway, the introductions over and done with, we settled into the dining room to get to know one another a little. The young children were quite delightful, playing in the far corners, though constantly casting shy glances to see if I was paying attention to their games. Medicine has a grand total of eleven offspring, which would put even the most diligent of my Catholic brethren to shame. His wife, the not inappropriately named Nesta, looks surprisingly well for it.

Over against one wall, standing on the floor in the absence of a mantelpiece, I spotted a framed photograph, which turned out to be of their first-born. Looking at his mortar-boarded head above gown-draped shoulders, his face a personification of pride, his hands clutching just the sort of fake scroll I posed with for my own graduation at Cambridge, I found myself quite at a loss. 'What's this?' I clearly recall asking, though it was perfectly obvious to the dumbest ass what it was. I'd already been told that the lad has qualified in law. He is apparently settling into the equivalent of a pupillage in chambers in the capital. I just don't think it really sank in till I saw that photograph. *Why?* I work with his father and have great respect for his intelligence and integrity, yet I couldn't square the idea that the son might be a barrister just like any silk we read about in the papers back home. More than anything, I'm glad I made the trip for that humbling revelation of my own prejudices.

It was also very revealing to see Medicine amongst his family, the perpetually joshing side to him that I see in the field giving way to a slightly stern but clearly devoted paternalism. Of a sudden, the subordinate light-keeper, one of our own 'boys' – just the sort of fellow to whose backside 'Bar Fly' would think nothing of delivering a swift kick – was transformed into the adored, respected father. I began to get a real sense of what motivates him to work so far away: everything for the family. That, too, was very humbling, and peculiarly sad. Seeing him there, a fully rounded man like any other, his youngest children clambering over him, hearing his throaty laugh at their less than subtle attempts to gain my attention, I resolved never again to use the ubiquitous 'boy' by which we whites habitually refer to our African workers.

Anyhow, you won't be much interested in any of that – a long way from your Surrey suburbs. Nesta spends a good deal of her time making lace, which she sells at market in K— once a month or so. I was treated to a perusal of the current stock, and jolly lovely it was too: everything from napkins to huge tablecloths. A surface mail parcel will arrive with you in the next few months which I should be glad if you would store. I have the idea that these will make the perfect present for someone somewhere at some point.

I was thoroughly spoiled for my stay: chicken with the mealie-meal. To judge by some of the children's comments, this was a rarity in my honour, which made me feel distinctly unworthy. I passed a restless night on the floor next to Medicine's recumbent and loudly snoring form (some things about him do not change from field to home). We were roused by Nesta well before first light, in order that we might catch the one bus back to K—, which has been known to come past at such an ungodly hour. As we set off she presented me with my very own loofah, a crop of which I had been surprised to find growing on a tree behind the compound when I was shown around the evening before. I was greatly touched by the gift and promised faithfully to dry it out and use it. I assured her I shall think of her every time I scrub my back in the bath, an assertion which provoked a delightful bout of giggling.

Medicine and I then stumbled the ten minutes to the main track in the pitch black, the only light that from the extraordinary Milky Way (a dense rash of a million bright, bright stars, nothing like the poor cousin we might see in England's murky skies), and settled down on a rock to await events.

I'm not sure how well I am able to convey the next part. Gradually the dawn eased itself across the sky and the hoots and calls of the night started to subside. As it got light, all I could see was sparse bush stretching in every direction. Medicine's village was out of sight, and for a time we might well have been the only two men on earth. Peace like it I have never known. Then, ever so quietly at first, we could hear the snort and growl of an engine. I exaggerate not when I tell you that for the best part of an *hour* the sound of that bus waxed and waned, one minute so loud you thought it must soon be upon you, the next growing so faint that you doubted you could really hear it at all. And, all the while, absolutely no evidence of any bus could be seen along the entire ribbon of dirt road weaving its way through the low hills to the horizon. At one point, straining my eyes in an effort to catch a glimpse of it, I made out in the distance the figure of a woman walking along the track, bright sarong wrapped round her, a gourd balanced on her head, one arm raised to steady it. The sun was well up by then and she was shimmering in heat haze, one moment clear, the next a blur. I watched her silently for some time, Medicine humming softly to himself at my side, and I will swear, for all her walking, she came neither nearer nor further away. She was still the same sized, gently strolling, shimmering figure, when finally the bus hove into view and, displaying a far greater respect for the laws of physics, proceeded over the ensuing ten minutes to reach our rock.

I cannot fully explain these unearthly things. I merely recount what I saw and heard (none of which, I should say, caused Medicine the slightest perturbation). No doubt you will conclude that I have been touched by the sun. All I can say is that it seems to me absolutely the epitome of this maddeningly beautiful country.

All of which might be causing you to wonder about my earlier comment *viz* both loving and hating her. Well, not long after rejoining the D.O.S. party, my fortunes took a turn for the worse. I came down with an awful 'flu, aching to my core, absolutely prostrate, pains splitting my head, fever so high I was most often delirious. All the aspirins in the world had no effect. When capable, I had but one thought: malaria. Despite their cheery expressions and their, 'How are you, old man?'s, I could see in their eyes that the others thought so too. It seemed to take months (two days, in fact) to get me shipped back to K—. I passed this time in a bleary haze, soaked in sweat, shivering as though I were in the Arctic rather than roasting under an African sun, surfacing from confused amalgams of past and present into lucid moments in which my only thought was that I should never see England again. I don't mind admitting that at these times I was reduced to tears, the more so once I had finally apprehended the disconcerting fact that Urquhart had been detailed to stay at my side whilst we awaited my evacuation. Even Umbi's arrival produced only temporary relief – the journey back threatened to finish what the fever had failed to accomplish. Urquhart ordered frequent stops simply to get water past my lips, such was the incessant jolting from the road. Every bump and lurch sent lances through my head, making me so sick that I'd thoroughly messed the truck and my clothes were quite beyond salvage by the time we reached K—.

To cut a long story short, what with the time it took to arrange my evacuation, the worst of the fever burned itself out within a day of reaching K—, leaving me weak as a kitten but otherwise alive and well. The medico pronounced it some sort of viral fever (what it did to my insides I dare not say). I spent close to three weeks convalescing at Hildred's before I was deemed fit enough to go back up-country.

No sooner did I rejoin the party than I developed this large and painful boil on the groin. Feeling otherwise well, I ignored it for several days, eager to get on with the next tranche of triangulation. But the lack of attention had absolutely no effect in causing it to shrink away. In the end, after an embarrassing session with a reproachful Collingwood (who more or less accused me of an illicit visit to a house of ill-repute), I was packed back off to K— to be put in front of the same medico. He incised it to let out the 'pus', which turned out to be a large, fat, white worm. The sight of it wriggling between the blades of the medico's forceps caused me the most frightful shiver down my spine. The locals apparently call it a 'doodoo mbaya' (bad insect) but the quack called it the larva of the mango fly, which is very partial to laying its eggs in clothing spread out on the ground to dry, thence to burrow under one's skin.

The upshot of all this is that I've done practically no surveying since returning. This has been doubly frustrating because while I was swanning around in England, the party here took delivery of the very

latest in equipment. It's called a Tellurometer, and by all accounts it is
set to turn the whole business of mapping on its head. Humphries
trialled it in Kenya last year and it compared more than favourably
with our current trusty but time-consuming and labour-intensive
methods. I shan't pretend to understand every last thing about it, but
essentially it sends out a beam of X-waves or micro-rays or some such
nonsense, bouncing them back from a distant target. There's a fancy
electronic calculation involved: from the time it takes to get its signal
back it can measure the distance between it and the target down to the
nearest eighth of an inch or so. Put it in place of a theodolite,
substitute the target for a light source, and you get a direct, electronic
measurement of the miles between. It works in all weathers, there's no
need to be able to *see* a distant hill, it dispenses with tedious angular
computations, and in short, the days of triangulation as we know it are
numbered. As if that wasn't enough, each set comes equipped with a
two-way radio telephone, so one can speak directly to one's 'light
party' sixty miles away. No more Morse on the lamps. No more
frustrating hanging around wondering what in blue blazes is going on
across the other side of the triangle. I'm itching to have a go. Medicine
has been out with 'Bar Fly' and is positively raving about it. I think he
had a moment of dismay – an end to his signalling with Baya – but I
gather the pair of them now carry out their long-distance arguments
over the telephone and that this has tickled him a bright shade of puce.
Whether said Tellurometer is all it's made out to be, time alone will
tell, but it's causing us a good deal of excitement in the mean time.

All of which makes the current uncertainty over our work doubly
frustrating. In the past few months the country has witnessed some
highly unpleasant incidents at the hands of the T.A.N.A. – you'll
remember the articles in the foreign pages I showed you over the
summer? I think they've been encouraged by last year's events in the
Gold Coast, or Ghana as it now is. Prior to my homecoming, the
T.A.N.A. was merely a thorn in the side of the government, organizing
demonstrations and strikes in support of the independence campaign.
But thorns, at their worst, cause only pricks. In the last month alone
we've had news of two explosions – one at an oil depot outside the
capital, the other wrecking a railway goods yard – and of the deaths of

two district policemen killed in a shoot-out in the rural territories to the north. Several settler farms have been torched. The government here is trying to hush these things up, barely a word in the papers. We only got to hear because Hildred, as head of a civil service department, receives security bulletins. He sent word with the last transport: those two officers died not forty miles from here. Hildred thinks we should decamp to K— for a time, at least until this bout of nationalist agitation has subsided. Collingwood, who was surveying along the Kenyan border during the height of the Mau Mau uprisings, has seen it all before. His judgement is we should carry on as normal for the time being. To scuttle back to K—, in his opinion, would only strengthen the oft-encountered suspicion that we are in some way agents of the government and that our surveying is a cover for being up to no good. It's an uphill struggle to convince the local chiefs of our benign intent as it is. Urquhart and I are happy enough to go along with him for the time being ('Bar Fly' is predictably belligerent, the BF, oiling his rifle at regular intervals and talking loudly about what any T.A.N.A. 'trouble-makers' can expect should they stray into his sights). But Collingwood lost one of his N.C.O.s to the Mau Mau and I don't think it'll take too much more for him to toe Hildred's line. What with all this, plus influenza and mango fly larvae, I'm beginning to wonder if I shall ever get to have a go with the Tellurometer.

Rereading the above, I see I've struck an unnecessarily gloomy note – the result of having too much time to think, I shouldn't wonder. Despite the troubles, life continues on much as before, in fact. I've been confined to camp for the past fortnight, while my groin heals, and I'm thoroughly lulled by the daily routine. To break the boredom, and to ease myself back to full fitness, I've been undertaking daily hikes to the top of a nearby hill. Nothing too strenuous – it's a little under fifteen hundred feet and consequently not one that's been of any use for our survey. But I'm glad my convalescence has brought me up here. On my very first ascent I discovered three graves, long mounds of stone, lying in parallel just in the lee of the summit. The weather-worn wooden crosses revealed these to be of three missionary priests who died hereabouts in 1883. From the dates, I found that the youngest, Fr Sebastian, was just twenty-nine – not three years my senior. There's no indication as to how they came to meet their ends, though one should think, from the fact that they died within a month of each other, that an outbreak of some disease must have been responsible. And who, I ask myself, would have struggled up fifteen hundred feet to lay them to rest in this spot? The discovery of the graves – for all I know I am the first European to happen across them in the intervening lifetime – set me on a long meditation: pondering their lives, their histories, how they came to be here, what they might have accomplished, how they felt about this country, whether they are now completely forgotten or whether there might be some ageing niece or nephew deep in the heart of England, who occasionally remembers – on an anniversary, or birthday, or some such – the favourite uncle who became a man of the cloth and went out to spread the Faith, never to return. I noted their names in my diary with the no doubt fanciful notion that when next on home leave, I might look them up in an old Catholic Directory, perhaps track down family members, bring them news of their relatives' last resting place. I doubt I shall ever get round to doing so, or if I do, that I should have much in the way of luck.

But what a resting place! The more time I spend here, the more I can understand the labour of love of that ancient undertaker. I've taken to sitting on the summit for hours at a time, gazing out over the plains, my leisure allowing a heightened pleasure in the vast, beautiful land sprawling below. It is from here that I write this letter. In the far distance, I can see the railway line running across the savannah. Over recent days I've quite by chance observed a curious thing. During the day, at least twice as many trains run west to east, heading for the coast, as come back the other way. I've studied this carefully over a number of hours, sometimes in the morning, sometimes in the afternoon, and always it is the same. Whether there is some inexhaustible reserve of locomotives in the interior which daily feeds this eastward migration, never needing replenishment, or whether the night traffic predominates in the opposite direction, I cannot say. Logic dictates the latter, but increasingly in this country I have the fancy that the former may in fact be the case. Either way, recording these observations for you brings me to the realization that throughout the writing of this letter I have been attempting to answer for myself one

Wednesday 5 March, on board the 11.27 CrossCountry train to Edinburgh, various points Birmingham to Crewe

Whether the effect of food, the long hours travelling, or the stuffy air on the train, I cannot say, but after my lunch I soon drifted off. I'm not sure how long I slept; I neglected to look at the time when I awoke, so disorientated was I by the sight that greeted me.

Whereas I had closed my eyes on a pleasing rural scene, they opened on to a grim, orange-grey, subterranean world. A foot or two from me, on the other side of the window, a mass of people teemed, every individual going in a different direction, colliding with or side-stepping their fellows according to their agility. Faces flashed in and out of my field of vision, some nonchalant, others startled, hurried. Coming to a little, I realised we were in a station. The train was at a stand-still, muffled announcements echoed, shouts went up. Somewhere in the coach behind me a man was singing in an unknown tongue. But outside there was no sky. The light was fluorescent, the platform roofed by a low concrete ceiling, parallel pipework snaking across its underside. My first thought was that I was on the Underground, that somehow I had ended up in London. But a moment later and my confusion was resolved. Through the thinning crowd I caught sight of a sign affixed to one of the numerous concrete pillars, which informed me that we had arrived at Birmingham New Street.

It didn't take long to get underway again, our train creeping blindly into the brightness of daylight. Sluggishly at first, then gaining confidence, we made our way along the sunken embankment leading out of the station and on into the northern reaches of Birmingham, passing neon signs advertising shopping arcades above our heads: The Palisades, The Pavilion. Gradually we hauled ourselves up above ground level and I was afforded an uninspiring view across the city, buildings and roads stretching as far as the eye could see, dirty brick warehouses standing forlornly alongside the tracks, their smashed windows an eloquent admission of defeat. I needed no encouragement to return to my reading.

I don't mind admitting that of all Laurance's letters, that one was the hardest. To begin with it was pleasant enough reading. I was plunged into memories of that first full summer he spent at Surbiton Drive. It was odd at first, for us both, him pitching up out of the blue like that, hauling his trunk inside and reclaiming the spare room. He was brown as a walnut, far leaner than I remembered, his dark curly hair considerably lightened. I can remember looking at him, thinking: I don't know this fellow at all. And the change wasn't just physical. He seemed to give off an aura of unimaginable experience, and for the first few days he was restless, appeared unutterably bored. I tried to make him welcome but it was difficult not to think that it was me he was in some way irritated by. It was, of course, merely a general process of readjustment to London life after so long in the African bush.

And I had my own adjusting to do as well. I had become thoroughly used to having the place to myself, had become rather set in my ways. There were countless things that jarred. Perhaps under the influence of his surveying colleagues, Laurance had taken up cigarettes: the flat quickly became tainted with the smell of stale tobacco. And whereas before going to Africa he would sleep in late, he now rose with the lark. I would stumble bleary-eyed from my bedroom, the fact of his presence momentarily forgotten, open the bathroom door and be confronted by the spectacle of Laurance, fresh from his morning bath, cleaning his teeth at the sink, clad not in a dressing gown but in a towel wrapped round his waist. Coming home after work, I would walk into an oven – he insisted on having the fire on the whole day, protesting that despite the warmish English summer, compared with Africa it was decidedly chilly. But for all these initial difficulties, after a while he seemed to acclimatize – and for my part I did too. There was a specific turning point, roughly a week after his return. I've no idea why he left it so long – perhaps he'd procrastinated over unpacking – but I got back one evening to find him standing by the gas fire in the lounge, as though waiting for me, a whisky tumbler in his hand.

'What d'you think, then?'

I followed the direction of his nod. For a moment I couldn't see what he meant: there were the silver-plated candlesticks, the photograph of my parents, the one of me with my squadron. But leaning against the wall next to the wooden-cased carriage clock on the mantelpiece there was a new ornament, a long, thin, mournful African face, fashioned from a block of ebony.

'One of my boys made it – carved it by hand.'

'Splendid,' I told him. And it was, too, glistening subtly in the lamplight. The expression frozen on the face was somehow moving, striking me for some reason as ineffably sad.

'Glad you like it.' He took a sip of whisky. 'It's a present. A souvenir from Africa.'

Thereafter, things got on to a more normal footing. We resumed our evenings out, rediscovered our rivalry at the chess board. Friday nights became something of a ritual, eating fish and chip suppers while we listened to the exceptionally entertaining cluster of programmes on the Home Service: first the news, then *Pick of the Week*, followed directly by Laurance's favourite, *Bushwhackers*, with the *Goon Show* and *The Verdict of the Court* filling the hour and a quarter before the current affairs slot. He started to accompany me to the twice-weekly nets and soon became a popular addition to the loose confederacy of the Directorate cricket club – as much in the pub after matches as on the field of play, though his abilities with the bat were welcome too. In fact, as I think of it, therein lay Laurance's particular charm. As a rule, returned surveyors didn't mix with the rank and file staff at HQ. Some of my fellow players started out being rather in awe of him. But though he could easily have, he never put on airs and graces, he would throw his hand in with the rest of us. I remember feeling strangely proud when, after a fortnight or so, one or two of the others delivered their verdicts, taking me to one side, supping at their pints, nodding in Laurance's direction, saying, 'Nice chap, that friend of yours.' For those couple of months when Laurance was around, there was undoubtedly an added dimension to life. It was a fine summer, just as he remarked at the start of that letter.

But as I turned the pages, reading about the difficulties he'd encountered on his return to Africa, I was overtaken by a mounting sense of foreboding. This was the one. At the foot of every page my concentration wavered, my mind lost in recollections of the day the letter poisoned my life.

Not that I knew it at the time. In fact, that March evening in 1960, while I searched somewhat drunkenly through my letter rack, trying to discover those very sheets among the collection of airmail paper wedged in the back slot, such a thought couldn't have been further from my mind. It had been a wonderful winter. I had scarcely noticed 1959 expire, giving way to the youthful promise of the new year, so wrapped up was I in life. Work was going well, of course. The changes in the Directorate's financial footing had hugely expanded my role in Special Projects. I now had little to do with the day-to-day business of mapping. I had my own office, next door but one to the director's. Not a week would go by without my meeting a delegation from this company, that ministry, some overseas government, discussing how the Directorate might help them. I was responsible for the generation of thousands of pounds' worth of work. They were some of my most exciting times.

But it was my life outside the office which consumed me. Wars could have erupted, governments fallen, sterling could have imploded, I doubt I would have noticed a thing. Save for a few notable occasions, I neglected my parents. What had till then been weekly visits dissolved into sporadic appearances, invariably when I had been able to persuade Helen to make the journey to Lisson Grove with me.

Helen, too, was remarkably happy. Even now, these decades later, I would like to think I could take some credit for this, and it still causes surprisingly powerful regret to remind myself of the true reasons. You see, on one of our earliest outings, she had confided in me her intention to leave the Directorate the moment her probationary six months were up. As anyone would, I reacted coolly to the news. I had no objection to escorting her out, showing her some of the local sights, taking in the occasional film, generally helping to make her remaining days in London bearable. She was vague as to what she intended to do and as far as I was concerned, if in a couple of months she was to disappear from the scene, there was absolutely no point in allowing myself to become in any way attached or otherwise fond of her. I don't mind admitting that this taxed my resolve; I found her beguiling from the word go. It was easy to forget just how young and inexperienced she was – her free and easy manner; her endearing, engaging laugh; her confidence, so inspiring in one three years my junior.

Though I had first met her shortly after she joined the Directorate, it was several months before I plucked up the courage to approach her again. In part this was for want of a suitable opportunity. We never seemed to bump into one another in the library, and though I sometimes used to see her across the canteen, she was invariably chatting and gossiping with her peers. She didn't seem to notice me. Additionally, of course, Laurance was back on his second summer's leave at the time and, as before, he spent almost the entire time at Surbiton Drive. We picked up where we'd left off the previous year and my free hours were largely spent in his company. Nevertheless, soon after he flew back out to Africa I attended a routine Whitley council meeting. There was some item on the agenda, I forget exactly what, which put me in mind of the young trainee cartographer from F Section. Whatever it was, it gave me the excuse to seek her out, and – rather to my surprise – she appeared delighted that I had done so. I remember feeling bolstered by her reaction. On an impulse I decided to stick my neck out. And the exhilaration when she agreed to a date! Before long we were seeing each other quite regularly.

It was a time of extremes for me. From the outset, Helen was in complete command. I was left constantly endeavouring to keep up. Yes, she would love a cycle ride. No, it was no longer convenient, would I prefer to sit in and play Scrabble instead? On second thoughts, she intended to take her sketch pad – and no one else – to Surbiton Lagoon, she hoped I didn't mind. I did, of course, but I went along with it every time, content to await her pleasure, such was the pleasure I found in her company. I learned her every gesture by heart: the perplexed shrug, the conciliatory grin, the hands waving as though they might just manage to fish the word she sought out of thin air. They rarely did, but I accepted those wordless explanations as to why she was putting me off as uncomplainingly as I greeted joyfully her smile of accession whenever she did firmly agree to an evening out.

I think I can be forgiven for reaching the conclusion I did when, towards the end of her first six months, she announced that she had, after all, decided to stay on at Tolworth. True, she had told me on several occasions of the interest she was finding in her photogrammetry attachment, how the discipline had gone a long way to remedying her dissatisfaction with cartography. But I was so struck with her that I assumed – foolishly, I can see that now – that I was in some way involved in her decision not to leave. Yet I don't believe I was entirely wrong. As the weather grew cold, as frost rimed the bare branches, she became more constant. She ceased her habit of cancelling every second or third engagement. We spent increasing amounts of time together, got little chess tournaments underway, best of ten, that sort of thing. On a few occasions we trekked up to town, shelling out two-and-six for seats in the gods at the Old Vic, where Richard Burton and the rest were engaged in their five-year programme staging Shakespeare's complete works. And, as if no longer concerned about the opinions of colleagues at work, she began to spend lunch breaks in my office, often arriving early in her eagerness to make the most of the hour together. To start with we would address each other formally for my secretary's benefit. But as time passed we abandoned any pretence, closing the door behind a stiffly exiting Margaret, Helen sometimes having to stifle a giggle until we were alone. We discovered – the result of a chance remark – a shared interest in bird life and we would often spend some while observing the skies out of my window. For days, I recall, she remained sceptical that Tolworth could yield anything of note after the plethora of species to be found in her native Lancashire. But eventually she did catch sight of one of the kestrels which I had assured her patrolled the skies above the woodlands surrounding the Directorate. I had such simple pleasure at her excitement as she watched the bird hanging motionless in the sky, its wings rigidly outstretched, fine adjustments effortlessly harnessing the airflow a hundred feet above our heads, as it conducted its patient search for winter nourishment. I think that at that moment I dropped what little remained of my guard and started to view Helen as someone of whom I could readily allow myself to grow fond.

I only showed her that letter because of her naïvety. We were in the lounge at Surbiton Drive – I can picture us, a March evening after work, not long after my birthday it would have been, sitting at either end of the hearth, somewhat inebriated. She was holding a gin and tonic, waving it about, the ice clinking against the glass as she recounted an experience that had taken place in photogrammetry that day. I wasn't listening properly to begin with, more concerned that she didn't slop gin on the carpet. But I can recall the moment when she fully captured my attention.

'So there I was, scrolling through, painstakingly plotting the course of this river, when I saw – John? – I actually *saw* a herd of elephants. Clear as day, frozen for ever in this great long line, heading down to the water.'

While I could appreciate the charm of this, her first glimpse of real, living (illusory, fossilised) elephants, I was ill-prepared for her subsequent extrapolation. Of course, we were both rather drunk, and I suppose it was on this basis that I allowed her such a lengthy flight of fancy. I listened as she unveiled the fantasies that preoccupied her during those long hours in the darkened photogrammetry room. I do not intend to do her a disservice if I say that her notions were hopelessly romantic – lots of stuff about how she dreamed of voyaging beyond these shores, of experiencing life in far-off lands. And she thought she knew how she'd do it, too: she'd learned of the scheme whereby a select few cartographers were sent abroad to help train local staff. Leave aside the fact that she was a woman, that the only Directorate personnel to go overseas in those days were of the less fair sex. Nor did I take any comfort from the knowledge that candidates were required to pass the first part of the chartered surveyors' exams prior to departure. I had too good a knowledge of Helen's character by then to think that would pose her any problems. Ignore also the fact that, for the likes of us, foreign travel was still the exception to the rule (it was some years later that Thomas Cook started marketing excursions to the Spanish island of Majorca; till then a British seaside resort was the limit of most people's holiday expectations). No, what was most disconcerting about Helen's view of the world was the depth of her ignorance. From the way she was talking – under the influence as she was – it appeared that she had given scant consideration to the practicalities. As far as she was concerned, life in another country would be one long adventure: new sights, new smells, new cultures to experience. Not a thought to the discomfort, the loneliness, the strange food, the stranger customs. Least of all to disease, to danger.

When she finally finished pouring her heart out, I think I was lost for words, staring into her intense, glittering eyes. At a stroke I'd been transported from a cosy evening in the company of the woman I held in such store to an altogether more bleak vision: solitary lunch hours, returning nightly to my empty flat, save for weekends when I would travel to my parents, the only people to whom I could recount the day-by-day story of my life. I would receive more airmail letters to add to my collection and after a few months she would be thoroughly lost, in love with something else, would never return to this life at Tolworth. These were the selfish considerations, of course. But what was uppermost in my mind was the need to save her from bitter disillusion.

My only thought was of dissuasion. She was being starry-eyed. How seductive the foreign can appear when viewed from the security of one's homeland. After an awkward few minutes of flannel and flounder, I crossed to my desk, rooting hurriedly through my letter rack. Eventually I found what I was looking for. I can clearly recall crossing the room, holding Laurance's letter out to her, inviting her in no uncertain terms to read it before she came to any hasty decisions. I settled myself back in my chair and sat in silence, running my finger round and round the rim of my tumbler, staring into the flickering fire, while Helen read the letter from Laurance which had so chilled my spine with his talk of life-threatening disease, of murderous African nationalists, and of worms that burrow deep beneath your skin, feeding on your blood while they metamorphose into grotesque flies.

The journey from Birmingham to Crewe has been appalling, an unremitting, grey urban sprawl, city merging into town into city again, never a hint of green between. I find myself beginning to question Mrs Bryant's enthusiastic endorsement of the north as a picturesque region. At the time she seemed so confident, yet as mile after mile of decaying industrial zone slips past outside the train, I begin to wonder whether her judgement has been somehow influenced by the associated memories. She and her husband used to make annual pilgrimages north. The realisation that they will never share such undoubtedly happy times again may well have led her to illusory recollections. Even the most ugly, unattractive place could conceivably be remembered as beautiful if the circumstances in which one found oneself there were sufficiently joyous. It seems to me that to view anything through rose-tinted spectacles – to try to project on to reality something which it is not – is a deceit. It can only lead to disappointment and ultimately despair.

Despite the depressing nature of the landscape, I find myself unable to return to my correspondence file. There are few letters remaining, that I do know. One consequence of the bliss I felt when all was well between Helen and me was that I neglected my correspondence with Laurance. I never knew if he was hurt by this – I suspect not. He had, it seemed to me, made his choice by then, crossed the boundary that divides those who merely work in a foreign land from those who immerse themselves in it. From that point on, I imagine, communication from home was of less and less importance to him. And despite the convivial times we spent together during his periods of leave, despite the pleasure and enhancement I found in his company, I realise – with the benefit of hindsight – that we never really knew one another. Not face to face, at least. As he put it, some things are easier to write than to say out loud, and in my view that devalues the sentiment. If one truly believes something, if one is truly affectionate towards another, then one finds the courage to say so. I do not believe that one can ever know someone from their written words, a conclusion I would dearly love never to have reached but none the less one which I am sure Helen would also endorse.

Contemplating his letter, with that parenthetical reference to my having taken his catch, I realise that one of the few things which Laurance and I properly shared was a love of the game of cricket. His home leave was usually in the summer and on several occasions I took the day off to accompany him to a test at Lords or the Oval. And we both played. Outside of my professional life cricket was the one arena in which I rose a little above the average. Fairly accurate line and length at a medium pace, with an inconsistent ability to swing the ball given the right cloud cover, and useful enough with a bat to occupy the middle orders. The Directorate had a thriving club, at least until the late sixties, when it rather went into decline. We competed in the civil service evening league: home games were contested at Church Fields, Chessington, with adjournment afterwards to the Blackmoor's Head just across the green. There was a tremendous team spirit: there is something about adversity that cements people. We shared in the best of times, winning the league twice. We also suffered ignominious defeat, losing the play-off against our arch rivals Ordnance Survey at the end of the '62 season.

All of which is by the bye. The point is, cricket was one of the few things in which I felt myself to be on level terms with Laurance Wallace. He was an elegant player all right. I can still picture him batting for a scratch team of returned surveyors, striding down the wicket, prodding at a divot with the end of his bat, whirling nonchalantly around to resume his stance, taking delivery of a stinging in-swinger and dispatching it through the covers with an impossibly casual stroke of his Gray Nicholls. Whereas I would have run hard until the boundary was assured, Laurance merely ambled a few paces then grinned at the scurrying non-striker before returning to his crease, the haring fielder all the while struggling to catch the red blur of the ball before it crossed the rope with a sprightly upward hop. Nevertheless, for all his style and panache, on the field of play I was Laurance's equal.

Mostly we were on the same side and I would find myself clapping his back, even putting an arm briefly around his shoulders, in celebration of his latest wicket-shattering throw. But there were a few occasions when a collection of surveyors would get together and take on the HQ 'A'. I never succeeded in bowling him, but twice I sent him back to the pavilion by taking his catch. The incident to which he referred in that letter was straightforward enough, an uncontested snatch of the ball from the air as it raced towards me at mid-wicket. The second time was a couple of years later, the 1960 season – the summer before the 'Venice' Christmas party. The game was evenly poised, the surveyors down to their last wicket but with only nine runs to get. Laurance, number two in the order, was threatening to carry his bat and take the match into the bargain. As the fielding side, we were on the defensive, pushed back, trying to save every run. The situation was made worse by the fact that we had played out our best bowlers in an attempt to wrest a decisive victory earlier in the innings. It was a computer by the name of Butterworth who was bowling and his ponderous deliveries were causing Laurance no difficulty. Already he had sent two balls over the long-leg boundary with insolent pull shots.

Our captain, desperate to plug the leak, dispatched me to the rope. I saw Laurance look around, tug at a glove, then hitch his box into a more comfortable position, and I am certain that he noted my presence. As he settled down to take strike again I allowed myself a glance towards Helen. She was shivering a little, I could see, in the descending evening cool, standing back from the boundary not twenty yards from me. I recall smiling at her, hoping to offer some encouragement – whatever the outcome, the game would soon be over – hoping also to convey my gratitude that she had turned out to watch. Cricket was one of her least favourite ways of passing a Sunday afternoon but once or twice that season she condescended to accompany me. My smile was wasted. She never acknowledged my presence, staring ahead, her arms wrapped round her body, attention focused on the drama being played out in the centre.

Given a more capable bowler, the captain might have set a trap. Laurance displayed a blithe arrogance at the crease, never believing that he would be caught out. He had already demonstrated his fondness for the satisfying thwack of the pull, and an intelligent bowler might have sent him a short leg-side delivery, hoping to tempt him into improvident action. Butterworth was no such talent. He lumbered up to the crease, disappeared momentarily from my sight behind the umpire, and emerged to chuck a loose ball slightly to off, which pitched mid-way along the wicket, rising languorously on its way towards the batsman. I watched incredulously as Laurance, with no conceivable reason to be reckless, stepped purposefully across his wicket – way past his stumps – positioning himself so that the delivery was well to his leg. His bat swung. By the time the crack of contact reached me I was watching the ball soaring skywards, its trajectory taking it on an inexorable path to me at long leg.

I never took my eyes from it. I was aware of strangled cries from my team, 'Catch it! Catch it!' The ball reached the apex of its climb. I ran forward a little way, then back again, neck craning, trying to gauge its likely landing. For what seemed like an eternity, it hung in the air. The final seconds passed in an accelerated blur. Suddenly it was plummeting towards me. I was too far back, started to run forward – I wasn't going to get there. Hands cupped, stretching skywards, I lunged, my balance going at the same moment. The leather mass hurtled in, slapping against the heels of my palms with a stinging pain. I clenched them together but as I fell the ball slithered out of my grasp, bumping off my forearm and flying free even as I collapsed on top of it. I lay there, winded, the hard ball pressing against me, trapped between my chest and the unyielding ground. I twisted my arm, hidden from the rest of the field by my torso, grasped the cool leather, feeling the roughness of the seam against my skin. My fingers closed around it, then I hauled myself to my feet, holding the ball aloft, a smile on my face, my team-mates' cheers ringing in my ears.

I watched as Laurance shook his head, tucked his bat beneath his arm, and started the long, defeated walk from the crease. And that was it. A small thing. Only a game. To give him his due, he never questioned the honesty of the catch. But, although I couldn't see it at the time, the greater victory was already his.

As I turned to leave the field, my delighted team-mates' footfalls thudding as they raced to congratulate me, I saw Helen, her back turned to me, walking slowly towards our makeshift pavilion, the irregular mound of bags and jackets heaped outside the Blackmoor's Head. She never once looked back at me in my moment of triumph.

Just outside Crewe we pass sidings crowded with ageing coaches bearing the faded livery of the old Network SouthEast. I imagine the reason that they are so far from home has to do with refurbishment. In time, thoroughly valeted and sporting the bright logos of one of the new privatised train operating companies, they will wend their way back down south to resume their duties ferrying commuters between London and its suburbs. It strikes me as a sensible economy. Presumably all that's required is some cosmetic reinvention before they slot into the new order

'The wind of change is blowing through the continent. Whether we like it or not, this growth of national consciousness is a political fact.'

British Prime Minister Harold Macmillan,
Speech to the South African Parliament, 3rd February 1960.

Helen paused, satisfying herself that the narrow side corridor was deserted. Tightening her grip on the box files and map folder, she leaned an elbow on the handle, at the same time pressing her shoulder against the door, slipping quietly inside her photogrammetry room as it opened. She was being faintly ridiculous: this was where she was meant to be, after all. This was what she was *meant* to be doing. Sort of. Granted, Mr Stevens remained an indulgent supervisor, but she was supposed to be concentrating on proper work. The delicious days of her training, in which she'd been free to practise plotting from any old material she chose – so long as she gained experience in dealing with a wide variety of terrain – were long gone. To be caught wasting time in this fashion could give rise to problems.

Not that she could remember the last occasion when anyone had checked up on her. She had slotted seamlessly into the life of the photogrammetry section, her enthusiasm for the task resulting in faster than average progress towards competence – something of which Mr Stevens had repeatedly informed her in the days when he'd still entertained ideas of dating her. Before long she'd been accepted as one of the team, her work passed uncritically by the supervisors, thence to be sent out to the cartographic sections, her novitiate status quickly an irrelevance. A few hours spent now on diversionary activity wouldn't unduly affect her schedule. She was ahead of herself anyway, her current project – plotting a block of South Georgia – made easy by the undeveloped nature of the gorse-and-grass landscape and the unambitious attempts on the part of the island to throw up hills. Bumping her bottom against the door, she shut it firmly behind her, its solid clunk leaving her suddenly secure, any chance of discovery shut out along with the rest of the Directorate.

She placed the files and folder on the table and went to switch on the Zeiss. A quiet hum filled the room, gently enveloping her, making her feel safe in the utter normality of the moment. Opening the folder, she extracted the weighty collection of maps, each as large as an opened-out broadsheet, laying them carefully on the table-top in front of her. It took her some while to find what she was looking for – typically, the relevant sheet turned out to be close to the bottom of the pile. But eventually, there it was: a sudden condensation of black contours, brown shading to emphasise the topographical relief, and across it all, in a gentle arc, the stencilled label: *Mfubo Hills.* She let out a little sigh of satisfaction, smoothing the cool, thick paper of the map sheet with her palms. Suddenly wishing to postpone the moment, and wanting to be completely comfortable for the task ahead, she collected a wooden stool from the corner of the room before continuing her quest.

There'd been no identification of the actual hill in the letter, but it shouldn't be too difficult to track down. She turned her attention to one of the box files, cross-referencing the map sheet number with the contents detailed on the file's spine before opening it. Inside, she was confronted with an untidy heap of documents and pocket-books, all clamped together by a sprung metal arm. She prised it back; it creaked slightly, a half-hearted protest at being disturbed after so long tensed in the one position. Sliding her hands down either side of the jumble of documentation, she lifted it out *en masse*, spending the next few minutes sorting the slim, cloth-bound pocket-books from the paper-clipped sheaves of papers. Finally she was left with a neat stack of twelve books, their scuffed covers hinting tantalisingly at their pasts. She tried to imagine the surveyors, reclining on their canvas chairs of an evening, gathered around a crackling fire, the African sky overhead pitch-black save for its speckling stars, these selfsame brown book covers resting on their laps as they wrote their diaries, pens scratching softly at the paper while strange and chilling cries echoed out from the surrounding bush and the shadowy figures of dark-skinned natives criss-crossed in the background, just beyond the firelight, as they prepared the supper, fetched refills of whisky and soda, carried stores in readiness for the following day's safari.

J. M. Urquhart: Monthly Diary, September 1958. She put the top notebook to one side. *Capt. P. Collingwood: Monthly Diary, August 1958.* It joined the first. *L. D. Wallace: Monthly Diary, October 1958.* She stared at the words scrawled on the white square affixed to the cover, unable for a moment to comprehend that this was actually it, third in the pile; that it had contrived to be near the top – eager to the discovered – when she'd fully expected it to be the very last one she came to. Taking the pocket-book from the stack, she held it for a long while, anticipation tingling in her stomach, her breathing quickening. Even though she'd known logically that it would be here, the very fact of having it in her hands . . .

Fighting down an inexplicable urge to shove the whole lot back in the box file and return it all to the library, she rested the book in a clear patch on the table. She opened it at the first page, seeing the familiar neat writing, the long looping tails from the terminal letters connecting one word to the next, forming chains two, three, four words in length.

K—, 1958.

> 1st *October:* All clear from Dr Forsyth so expect return camp next transport. Groin still devilish sore. Tedious day moping around Hildred's, no one bar servants for company. He's got them well trained. Tried to persuade 'house-boy' (Joseph; forty-five if he's a day!) to have tea with me. Went wide-eyed and backed out of room before I could inflict irreparable damage on continuing job prospects.
>
> Weather exceedingly grim.

2ⁿᵈ & 3ʳᵈ October: ditto!

4ᵗʰ October: At last, Umbi heading up-country. Spared having to help load lorry on grounds of wound. Pleasant enough journey, Umbi in good spirits. Had to feign sleep after a while – not his fault; still well below par and not able to cope with his constant prattle. Pouring with rain; flooding in places made going v. slow. Arrived camp late, U. and C. out in field, B. at base. Passable evening all things considered. One too many sun-downers but nothing to get up for for at least next fortnight – Forsyth clear enough on that score. No confidence in own needlework.

MFUBO BASE.

5ᵗʰ October: First full day back at camp. B. off early, aiming link with U. NW of T73, though how far he'll get in present conditions God only knows. Glad to be on my own. M. has misfortune to be B.'s head light-man this trip – gave me very old-fashioned look when setting out, poor chap. Still, Baya with U. so he should get some fun out of it given half a chance. Caught up with some of the backlog of calculations in absence of anything more diverting.

6ᵗʰ October: Still behind with paperwork but couldn't raise game. Better weather so went for a stroll to get groin used to the idea. Prosper tried to persuade me to take rifle but heart not in it. Pleasant sensation of rediscovery. Easy to become blasé about this place what with work routine, &c. Beautiful moment deep in bush – not being especially careful but stumbled across group of impala all the same. Good ten minutes observing before they got wind of me – absolutely charmed by their huge eyes and dainty nibbling. Mother nuzzling young. Looked so at peace – strange to think that all the while their every sense is on the alert for danger. Glad didn't take gun.

7ᵗʰ October: C. back, successful trip. Weather held in his sector and he got good data from both theodolite and Tellurometer. Reckons comparison better than fair – bears out Humphries' results. Cracked on with paperwork under C.'s watchful eye. U. still out come nightfall. Solemn evening with C., reminiscing.

8ᵗʰ October: Groin healing well, definitely stronger. Scattered showers only. Long walk, took in hill. Missionary graves, 1883: Frs Augustus, Ignatius, Sebastian – Jesuits or I'm a Dutchman. Back at camp evening. No sign of U. but lots of fording coming from his end and rivers up at present. C. distant. Needs holiday in my humble.

9ᵗʰ October: Grim weather again, cooped up in tent, restless. Bedraggled B. rolled in around 3 p.m., unable to get to his section due to flooding. *Still* no sign U. – B. had no contact while out either. C. a little twitched, as are all. Pleased to see M. back; rather guilty to have moment of gratitude that he was with B.'s party after all. Tense evening. C. decided to set off after U. in a.m. T.A.N.A. troubles uppermost in all minds, Hildred's recent letter about murdered police especially.

10ᵗʰ October: Fitful night, partly tattoo of rain on tent, partly concern about U. Up early. C. looked awful but set off first light. B. and I tussled at backgammon – altogether more appealing prospect than admin. Demolished couple of bottles in evening.

11ᵗʰ October: Hung over; queer mood in camp. Walked again, stayed out most of day in spite of overcast. Took rifle more for safety's sake than in expectation of bagging anything. Huge relief evening, C. bringing back rather sheepish U. and all men more or less unscathed. Bloody fool got wrapped up in job, went way too far in difficult country and cut self off from supply dump. Lost most food 'on heads' while fording torrential river. Entire party have been dragging themselves back, nothing to eat past 3 days, getting weaker all the while. Managed to regain stores dump otherwise it could have got nasty. Two porters with infected feet, one in quite bad shape – Penicillin commenced immediately. Sobering, quite how easily this country can turn against one.

C. gave U. rocket in front of us all – respect for bush, taking stupid risks, &c. Gave Baya a severe ticking off, too, though what in hell's name *he* was supposed to do about it I don't know. Long discussion over serious amt. whisky evening: C. deeply troubled by Hildred's letter, thinks we should head back K—. Business with U. has put wind up him all right – had an N.C.O. meet untimely end at the hands of machete-wielding Mau Mau in '53. U. putting in lots of effort to change his mind – thinks it's all his fault, I suppose. Kept out of it myself, damned depressing all round.

12ᵗʰ October: Better day, strong sun, no clouds. C. seems to have slept it off, determined now to stay, at least for time being. Finally dispatched last of my paperwork. Climbed hill in celebration – very hot. Odd thing with trains.

13ᵗʰ October: B. and C. out with full-strength parties. U. and I confined to barracks pro tem, even though groin pretty much mended. M. with B.'s party again and none too pleased about it either. Took U. up hill – he confirmed trains all one way, more or less. Relief. Thought I was going mad.

14ᵗʰ October: Am going mad, or at least shall do if I don't get to do something soon. Camp-fever setting in. Leg now completely back to form, not even a twinge on climb. Half a mind to muster party and trek off in any case and to hell with C. Well behind with my section and not getting anywhere sat here twiddling thumbs. Mentioned idea to U. who practically had fit: quickest way to get C. to decamp and high-tail it back to K—. Fair point. Caught up with neglected correspondence, letters to A. and J. Took 5/- off U. over few hands poker in evening.

Helen closed the book and sat back on her stool. Not a single mention of which hill it was. She'd read countless monthly diaries in the course of her time in photogrammetry – checking descriptions of trig points, confirming altitude data with original observations – and never once had she known a surveyor fail to give exhaustive details of any land feature they happened across. Even if it wasn't part of their chain, they couldn't seem to resist shooting off azimuths at the very least. That was in the nature of surveyors, after all, the urge to describe the world in terms of numbers, angles. Yet this man could go on for pages, so it seemed, without ever once mentioning anything about the landscape. It was charming, of course, his entries bringing back vivid memories of the letter John had shown her. She hadn't followed all the ins and outs of the days' events, and in general his writing seemed less evocative than that in his letter. But nevertheless, there was the odd moment – those impala out in the bush – which stood out from the minutiae of camp life. She resolved to find out something about impala, at the very least what they looked like, from an encyclopaedia, or back issues of *National Geographic* in the public library.

But she was no nearer finding out what she wanted to know. Putting the diary down with a reluctant sigh, she gathered up the sprawled papers and notebooks and returned them to the box file. She let the sprung clip snap back on them, the impact flushing out a haze of startled dust. Taking the second file, she started the long trawl through until at last she found the aerial photographs corresponding to the map sheet of the Mfubo Hills.

That must be it, surely. She pressed her forehead slightly harder against the Bakelite eyepieces, willing her eyes to absorb the geography on which she gazed. Below her stretched an African landscape, black and white and grey, the tiny, low trees of the open bush clear to see. To the left, the flat ground erupted and heaved, the south-eastern Mfubo Hills stretching up, reaching out to her; stark, dark cols, scree tumbling off sharp ridges. The southern-most hill stood a little apart from the rest of the group, a rounded runt compared with the towering, angular masses of rock of the main range. Consulting the map, she cross-referenced the summit as 1,468 feet – almost certainly the hill Laurance had referred to.

She searched around, trying to discern any evidence of the base camp. By rights it should be located somewhere nearby. The vegetation pattern of the bush continued uninterrupted right to the point where the fertile soil of the plain was suddenly breached and penetrated by the hard, barren, upthrusting rock. No tents, no stores dumps, not even the charred ring of fire-break by which she so often located camps on other blocks. Leaving the Zeiss for a moment, she returned to the photography file, finding that the RAF had flown this particular strip in March '57, presumably well before the base had been established.

Gazing down the binoculars again, she scrutinised the hill, straining to pick out any nuances. What altitude had the plane been at? A good few thousand feet too high for the resolution she required. Almost at the moment she decided simply to accept that this must be it, she saw them: three minute grey-white flecks, no bigger than splinters, forming a little III just off the summit. No further proof was required. This was his hill.

Suddenly animated, she crossed the room and switched off the overhead light. The faint glow from the Zeiss guided her back to position. Swallowing self-consciously, she settled herself down and turned on the cursor, the tiny scars of the graves sharper now for the ambient blackness in the room. With practised hand movements she brought the little bright speck to a gentle landing on the top of the hill, exhaling slowly as if the very act of breathing would transport her thousands of miles away. Mentally, she tried to lower herself into the model landscape below, silently reciting remembered phrases from that letter, trying to transpose her viewpoint so that she was no longer looking down on the mountain but was rather sitting, just as he had sat eighteen months before, writing the letter. Yet he himself had been there a year and a half after these photographs were taken . . .

The mismatch of time dislocated her, jerked her back to the reality of her photogrammetry room, the drone of the plotter. Her forehead wrinkled against the moulding of the eyepieces. Gazing down on the plain, she endeavoured again to immerse herself in the scene. But for all her efforts, it was a hollow exercise. She had hoped, armed with the words of one who had actually been there, that she would achieve what had always eluded her, the rotation of her point of view through ninety degrees, the transformation from observer to participant, breathing the humid air, feeling the warm whisper of wind, watching the circling of buzzards high above a kill, waiting for the moment when their descent would tell of the lions' satiety. But it was no good, nothing could alter the fact that she was merely peering down at that part of the world, wasn't actually *in* it. *Illusion, illusion, illusion*, that's what Mr Stevens said of photogrammetry. Despite her huge effort of will, he was right.

She was half-way to the light switch when the knock came at the door. She froze in the darkness, her heart startled into a gallop. For a split second she toyed with the idea of hiding, of stealing swiftly to the dead space which would be formed by the door swinging open into the room. Whoever was there would quickly satisfy themselves that it was empty, would go on their way.

'Hello?'

The door handle squeaked and a wedge of light forced its way into the room.

'Helen?'

'John!' She laughed with relief at the sight of his owlish expression as he struggled to accommodate the dark interior. 'What are you doing here?'

He stepped inside, holding the door ajar behind him. 'Do you mind if I put the light on?'

'Please.' She turned without waiting and was already perched on her stool by the time the harsh electric glare burst from the strip light. She squinted at her watch, thinking that time might have flown and that the lunch hour must be upon them. It was ten to eleven.

She looked up quizzically, finding John hovering irresolutely by the light switch.

'Is everything all right?'

'Yes – it's nothing like that.' He cocked his head on one side. 'I was after some T— maps, that's all. Maureen said they were booked out to you.'

'Oh.' She swivelled on her stool, turning to face the map sheets spread over the table. She started to gather them, quickly burying the Mfubo Hills among the rest. For the briefest of moments she wished she still had long hair, something to hide the rising colour she could feel burning her cheeks.

'If you're in the middle of something . . .'

'No, no.'

'I could come back.'

'No, look, here – take them.'

Try as she might, she couldn't get the maps to form a neat pile, their edges sticking out to varying degrees. John was standing behind her now. She attempted to return them to the folder anyway; a couple of corners caught, dog-earing back.

'Careful!'

'All right!' She took a deep breath. 'Sorry.'

'There's no hurry.'

In the ensuing silence, she managed finally to guide the bundle back inside the folder. In his lack of help she could sense John's reproach. An irrational guilt pervaded her: of all the people to find her. She shouldn't have drawn the material officially. She was a frequent enough visitor to the library, she could have sneaked them out unnoticed. But she had to go and do things by the book.

'I thought you were working on the Falklands?'

She closed the flap at the end of the folder and turned to face him, holding it out, smiling nonchalantly.

'I am. Mr Stevens suggested it. Said my contouring still wasn't up to scratch on mountainous terrain.' She rolled her eyes. 'Practise, practise, practise. That's what he always says.'

Her light-hearted laugh was swallowed by the hush.

John took the folder. 'Still all right for lunch?'

She nodded, alarmed to feel tears prickle her eyes.

'I'll pick you up, shall I?'

'I'll come to your office.' She couldn't bear the thought of him turning up here again, repeating his entrance.

'Right you are.' He half-smiled then leaned down to kiss her.

The edge of the map folder nudged her breasts. His lips felt dry, taut. He'd been sucking a peppermint.

He disengaged, straightening up. 'Right. See you then, then.'

She nodded, managing a 'Yes' from the depths of the pit she felt herself to be in. She watched him silently as he crossed to the door, his gait awkward, as though aware of her eyes on his back. He'd got his hand on the handle when a thought struck her.

'Are you back in the library, then?'

He turned, frowning. 'No, I'll be in the office . . .'

As if noting the direction of her gaze, he looked down at the map folder in his hands. 'Oh, that!' He laughed, a brittle sound. 'No, the brigadier wants these.'

'The brigadier?'

He nodded again.

'What on earth for?'

He stared at her for an unnaturally long time, looking for all the world as though it was the first time the question had occurred to him.

'Do you know, I really haven't the faintest idea.'

c/o Overseas Surveys,
P.O. Box 152,
L—,
M—.
4th February 1959

My dear John,

I really am the most hopeless case, aren't I? Firstly, heartfelt thanks for yours of November last, which, had I had even the basic courtesy to inform you of my change of location, would have reached me a good deal sooner than it did. As you'll by now have gathered, after collecting a prodigious number of postmarks in its meandering around the continent, it eventually caught up with me here and your news was as avidly devoured and appreciated as ever. All except the bit about the increase in the rent. No doubt you've argued till you're blue in the face, but are you sure he can get away with such a hike? I shall adjust my banker's orders accordingly, though by now you'll be thinking the worst of me as I shall be a fair way in arrears on the difference. I'm not immediately in a position to make good the deficit: things are rather tight, no idea where the money goes. Life out here is certainly cheap enough but there are the inevitable commitments back home which swallow the greater proportion. Anyhow, that's no concern of yours, whereas the continued sweetness of our esteemed landlord most certainly is. I can do nothing but offer my sincerest apologies and promise a cheque for what I reckon to be the difference once next month's pay goes in.

Assuming we're still on speaking terms, I shall go on to recount the events of the last few months. From your comments you've clearly been keeping abreast of developments in T— and I'm sorry to confirm that it really has been the most dreadful time. In fact I'm not at all sure I should have felt up to writing much before now in any case. We left in a hell of a rush in the end – widespread unrest throughout the country and two settler farms to the east of the Mfubos put to the torch, the men slashed to pieces and the womenfolk spared to live out a ghastly future. Some of the things they endured I cannot begin to speak of. We spent an interminable time back in K—, holed up with Hildred, who was like a cat on a hot tin roof, charging about issuing orders one day, countermanding them the next. He's civil service as opposed to ex-military, unlike many of the D.O.s, and I think he'd have given anything to be able to blink his eyes and find himself on a bowling green near Dover instead of being in the middle of a crisis out here (a sort of inverse Drake). We were the least of his worries, of course, and we rather languished, waiting for London to creak into life and come up with some sort of decision as to our immediate futures. Meanwhile we tried to make the best of it, tying up loose ends and generally wrapping up the paperwork for the sections of the chain we had managed to complete. My heart really wasn't in it.

K— was a pretty miserable place, the atmosphere in the bars the antithesis of that which we had come to know. I found myself somewhat embarrassed by our temporariness as D.O.S. surveyors: at the first sign of difficulty, back we scuttle to the haven of the town and await our marching orders to a quieter corner of the ever-diminishing empire. The poor sops who've made their lives out here, for whom getting out would mean abandoning everything they've worked for – well, you can imagine.

I have to say, by the time H.Q. finally came through with the orders to transfer here to M—, the spate of troubles had more or less fizzled out – at least for the time being. But there was no sign of a corresponding return to good humour amongst the local white community. I think it has served to hammer home the inevitability of change. Please God there'll be no more bloodshed, but in my opinion T— is on a headlong course to independence and the only question is the speed and smoothness of the transition. The bitter irony is that further unrest is likely to slow it down rather than the converse. Allohya is out of gaol and is presently in direct talks with the colonial government, but you can bet your last shilling that at the first sign of more trouble he'll be back behind bars. As I write – from what news we get to hear – he's got a firm grip on the situation. But pessimistic commentators are already posing the question as to how long he can keep the more militant factions reined in.

All of which is just so much politics and leaves me cold. My first concern is with the personal tragedies, which came home all too forcefully in the final days as we broke camp and prepared to head back to K—. The day after we got news of the first farm to come under attack, Umbi turned up – apparently ignorant of the deterioration in the situation – with more supplies (unnecessary, though he wasn't to know that) and the post. Usually this is exclusively for us surveyors and as it happened I was sorting it out myself – four piles, mine the least weighty. In the middle of it all I came across a telegram and I was half-way to dropping it on one heap or other before the fact sank in that it was addressed to Medicine Usai.

Now, although the men only rarely get mail, I didn't think much of it to start with. He'd had one the year before, announcing the uneventful arrival of son number six or something, so I merely put it to one side. Once I'd finished distributing the rest, I ambled off to find him. I still have this vision – like a motion picture in my head – of walking through the camp, wading through a great crowd of the native chaps going about the business of breaking camp, blank, incurious looks being thrown my way, the sea of bodies parting in my path, leaving me direct sight of him, squatting on his heels beside the kitchen tent, whittling away at some wooden toy that was his current project, looking up, his face – which the moment before had been the epitome of concentration – splitting into a grin and the familiar greeting, 'Massa Laurents!' ringing out. He was still smiling when I handed him the telegram. His expression only changed when he registered that it wasn't something of my own which I'd come to show him – that it was addressed to him. It was only at that moment, seeing the puzzled concern descend across his features, that I got the first inkling that all might not be well. It took him an eternity to get the damn thing open and a second eternity to absorb the contents. Meanwhile I was 'floating' there, suddenly feeling somewhat detached from the situation, scrutinizing his face for any hint of what news it contained. I remember the unabated clatter and chatter of the men, and having the distinctly odd thought that they should give it a rest, give him some peace in which to read.

In the end, he handed the telegram back to me. I've absolutely no idea why I did this, but I stood there and read it out loud. I can only think that in the shock of the moment I assumed he wanted me to read it for him. That I regret most of all.

You know how these things are worded – no room for more than the most essential of information. 'Return statim. T.A.N.A. riot. Churchill grave. George.' My first thought was that our own Winnie was in some way ill and I couldn't get over the preposterousness of someone having sent a telegram to Medicine to that effect. I almost laughed and I can only thank God that the following sequence of thoughts took place swiftly enough to prevent me from so doing: Who is George? George is Medicine's son. How strange that he should be using Latin. George is Medicine's son who's studying medicine. Churchill is his brother, the barrister's pupil, whose mortar-boarded countenance beams out into their dining room hut from his graduation photograph propped against the wall.

Collingwood was a disgrace, in my view. It's true, the preceding weeks had taken a considerable toll on him and I can only put it down to the strain. He kept bleating on about the poor farmer and his wretched wife upon whom, &c. Mind you, I'm not sure that I was any more coherent. I recall saying again and again that Medicine had nothing to do with any of that, that he'd been working for the Directorate for ten years, a fact of immeasurable importance to me at the time. I truly believe we might still be there to this day, repeating our respective points over and over, neither of us making any impression upon the other, but for the fact that at a certain juncture I was overcome by the image of Medicine whittling away on that bough, his face splitting into a grin at my approach. I cannot recall taking my leave of Collingwood. The very next memory I have is of packing Medicine into one of the Land Rovers, over-revving the engine and the wheels throwing up a great cloud of red dust which was all I could see as I glanced in the mirror to take a last look at camp.

Throughout that long drive Medicine was mostly silent, brooding on things. All he would tell me was that he knew Churchill had fallen in with a radical element in the capital. It seemed pretty clear that he'd ended up on the receiving end of 'police action' at a demonstration – almost a daily occurrence at the time. The news reports invariably ended with details of the number of police and activists injured or even killed. I was all for driving Medicine right to the capital but as we raced into K— he told me, very matter-of-factly, 'The bus station, Massa Laurents, I think it would be wise to go on from there alone.'

And that was the last I saw of him. Despite the unrest in the countryside, I was determined to travel out to his home at least once during our subsequent weeks of enforced idleness in K—, but Hildred vetoed the idea in no uncertain terms (the threat of house arrest seemed to roll all too easily from his tongue). It is still a source of considerable regret and sadness that I left without further word from Medicine beyond his distracted goodbye and his rather pathetic gratitude at the bus station. Suffice to say that for all I know Churchill might very well be dead.

Collingwood was apoplectic on my return to camp – tore an almighty strip off me practically as soon as I stepped down from the Land Rover. I'm quite sure you can hazard a guess as to the content of the dressing down. Can't remember much of it myself, I simply stood there wondering how much redder in the face he could get before bursting some vital blood vessel and becoming the latest casualty of the whole sordid affair.

The upshot is, it's taken me all this time to rebuild my respect for him. Since arriving here in M— he has gradually regained his composure, but I don't think he should ever go back: his nerves are shot to pieces. We've been sent to augment the survey party here and, even though the situation in T— is currently stable, London – in its infinite wisdom – has decreed that we shall be staying put till the end of the tour. All I can hope is that after the summer we might be able to return to T— and pick up where we left off – I for one am determined to do what I can to help put the country on a better footing.

You should be in no doubt that for a while I did seriously consider my position – the whole episode, start to finish, left the foulest taste in the mouth. But for the fact that I can see little to go back to England for, and I have a vague notion that I would be in some way deserting should I hand in my notice, I would be on the next flight home. However, at time of writing, I am trying to knuckle down and am struggling to recapture my enthusiasm for the business of surveying, of which there is plenty to do out here.

I've written upwards of a dozen letters to Medicine, all of which have so far been posted in the wastepaper basket. For all that I wasn't in the slightest bit involved, I'm as responsible as the next Briton, and the camaraderie of more than a year in the field together is as naught. There's too much of a gulf; my skin puts me firmly on one side of all this, just as his puts him on the other. Which, I now appreciate, also goes a long way to explain Collingwood's behaviour at the time – and Hildred's absolute refusal to countenance my trip to see the one African family in which we could surely place our trust. Damnable, bloody, stupid business.

Anyhow, you should be assured that my frayed nerves are gradually healing. We're stationed on the coast. No hills, so the work is all Tellurometer traverses from 77′ towers which we assemble, survey from, dismantle and move on in a slow but comforting daily rhythm. Our base camp is near the shore and I spend most of my time there wandering the beaches, the waves of the aquamarine Indian Ocean soothing me much as they soothe the troubled continent against which they lap. It's tranquil, but it isn't home. I'm not sure where home is. The closest I've got to it, I now realize, is sitting at sunset outside a collection of tents in the massive shadows cast by the Mfubo Hills. At time of writing I simply don't know that I shall return there, yet anywhere else I think of comes a poor second.

All of which should make me consider you lucky. You sound so very content with your life, and I'm certainly looking forward to returning for a couple of months in the summer. In some ways, I envy your lot, yet I do not want it for myself. Just as well, really, as I cannot see how I should have it. But that is a story for another day. Presently I'm simply too tired.

Write to me at the above address if you can find the stomach for it. I realize I must be turning into the dreariest of correspondents and

Wednesday 5 March, half-past four, Preston station

Foolishly, I can now see, I have been dangerously absorbed in the past. This realisation forced itself upon me with my arrival here in Preston which, I was shocked to discover, unfolding the map as we approached the station, is close enough to my destination to appear on my Travelmaster of northern England. The bulk of my journey is now behind me, a brace of twenty-five-minute hops with a four-minute connection at Blackburn all that remains before I reach Clitheroe, thence to take the bus to Dunsop Bridge. Why had I given no thought to the end of my journey? Why had I allowed myself to become so wrapped up in what has long since gone? I suppose it was the notion of the hundreds of miles still to travel that made me so complacent, that prevented me, earlier in the day, from considering my somewhat delicate position. With so much time to ponder the problem, there seemed no need to trouble myself with it for a while.

But the fact remains – and it is all too stark now that I am nearly there – I have absolutely no idea where I am to stay when finally I reach the village that is my destination, nor whether Helen will be there to receive me as I hope.

Information, planning. *First a plan.* Stepping out on to the platform, heavy rain drubbing noisily on the roof high above my head, the temperature uncomfortably cold after the carefully regulated environment of the train, a chill breeze somehow infiltrating the enormous warehouse that is Preston station, the echoing tannoys, the bustle of people – all these things served to sober me up, drunk as I have been on reminiscence and recollection. I had to pull myself together.

Fortunately, my connection here is leisurely and Preston

station proved to be as well-endowed with telecommunications facilities as was Reading. On one of the far platforms I spied a phone box and I made my way directly there, pausing only to confirm, on one of the numerous television monitors, the platform for my next train (heading for Colne, though I shall alight at Blackburn) in thirty minutes' time.

I put in a call to Mrs Bryant at her home. Within a few seconds of her answering, I could tell it was a bad moment; her voice was querulous, upset even. Before I could speak, she reminded me: Wednesday is Mr Bryant's bath day, the care assistants were there already. In the background I could hear him shouting, the words (if that is what they should be called) unintelligible. Brushing aside my natural disinclination to be an inconvenience, I nevertheless pressed Mrs Bryant for the information I required.

'Was there a second post, any phone message?'

She hesitated, probably distracted by the battle going on in the downstairs bathroom.

'No post, one call, from the builders. They've got a date for starting work on the conservatory.'

There was something of a pause while I digested this news – strangely unconnected to me, as though she had imparted something to do with my distant past rather than something intimately involved with my present. In the gap, while I tried to formulate something to say, Mr Bryant's muffled bellowing continued unabated. And I was aware of another sound, which at first I mistook – although logic dictated it simply couldn't have been – for the noise of Mrs Bryant's duster, rubbing, rubbing, rubbing as she polished furiously the surface of the desk in my lounge. After a few moments I realised that what I was hearing was the noise of her rapid, shallow breaths.

'Thank you, Mrs B.,' I told her. 'In that case, I'll not keep you any longer.'

She didn't reply so I went on to make a clumsy attempt at terminating the call. Midway through my goodbyes I heard her say, all of a rush, 'Oh, Mr Hopkins, where are you now?'

I smiled at her sudden reanimation. 'Preston, Mrs Bryant. And it's raining – hard. But I'm getting there.'

That seemed to settle her and we managed to sign off with some semblance of normality. As I replaced the handset and scooped the unused coins from the little drawer, I tried to picture the scene at her home. Children may hate bathing but at least a parent has the size and authority to compel it. Wednesday is Mrs Bryant's most distressing day. She once tried to explain it to me, as the doctor had explained it to her: some sort of deficit caused by damage to the brain, a lack of control, a lack of comprehension, an inability to remember from one week to the next. *I've got to think of him as a little child.* Under such circumstances, being lowered by means of a hoist into a tub of water can apparently be a terrifying experience. And each time it occurs it is as unnerving as ever. I found it hard to understand myself, and in truth I think Mrs Bryant still does.

Walking back along the platform, I tried to think what to do about my predicament. There would be no word from Helen now, not before I turn up at her door, if indeed it is still her door. This is my own fault, though I can see no way in which it could have been avoided. Walking over the footbridge, back to where my next train should depart in twenty minutes, I turned the question over in my mind. I could not, of course, have written saying that I was coming all this way specifically to visit her. Besides anything else, that might have invited an outright rejection of my plan, a decision which I could quite conceive of her making in a rush and later coming to regret. So, writing that letter, I had dissembled a little, something about a centre of Britain project for the millennium on which I was now engaged. I would be visiting her area, a matter of research, reconnaissance. Perhaps I could call in? At the time of writing, I had been sure both that she would put pen to paper prior to my departure and that her response would be in my favour. Who would be able to say, *No, you can't come*, to an old friend who would be in their vicinity in any case? Now I can see things differently. It was, after all, a casual, incidental proposal. Perhaps she hoped that, if she simply made no reply, the idea might quietly be forgotten on both sides.

Preston station is of a certain age. Something about the architecture – the huge, metal columns, thick as ancient tree trunks, supporting a high, arching roof underslung with a network of great girders, the whole painted in red and black – puts one in mind of the Victorian era. The station has not worn well. As I walk, heading for a branch of QuickSnack which I spotted half-way along the platform, rivulets of rainwater pour from the leaking roof, forming large, dank pools on the tarmac underfoot. Here and there television sets, their brackets screwed into the venerable brickwork of the platform buildings, detail the progress or otherwise of various services. These days, I imagine, what investment is available is directed mainly at installing such items of communication equipment. The fabric of the buildings has to look after itself. It must surely be only a matter of time before a leak is sprung directly above a monitor, the resulting downpour shorting the electronics. That strikes me as rather dismal, hopeless even, and I arrive at the cafeteria in a gloomy state of mind.

I order myself a cup of tea, glancing at the newspapers ranged on a stand by the counter while the woman busies herself with the urn. The *Evening Post* announces, in a bold banner headline, that Preston's spy-cameras are to go ahead. My tea ready, I take myself to a window seat, prepared to sit out the remaining quarter of an hour before my next train leaves.

It now seems to me the height of folly to try to complete my journey in the space of the one day. I have no way of knowing whether there will be any accommodation for me in Dunsop Bridge, and the bus I am due to take is the very last service. I might end up stranded. I really have no choice but to stay overnight in Clitheroe, making the final leg of my trip tomorrow when at best I may have received some word, via Mrs Bryant, from Helen. Or when, at the very least, I shall have the ability to get back from Dunsop Bridge, back to the relay of trains which will carry me home again.

The matter resolved, albeit somewhat unsatisfactorily, I settle down to sup my tea, my mind – now that the concerns of the immediate future have been resolved – turning once more, unstoppably, to the past. I managed to finish reading the last letter I ever received from Laurance before we arrived in Preston. Somewhere in the swirl of conflicting emotions it aroused, a wry memory came back to me. When I wrote to him, I well knew what had been going on. Aside from anything else, I was still in the habit of reading his monthly diaries. I was perfectly aware that he'd been evacuated to M— when I sent my letter to his old address. It wasn't that I didn't want it to reach him. On the contrary. But I recall thinking at the time: if he hasn't had the decency to tell me, I shall act as though I don't know. When I eventually received his reply, I was chastened. I'd had no idea quite how intimately he'd been involved with events. I felt foolish, guilty. I knew how fond he was of his light-keeper, Medicine Usai (*that's* the surname). The very last thing he'd have felt like doing was to write with a change of address.

We had another fine summer in '59. If anything we eased ourselves back into the swing of things more quickly than the year before. Laurance seemed to throw himself into London life with abandon. He was full of good humour – sometimes, it seemed, almost overly so. Once more, he went down a storm at the cricket club. And he taught me to play backgammon – a game I had always associated with the moneyed classes but one to which, when introduced, I rapidly warmed. It became our little obsession that summer; if anything I was the one goading Laurance into just one more game, when perhaps he was thinking of turning in and I certainly should have been.

On a few occasions I glimpsed a more serious side to him, one I'd not seen before. It would usually be late in the evening, sitting in the lounge at Surbiton Drive, as we took turns shaking the dice, clicking our counters round the backgammon board, trying our damnedest to pounce on the other's unprotected pieces while at the same time endeavouring to keep our own men safe.

Laurance would invariably be weighing into a bottle of whisky and, although I would indulge in a gin and tonic or two, I like to think that my relatively clear head helped me hold my own against someone so much more experienced in the art of what Laurance termed 'gammonage'. At such times he would abandon his somewhat enforced gaiety and really get down to the task at hand. And from time to time, perhaps because of the whisky, perhaps a result of the lateness of the hour, he would begin to tell me something of his experiences in T— at the height of the troubles. Naturally, this was all very well for him, being utterly *au fait* with the tactics of backgammon as he was. He could chatter to his heart's content and still calculate in a split second the most advantageous moves to make with his latest roll of the dice. But for a relative novice such as myself, concentration was all.

So it was one August evening. The situation in T— had remained settled over the summer and it was only a few days before Laurance was due to fly back out to join his reconstituted party. Leapfrogging his more senior colleagues, he was to be made one of the youngest party leaders, a recommendation originating from the retired Capt. Collingwood and as much a surprise to Laurance as it was to anyone. We were on the final game in a series of seven, even-Stevens and everything to play for. I was in the marginally better position, with the vast majority of my pieces home and only a couple left to get past the remainder of his men. I can't remember exactly what I'd thrown, a five and a six quite possibly, but whatever it was, I was struggling. Laurance appeared to be doing his best to distract me, going on about the weeks they'd spent cooped up at the District Officer's in K— before being flown out.

'It was all very tedious,' he told me. 'I'd usually kill time hanging around Hildred's office.'

'Really?' I could see I had no option but to move my outlying counters, yet in so doing they would both inevitably become exposed.

'Poor fool was quite out of his depth, trying to make sense

of conflicting reports about where the rebels had gone to ground.'

'I see.' I really was in a corner. With both my counters exposed, it would take just one lucky throw of the dice for Laurance to pounce and send at least one of my pieces back to the start. He wasn't far behind. Such a set-back might very well give him the game.

'Not much of a tactician, Hildred. Used to get in a hell of a lather over how best to organise his men. The nationalists were past-masters at melting away into the hills at the first sign of trouble – locals, of course, so they had the lie of the land.'

Despite his chattering, I'd arrived at my plan. Best to use the combined dice score to get one man home to safety. The other would have to take his chances, but at least with only one counter left exposed Laurance would be very lucky indeed to score a direct hit. I made my move.

He gathered up the dice, dropped them into the shaker. After a brief rattle he flicked his wrist, sending the numbered cubes spewing across the felt.

'He used to plan the operations down to the minutest detail.' Laurance's voice had taken on a more distant note as he considered his options. I myself was making rapid calculations, trying to see if he would be able to land any of his counters on mine.

'Had some very comprehensive maps with which to do so, too.'

He couldn't do it! I'd been through every combination in my head, and whatever counters Laurance moved, none could get my last remaining piece.

'Which quite surprised me.' With a defeated air, Laurance picked up one of his men and marched it a little nearer its home. He still had four others in the field. The advantage was mine. I gathered the dice.

'I thought all the existing mapping was completely wrong.'

I was about to roll my next go. Something about his tone of voice caused me to stop.

'Sorry?'

'The old maps – they're completely wrong. I couldn't think where Hildred'd got his from.'

I inverted the shaker, heard the dice spill out with a dull thud on to the backgammon board. I ignored them, holding Laurance's gaze.

'Did you ask him?'

He nodded, took a gulp of whisky, never taking his eyes off me. 'Quite coy about it at first. Eventually he caved in. Seems there's some geographical section attached to the army – they supply mapping for any trouble spots anywhere in the empire, help suppress insurrection.'

His stare was making me quite uncomfortable – he hated to lose and I can only think that he knew the game was up. I shook my head and looked down at the board. My dice were showing double five! Last man home and two off the board in one fell swoop! I started to move my pieces.

'What none of us could understand was, where in hell does this geographical section get its maps from? If someone's got such good coverage of the country already, what's the point in us surveying it all over again?'

I tapped my final counter home then started the inexorable process of winning the seventh and final game, and that evening's series to boot.

'I'm terribly sorry, Laurance,' I told him. 'I really haven't the faintest idea.'

I never received another letter from Laurance Wallace. Shortly after he left that summer, Helen and I started to go steady and I immersed myself in her company. I suspect that was why I never seemed to find the time to write. Every now and again, though, I would fish his latest monthly diaries out of the library and keep track of his progress. Bit by bit he and the others worked their way westwards, charting the interior of the country, heading all the while for the Great Lakes and the Arc of the Thirtieth. One thing I did learn, however indirectly: Laurance got a new head light-keeper. The man, Medicine Usai, who had performed that role before the troubles, wasn't mentioned again.

The summer of the following year – 1960, the last summer we spent at Surbiton Drive – was altogether different. Laurance was subdued. In part, I imagine this was because things were becoming troubled in T— yet again. The pace of progress towards independence was too slow for some nationalists and further unrest was brewing. There was uncertainty as to whether he would be allowed to return to the country for his next tour.

In part, though, his change of mood might have been down to me. I couldn't spare so much time to entertain him. There was Helen to think of, after all. Helen, typically, was very thoughtful, concerned that Laurance shouldn't be left out in the cold. I lost count of the number of evenings the three of us spent together. Indeed, on occasion, I had to explain quite forcefully to her that I didn't think it would be too inhospitable for us to go out on our own. Laurance, to his credit, seemed to detect the tensions. For the first time since we'd started sharing the flat, he went on a lengthy trip back to Cambridge to see his family. The break was a great relief to me. Helen and I could slip back into our habitual ways. Yet even though he stayed away for three weeks, Helen remained rather volatile and ill at ease. At the time I assumed it was because she knew he would inevitably return. I tried to encourage her to forget about him.

When he did come back, he was even more gloomy. Despite all the efforts we made to make him feel welcome, he remained distracted. I imagine it is an altogether different kettle of fish playing friendly threesomes at Scrabble when one thrives on the direct head-to-head of the chess or backgammon board. He did still come to cricket, at least. That summer I caught him out, a glorious end to a thrilling and evenly balanced match. Nevertheless, I wasn't sorry when the end of August drew near and the time came for him to fly out to Africa.

Once I had the flat to myself again, I hoped that Helen and I would get things back on an even keel. Instead, one obstacle was exchanged for another. Earlier in the year she'd got herself on to the decorating committee for the Christmas party. To start with there hadn't been much to do, a bit of initial planning, drumming up support, deciding on the theme. But as the summer drew to a close the work started in earnest, and, if it's not unkind to say so, she became somewhat obsessed by it. Sometimes we hardly saw each other from one end of the week to the next, so wrapped up in painting was she. Mind you, the effort was well worth it. The decorations that year were superb, everybody said so: tremendously life-like representations of Venetian canals, the square of St Mark's. Even the canteen was transformed into what I was assured was a quintessentially Italian café. Nevertheless, as Christmas drew near, I began to look forward to a return to normality, began to relish the prospect of having her to myself again. Early in December, the situation in T— erupted, demonstrations and strikes paralysed the country, and I learned from the brigadier's office that the survey party was being pulled out. There was no transfer to another country this time; the surveyors were coming home. I received the news with a heavy heart. Laurance would be back in the flat for Christmas. It seemed I wasn't to have Helen to myself again for a while longer still.

Time marches on; the Colne train will be leaving in a few minutes. I drain the last of my tea, the sediment at the bottom of the polystyrene cup bitter on my tongue. As I stand, prepared to leave the QuickSnack, I notice something which completely escaped me when I came in, preoccupied with the prospect of refreshment as I was. In the middle of the small room is one of those tree-trunk-thick pillars, a massive, solemn column piercing the low glass ceiling of the cafeteria, towering onwards to meet the old station roof scores of feet above. Its huge solidity makes the construction of the QuickSnack appear flimsy, the plastic panelled walls insubstantial, the thin frames of the windows cheap and tawdry. The cafeteria strikes me as an add-on, a pathetic structure clinging to a leg of the Victorian edifice in which it is contained. Leaving my cup on the side, I pick up my suitcase and briefcase, and make my way outside once more, steeling myself for the final travelling ahead.

1,500 AFRICANS HELD BY POLICE
T—, 12th May 1960

Police cordoned off a T— village to-day after an African radio operator in a police car had been murdered last night while on patrol.

More than 1,500 Africans have been detained for interrogation. The police vehicle was severely damaged and two members of the patrol are still missing.
– Reuter.

'More tea, Helen?'

Mrs Hopkins raised the cosy-covered pot an inch or two, her free hand coming to rest on top in an intimation of the act of pouring.

'Thank you.'

Helen smiled into the silence, pushing her cup and saucer a little way across the table towards John's mother. As she watched the brown liquid streaming from the spout, a memory came unbidden. She was a child, her mother was re-enacting a favourite radio sketch, miming the very same act in a moment of playfulness during an otherwise austere supper. She could almost hear her voice, could almost see her eyes twinkling as she attempted to emulate the sound effects. *Tea, madam? . . . Glug-glug-glug . . . Milk, madam? . . . glug-glug-glug . . . Sugar, madam? . . . plop-plop-plop . . . Anything else, madam?* And Helen, delighted, hardly able to contain herself long enough before coming in with the punch line, *Yes! A cup, please!* Then her father, an exaggerated sigh: *Miriam! Do we have to?*

'Thank you,' she said again, retrieving her tea. Mrs Hopkins sat back, wearing a look of quiet satisfaction.

The silence continued awkwardly, punctuated only by a single quiet chime from the mantelpiece clock. Helen took a sip of her tea, her swallow sounding absurdly loud and gristly. She couldn't help herself, stole a glance over the rim of her cup: half-past three. Another half-hour before they could invoke the trains and decently make their escape. She looked at John's father, brooding in his chair at the head of the table. In the six or seven trips she'd made here, the old man had spoken about as many words to her. At the other end of the table John was compressing crumbs of Battenburg into a ball on his plate. She watched him lift the last morsels of cake to his mouth, start to chew.

'So, have you been doing any painting?'

Mrs Hopkins's tone was bright, brave. Helen settled her cup on its saucer, caught the mother's eyes flicking towards her son as if seeking approval.

'No,' she told her. 'There never seems to be time. Or inspiration, at the moment.'

'Oh.' Mrs Hopkins appeared genuinely crestfallen.

'But I shall be soon.' She spoke in a rush, thankful to have remembered something with which to reward his mother's attempts to converse. Hardly art, but painting, yes. 'We're starting to plan the Christmas party. We had the first meeting last week.'

Seeing her puzzled look, Helen elaborated: 'I'm on the decorations committee.'

'It's a long way off, Christmas.'

The observation was indisputable. 'There'll be lots to do. We're going to turn the Directorate into a little Venice.'

Mr Hopkins wheezed out a humourless laugh. 'That's something, isn't it? Painting and decorating. Not tried that, have I?'

'It's not that sort of painting, dear.'

A further chuckle, devoid of mirth, catarrh rattling somewhere in his chest. The sound made Helen nauseous. Why did his wife *always* have to take the bait?

'John tells us things are going much better at work.'

The statement was intoned as a question and Helen mentally

squirmed. The subject was best avoided, but if Mrs Hopkins *insisted* on raising it.

'Thank you, yes.' She forced herself to sound breezy, casual. 'I'm still in photogrammetry and I'm still really enjoying it.'

A clearing of a throat from the head of the table.

'And what is it you do there again?' Mrs Hopkins ignored the warning signal.

'Well, it's rather complicated.' Helen glanced at John, hoping for rescue. He nodded encouragingly instead. 'I plot out features on aerial photographs, make a sort of guide for the people who actually draw the maps. You have to scale the distances, fix the heights, mark the contours.'

'I see.' Mrs Hopkins smiled, broke off eye contact, turned to her husband. 'More tea, dear?'

Mr Hopkins pushed his cup forward without a word. Then, shifting his attention from the crockery: 'So, you'll be keeping the job, will you? Stopping in it a while? Till something better comes along?'

'Yes.' She tried to keep the irritation out of her voice. 'Yes, I rather think I shall. Until something better comes along.'

She shouldn't have added that last bit. The silence descended again, as abruptly as if a plug had been pulled from a radio. Next to the fireplace, where a mean little pile of coal crackled its defiance at its current adversary, the unseasonable May chill, John's father's battered brown suitcases sat in reproachful stillness, admonishing her latest act of flippancy.

'That's good.' Mrs Hopkins, trying to rescue a situation of her own making.

'And how about you, Dad?' John, compounding it.

'Oh, yerss.' Mr Hopkins, drawling the affirmative in exaggerated sarcasm. 'Sold two brushes last week alone, I did.'

She stared into her tea. What wouldn't she give to be out of here, striding the Lisson Grove pavements, past the ranks of council back-to-backs, legs gulping long yards of distance, free, away.

'So you've given up on that idea of going overseas, then?'

She stared at Mrs Hopkins, a dozen replies jumbled in her head. This was impossible! Her tugging one way, him tugging the other, the pair of them straining hard enough to rend her apart. John said nothing, as per usual.

'If you'll excuse me?' She rose precipitately, no longer concerned to meet anyone's eye, nevertheless appending an untruth for politeness' sake: 'All this tea.'

'They're terribly fond of you.'

'Oh, yes!' She was walking briskly, angrily, John struggling to keep pace beside her. 'It's perfectly plain.' She abandoned irony: 'I don't know how you can stand it.'

'You have to make allowances. He's been through a lot.'

'So have many people, John. They don't go out of their way to make life miserable for others.'

Allowances! She was sick of making allowances: *Your father's tired, Helen; Your father's a lot on his plate just now; He doesn't enjoy it any more than you do, love; If only you'd behave yourself; He can't be showing favouritism now, in front of the other children, can he?* She quickened her step still further, craving the solitude of her dismal little room, the chance to be alone with her thoughts.

John, who had momentarily fallen behind, caught up, grabbed her elbow, bringing her to a halt, forcing her round to look at him.

'He doesn't mean any harm. You've got to understand.'

She shook her arm free. 'Oh, I understand, all right! You learn your trade, perfect the art of stringing a tennis racket. Then the war, out you go fighting fires, see horrific things, and all the thanks you get afterwards is a machine that does your job far faster than you ever could, and – heaven forfend! – better, too. So you're out of work, selling brushes door to door, only you're no good at that, so you take money off your only son. And when he brings a woman home, a woman who might eventually have some claim on his life, his money too; a woman who thinks she might, just *might*, leave the job she's so incredibly fortunate to have . . .'

She stopped short, horrified at her spat-out words. His face looked suddenly pale, his mouth half-open, the lock of Bryl-creemed hair flopped forward over his brow with the violence of their confrontation.

'I'm sorry.' She felt awkward, spoke the words quietly. She hadn't meant to hurt him. He'd been nothing but kind to her.

'Did you mean that?'

'Oh, John, I'm sorry. I really shouldn't –'

'No,' he waved a hand impatiently. 'I mean, what you said about having some claim? On my life?'

She was confused for a moment, took a second to recollect her own words, felt her heart lurch when she did.

'Well, that's how *he* sees it, isn't it? Her, too. It's obvious.'

He gathered the swathe of hair, smoothed it back with a sweep of his hand, never taking his eyes from her. 'But do *you*? Is that how you see it?'

She felt her shoulders sag. The day was an absolute disaster.

'I should very much like it if you did.'

'Oh, John, I don't know.' She lifted her arms, let them fall to her sides. 'I didn't mean anything by it, I wasn't really think-ing.'

Abruptly, before she could finish trying to explain, he took a step forward, his hands grasping hers. 'Helen?' His eyes looked strange, the pupils big black pools.

'Please, don't!' She slipped her fingers through his grip, panic rising in her breast. She took a deep breath, tried to speak more calmly. 'Don't.'

His head dropped, leaving her staring at the sharp parting, his dark hair combed perpendicularly away on either side of the strip of scalp. A bus thundered past, the slipstream buffeting them. The noise gradually subsided.

'It's not that I'm not fond of you. I'm simply not –'

'All right!'

Without looking at her he started to walk, calling over his shoulder, 'Let's get on, shall we? There's a train at twenty-five-past.'

*

She didn't see him the following week. Tucked away in the photogrammetry room, desultorily plotting great tracts of wind-swept Falklands moor, she wrestled with remorse. She was worthless. She hadn't meant to lead him on. He'd been nothing but thoroughly decent towards her. It was so difficult to resist – when she felt so alone, so friendless. But she couldn't, she really couldn't. In her heart of hearts, she'd known, could see now what a tremendous effort of deception it had taken to convince herself otherwise. She'd tried to give him the right idea, remaining decently distant, confining their intimate contact to the briefest of pecks on the cheek, the lips. From time to time, the self-deception wearing thin, she'd tried to back out of it, put him off from one suggested outing or other. But after a while the effort involved had come to seem pointless. He would persist, always managing to change her mind, persuade her to come out on another date. And why not? He was charming enough, in his way, pleasant company. There was no harm in it, no harm in playing along, so long as she didn't send any false signals, so long as she made it clear that this was nothing but an affair. As to anything else. Well, she couldn't. She simply couldn't.

She didn't expect more than a passing contact in the canteen now. Why should he? Why should he come here, seek her out in her darkened cupboard, ask her out again, after the way she'd disabused him, the way she'd dashed his hopes? The thought made her feel desolate, hollow. What did that mean? Didn't that mean *something*? That, after all, she was fond of him? That she might even. That perhaps she. But even as she entertained the prospect, something inside her recoiled, reared away. It wasn't just his father, though that would be reason enough. There was something about the thought of. She was marking time, that was all. This wasn't the place for her, wasn't the life she wanted for herself. She didn't know what she wanted, only that it wasn't this. She was simply going through the motions, saving a dozen pounds each month, dreaming again – in the way she'd dreamed in her bedroom in the White House – of something better, something exciting, something *other*. No, she'd hurt him terribly. He wouldn't come back. And if he did, and she gave in to the pale affection she undoubtedly felt, encouraged him again, raised his hopes once more? That would be the cruellest thing. Not long, now. She had over one hundred pounds saved. In a few months.

He came the following Tuesday, a timid tap on the photo-grammetry room door, then he was standing before her. She gathered her resolve.

'I was wondering, would you like to come round tonight? Play a game or two?'

'No, John, I –' A hand, waving, searching for inspiration, returning to her side empty, clutching nothing but air. 'No.'

'Scrabble, not chess. I'd really like you to.'

'*No*, John.'

'Look,' an edge to his voice. 'Forget the other day. I was being stupid. Of course you wouldn't. I mean. I don't know what I was thinking, really.'

A slow shake of her head.

'Please.'

Another shake.

A hand run through his hair. Then, completely unexpectedly, the baited hook, the fluttering sparrow flitting over the fields below.

'I've other letters, you know. From Laurance. I looked them out the other evening. I thought you might like to read them.'

Sir David and Lady Rosemary Wallace
The Lodge House, St Helen's Passage
Cambridge

8th May 1961

Dear Mr Hopkins,

I should like to thank you very much indeed for the consideration you showed towards Annette, Rosemary and me on Sunday last. Your kindness in extending hospitality for what was a difficult and unannounced visit was much appreciated.

I must also apologize for any embarrassment we may have caused you. As I tried to explain, we really had no idea of the situation. I can only extend my sincere apologies and emphasize once again that our visit was occasioned by quite exceptional circumstances in which, as I'm sure you will understand, we had no choice but to travel to London. I do not anticipate that we shall trouble you again in the future.

Although the news you had to impart was by no means welcome, it is certainly preferable to not knowing, to being prey to the dark imaginings that were dogging Rosemary's and my twilight hours. I speak only for my wife and myself in this, of course. Annette has remained as upset as she was, I'm afraid to say, and I would imagine that, for her, it is a moot point at present. We've had a doctor call on her, one of the best men in Cambridge, but beyond a mild sedative there's apparently nothing he can do.

Though Laurance is his own man, has his own life to lead, makes his own mistakes, as a parent, one can't but feel in some way responsible. That might sound preposterous, but perhaps in time you will understand. Actually, I rather wish I hadn't written that. I hope you are *never* in a position to understand. What I am trying to do is to apologize for him.

The very least I can do is to extend the invitation to call on us should you ever find yourself in Cambridge. Even if I am not at home, Rosemary would be delighted to repay your kind hospitality.

I hope you will not mind my writing to you like this.

Yours sincerely,

David Wallace

Wednesday 5 March, on board the 16.46 NorthWest train to Colne

This train is a tiny two-coach affair and it reminds me very much of a bus. There are the hand poles, complete with button pushes should one wish to request a stop (although, from the announcements, it would appear we are scheduled to call at all stations en route). The electric doors open inwards, rotating through ninety degrees at the same time as they slide apart. Boarding at Preston, my ticket was checked by a guard who was in fact more of a conductor, a ticket machine slung across the front of his chest by means of a harness. As I say, more like a bus, and no more so than in the noise, the abrupt sensation of actually *travelling*. It is a far cry from the plush comfort of the CrossCountry InterCity, with its hermetic interior insulating one from the clatter and judder of its high-speed passage through the world. On this brief leg of the trip, I am constantly reminded that I am sitting in a steel tube hurtling along at a lively rate over joints and junctions and uneven sections of the track.

Basic, if modern, rolling stock, then, but smart enough in its own way. The doors, for all their omnibus qualities, swoosh to and fro with a repressed hiss at the various minor stations at which we call, ushering passengers off and on. And whereas the massive, barrelling InterCity was kept at a rigidly controlled temperature, barely the right side of the line between comfort and chill, this little NorthWest train is gloriously warm – delightfully uninhibited in its heating – a draught of hot air blowing on me from a grille in the ceiling immediately above my head. I find myself rejoicing in this excess of temperature, which makes me realise the verge of coldness upon which I have been these past many hours.

I seem to have run into Preston's rush-hour, but despite the crowd I've secured myself a seat. Directly across the aisle from me sits a young woman. In front of her is a pram. I can just make out a pink-hatted head, which makes it a girl, unless I'm very much mistaken. Outside it is raining still and the windows are steamed up.

Whether it is the immediacy of the travelling experience – the bouncing, rattling, jolting, hissing train on which I now find myself – but all of a sudden I feel I am rushing headlong. After the hours of patient progress, churning my way through county after county, my journey is abruptly in its closing stages. My passage is being expedited accordingly, each mile appearing to flit past faster than did a dozen before.

This sense of urgency has imbued my reading with new vigour – I feel somehow that I should finish studying my correspondence file before I alight at Clitheroe, before my journey is all but at an end. But this train is not conducive to reading. There is the rocking and lurching, making it hard to focus on the written word. Also, the seats are shallow, clearly designed for economy of space rather than comfort, forcing one into an upright, perching posture, no depth at all in which to sit back and be supported whilst one tries to read. I imagine that the usual passengers, tired after their day's work, are happy enough to be conveyed, any old how, to their homes for the evening. But for someone such as myself, the situation is far from convenient.

Nevertheless, I have managed to finish the letter from Laurance's parents. Or rather, from his father. As with their unexpected visit to Surbiton Drive – the doorbell chiming just after my lunch, causing a surge of foolish hope in my breast – his wife played no part. I can still picture her, sitting on the sofa in the lounge of my flat – it was my flat by then – worrying the hem of her tweed skirt, fretting with a curl of hair, rotating her watch again and again as though it could never feel comfortable. And all the while hardly ever looking at me. And beside her, strangely calm and still – until my words caused her to start sobbing – the younger woman, Annette.

No, I have to say, reading Sir David's letter again actually caused me a moment of amusement – a welcome, if incongruent, oasis of humour in the otherwise haunting memories. The very thought, had I ever happened to find myself in Cambridge, of calling on Laurance's parents, only to find his father away on some diplomatic business or other. Well, delighted Lady Rosemary would not have been.

I say that their visit was unexpected, and in a way it was. Yet had I possessed even an ounce of foresight, I could perhaps have anticipated it. It had been some four years since one of those letters had dropped on the mat at Surbiton Drive. Neat handwriting, blue ink, Cambridge postmark. A month after Laurance's awkward departure, they started to appear again. I thought little of it, putting them on the shelf by the telephone, though in truth I might as well have thrown them in the bin. Oh, I knew he was once again in his beloved T—. That much I had suffered to discover. Had I scored out the English address, written in the details of the Overseas Survey PO box in K—, they would have reached him. But I hadn't the slightest intention of forwarding his mail any longer. Would I have done differently had I known the worry I would cause? In all honesty, even with the weary wisdom of my accumulated years, I very much doubt it. I owed no debt to those people. The messiness of their lives was no concern of mine. Besides which, I wasn't causing them any anguish. Any agony they endured – wondering why there was no word, no longer knowing where to write to him – was entirely his responsibility. I can only imagine that the last thing he thought he should do was to let his family know his whereabouts.

So, I placed letter after letter next to the telephone, making a little pile, and there they gathered their share of dust. They came sporadically to start with, weeks apart, the writer perhaps reluctant to pen another whilst anticipating the imminent arrival of a reply. Gradually, they came more frequently. There was never a return address, of that I can be sure. Had there been, I would have sent them back, *No longer known at this address*. The Wallaces would never have made their unexpected visit. Or perhaps they would. When trying to understand how things went so very wrong with one's life, one visits – or revisits – every significant place. I toyed with the idea of opening the envelopes once, of finding the identity of the sender, in order to redirect them. But I didn't have the nerve. Opening someone else's mail. At least, that was the excuse I fashioned for myself. But I think perhaps I simply wanted to forget him. Whatever the reason, I was certainly glad that the envelopes were all intact, those months later, when – almost as an afterthought – Sir David asked me to return them to their author.

After the awkward introductions, my sheer bewilderment at finding a knight of the realm on my Surrey suburban doorstep, I invited them inside. Sitting in the lounge, cups of tea served in hastily cleaned best china, I was told that they'd had no word from Laurance for many months. A cough from Lady Rosemary. Sorry, *Annette* had had no word from him for many months – his parents had long since habituated themselves to erratic communication. Could I shed any light on the matter? They didn't want to approach the Directorate officially. That would cause . . . embarrassment. But they were worried to distraction.

I'm afraid that the nerve was still red raw at the time. So I spared them no detail, telling his family what their kinsman had done. Not even Annette's crying made me moderate my story, gloss over the more troubling memories. It was only when she finally spoke out, interrupting me at the bitter climax, her uncultured voice grating the air like the scraping of fingernails on a blackboard, that I suddenly understood. Though not for a while longer did I learn the true extent of Laurance's inconstancy, his fecklessness, his betrayals.

A goods train, truck after truck laden with coal, overtakes us on the outside track as we start to slow. Brakes grinding, we come to a halt in another station. I've lost count. I wipe a porthole in the condensation until I can see the name on the platform. Lostock Hall.

A young couple get to their feet further along the carriage and make their exit through the door at the far end. I watch them through my irregular rectangle of clear glass, already beginning to mist up again, as they walk alongside the stationary train. They are sharing a laugh about something. He opens an umbrella. Hoisting it aloft, he wraps his other arm around her; she tucks her head in at the angle where his shoulder meets his neck.

The sight provokes a strangely lonely, melancholy feeling. This is the oddest thing about travelling. I would never have heard of a place called Lostock Hall – the possibility of its existence would never have crossed my mind – had I not made this journey. The nearest I would ever have got would have been if, alone in the quiet of my lounge one winter's evening, I had unfolded my Travel-master and chanced upon its little grey square nestling on the black line of the railway which connects Preston to Colne. And even then, I would never have known anything of the people who live here, would never have glimpsed even that moment of affection between woman and man. It is disconcerting. Over how many other grey blobs have my eyes roved as I peruse my maps? How many other umbrellas have been raised aloft against the March rain, the couples beneath encircling each other with comforting arms, she resting a weary head on his shoulder? And what if I were to come back, in a month, a year, half a lifetime? Would I see instead a solitary man, his umbrella broad enough for two, wending his way at the end of another long day to an empty home?

The train jolts, edging forward once more. As we gather pace we catch the couple, pass them, leave them to their lives. Turning from the window, I look at the hand steadying the correspondence file on my lap. My skin is creased, weathered, stretched thin over the bulbous knuckles. In places it is marked with coffee-coloured blotches – liver spots, a natural part of growing old, as my doctor cheerfully explained when I brought them to his attention.

Bringing this ageing hand to life, I return the file to my

briefcase. Blackburn isn't far away, the connection there my most demanding. Four minutes to locate and board the train that will take me as close as a railway can to my destination, Dunsop Bridge.

POLICE STONED IN T—
Disorders Spread to West

From Our Correspondent
T—, 1ˢᵗ December 1960

K— had a day of disturbances yesterday as news filtered through of last week's unrest among African crowds in Kanchingwea in the Northern Province. At a T.A.N.A. meeting in the Memorial Gardens Mr. E. B. Chipangale told a crowd of 1,700 that the nationalists would not be deterred by the 'shooting at Kanchingwea'.

Police used tear gas and batons to disperse the crowd after several officers were injured by flying stones. A company of the King's African Rifles was ordered from barracks to guard the European and Asian schools and the power station.

AIRCRAFT USED

Several hundred demonstrators were arrested in the town but the majority fled into the surrounding bush. There were later unconfirmed reports of attacks on farms in the region.

R.A.F. spotter aircraft, armed with anti-personnel bombs, overflew the Western Province but were hampered by low cloud. As of to-day the main airfield is also being guarded by troops.

The Northern Province, where last week demonstrators attacked the Kanchingwea and Dolphin Hill airfields and where police opened fire wounding six people and killing two, was still uneasy to-day. Increased troop movements were evident in the area but Government sources refused to confirm that plans were being laid to re-take the airfields. Transfer of soldiers from the Southern Highlands was described as a 'routine precaution'.

Once the applause that marked the end of the director's speech had died away, people began to leave the tables, drifting and sorting into groups. Helen went with John over to some chaps he knew from the cricket club. She had nothing to contribute to the conversation. That suited her. She was able, with a modicum of nodding and smiling, to convey the impression of rapt attention, between times observing the rest of the canteen over the shoulders of her various interlocutors.

After a while someone in the group by the record player managed to get it going and the energetic opening bars of 'Rock around the Clock' boomed out. There were plenty of people already the worse for wear. Within moments a smattering of couples was more or less jiving, the catering staff continuing to dismantle the trestle tables around them. The music altered the atmosphere, rendering things more anonymous, cloaking conversations, masking the squeak of shoes on polished floor. Casting a glance at John, with his red paper hat perched at an angle atop his head, seeing him engrossed in a discussion with Butterworth, she felt safe to slip away.

She made her move boldly. If he should look up, all he would see was someone on her way to the ladies'. Once the press of dancers was between them she slowed, trying to gauge where best to station herself. She chose an unpopulated stretch of the far wall, standing herself at the zinc counter of a two-dimensional bar, cups of piping coffee spread along it at irregular intervals, the somewhat unconvincing plumes of steam fixed motionlessly in the air above the cups' rims. That hadn't been her. To her side was the short figure of the Italian barman – stripy aproned, black bow-tied, dark mustachioed. She sent him a nod of greeting. He continued to stare sightlessly past her, out into the hall, apparently transfixed by the spectacle of his absentee customers dancing, their abandoned espressos cluttering his counter. That *had* been her – her own creation, one of many. No name, but on a whim she decided he might be an Antonio.

Turning her attention from the two- to the three-dimensional, she searched the crowded canteen – the café – until eventually she saw him. Leaning casually against a pillar, chatting with a couple of other surveyors whom she vaguely recognised. She watched him for a long while, swallowing drily from time to time, resting her back against the coarse strip of lining paper on which the mural was painted. Not once did he glance across, show any sign that he was aware of her standing there. His face was deeply tanned. His hair – curly, tangled, unruly – was boyish. A challenge. She longed to run her fingers through it, snag the knots, tease them out. At the very least she was determined they would have a conversation. The summer had been awful; she'd so wanted to ask him everything about Africa, hear of his experiences first-hand. But there was hardly ever the chance. John was always hovering, his scorn for her 'romantic notions' sufficiently well rehearsed to make raising the subject distinctly unwise. Laurance had somehow sensed the tensions too, she was sure. Not once did he volunteer anything about his life in T—. At one point John had speculated, as part of a general discussion about his co-tenant's mood, that he was depressed by the troubles out there. She wasn't convinced. Every now and then she would look up from the Scrabble board, her next go decided, only to find Laurance's eyes on her, his gaze lingering a fraction of a second before dropping to his own letters. It was almost as though he was willing her to ask. As though John was inhibiting him, too. His unexpected return these few months later, his coming along to the party – she was determined to find a way to speak to him alone, away from John's unspoken disapproval.

An eruption of unheard laughter, three surveyors grinning, turning slightly from one another, a hand raised in mock protest, eyes crinkling. She felt suddenly vulnerable, exposed, standing there like this, staring. Were they laughing at her? She looked away, feigning interest in the dancing, tapping a foot, tilting her shoulders in time with the beat.

Haley gave way to Presley, 'Ain't Nothing But a Hound Dog'. Who gave way to Miller, some big-band sound for the older ones, she didn't know its name. Dancers retired, others took their places. Between the shifting bodies she glimpsed John across the hall, still talking, red cracker hat still on his head. At that moment he cast a swift look around before engaging once again in conversation. He didn't see her.

Naked pillar, no surveyors. Distracted, she'd missed him going, missed a golden opportunity. Everywhere she looked her eyes met turned backs, twirling forms, established huddles.

Wednesday 5 March, on board the 17.16 NorthWest train to Clitheroe

A flurried four minutes at Blackburn – no time to form any impression of the station. The last leg of the relay and, in spite of my previous determination, I can read no more.

In part this is the fault of the woman opposite. Wrapped in a fleecy jacket emblazoned with the legend 'Tog24' on the left breast, she is ostensibly buried in a book herself. Yet when I opened my file, intending to study the few documents remaining, I distinctly saw her eyes shift, trying to see what it was I was holding. With anything else I wouldn't have minded, but the final items, as I remember, are far and away the most sensitive in the entire collection. I tried retaliating, staring pointedly at the cover of her paperback, illustrated with a picture of an old pocket watch, the name of the author – Japanese, at a guess – both unpronounceable and unfamiliar to me. But she remained unabashed. I contemplated changing seats but again this is a small carriage and I couldn't hope to disguise the motivation for my move. It would be unthinkably rude. I put my file away in my briefcase.

And in truth, I am relieved. I've often heard the cliché and now I can testify to its veracity: travelling is an intensely tiring business. I imagine that hitherto some form of nervous energy has kept me going. But now my journey is almost complete, my reserves seem to have deserted me. Fatigue floods every corner of my body. I am exhausted. I crave a lie-down. Yet try as I might, and I have tried, I cannot sleep.

My mind is teeming with regrets. Why did I never guess what might drive a man such as Laurance to espouse the lonely, estranged life of the overseas surveyor? Laurance, who could clearly have followed almost any profession he chose. (My explanation? He dazzled me, as he dazzled everyone else, with his easy charm, his laconic humour, the gift of his company.)

And why did I never press him, enquire into his background, where he came from, why he rarely returned there? (I can answer that easily: it wouldn't do to pry. In my youth, form, protocol, dictated every facet of conversation. What a friend chose to reveal was all you were ever to know.)

And why did I further entangle Helen in his wretched web? Drip-feed her letter after letter when it was so clear what was happening, her obsession with his raconteur's version of life in Africa? My only concern being that when all his letters were expended she would cease to come round, would cease to bother with me. (I don't think I need answer that.)

And all these regrets seem to crystallise in a single moment in the lounge of Surbiton Drive, the day I had a knight of the realm, and his odd family, for tea. The moment when, in the midst of my revelations concerning Laurance and Helen's elopement, the wretched girl, Annette, gave voice to the only intelligible sounds she made in my presence.

I had no proof. She was only ever introduced to me as Annette. All she ever said was, *No, oh, not Laurance!* Yet the moment her jarring accent shattered my narrative at its painful climax, I knew.

Within an hour of the Wallaces leaving, I put pen to paper. I wrote Helen numerous letters in the weeks that followed. Starting each one, my mind would be alive with exhilarating, vengeful images: the letter arriving some weeks later, her apprehension as she recognised my writing, the deepening look of puzzlement as she read. But no matter how carefully I crafted my lines, I could never truly picture the scenes I so wanted to follow: the anger clouding her features, her marching, airmail paper in hand, through some African house, confronting him on the verandah, waving the letter in his face, demanding an explanation. His tongue-tied capitulation, her tight-lipped departure, the endless flight, her ringing my doorbell. My magnanimous welcome home.

As I completed each one, signing off with the same, unvarying, 'Much love, John', all I could see was: her finishing reading the letter, handing it to him. Him bowing his head, studying my stilted words. Her waiting, arms folded, suspicion on her face. Him finishing it, looking up with a disarming grin, rattling off some charming, good-humoured, raconteur's pack of lies. Her look of relief. Him laughing. Her laughing. Her taking the letter back and tearing it in two.

I shouldn't have cared what she would make of it – at least I would have done all I could. I shouldn't have cared that she would dismiss me as a jealous, deluded fool. I shouldn't have cared that she wouldn't come running back, her brief flirtation with the exotic, the unknown, the illusory, an unmitigated disaster. But I did. And, in truth, I harboured a secret hope that their affair would destroy itself without my intervention – such a burden of illusion. Certainly I never suspected they would take things as far as they did.

Every single letter I wrote to her I screwed into a ball and posted in the bin.

Telegrams in Brief

T—, 14th December 1960. – Governor Sir Leonard Hodge to-day declared a State of Emergency following three weeks of rioting and unrest in the Northern and Western Provinces and the virtual breakdown of public order in the rural areas. Curfews will come into force from 6 p.m. and further restrictions on public assembly are to be enacted. – Reuter.

For a time, they strolled beside a Venetian canal. On the far bank, bright flowers in window boxes adorned tall terracotta- and ochre-coloured houses.

She was glad she'd decided to wear her hair loose, cheek-bones accentuated by the pixie-like style. And it was a good choice of dress, the plain green wool warm and practical, yet cut in such a way that it hugged her body – enticingly, not at all indecently. Absent-mindedly her fingers found the chain hanging from her neck, came to rest on the small medal dangling from it.

'Is that a Saint Christopher?'

She glanced at her companion, found his gaze to be fixed on her hand. She laughed.

'Yes! My mother gave it to me when I came down here.'

He smiled. 'You're of the Roman persuasion, then?'

She nodded.

'Same here.'

She looked at him anew, raising her eyebrows.

'Oh, yes.' He laughed. 'Not practising, though. Can't remember the last time I went to mass.'

'How funny! Neither can I. I mean . . .'

She bit her lip. God! Why did she have to sound so crass, so stupid? She'd killed the conversation. Laurance fell silent, staring down at his feet as he walked. His stride was long, relaxed. Her footsteps seemed hurried in comparison. This was awful; she wanted to be bright, interesting. He must be regretting ever suggesting they leave the party. She tried to think of something else to say. Her mind was blank. They passed a gondola, the gondolier frozen in the act of propelling his craft forward, his passengers staring fixedly, evidently overcome with the beauty of the exotic city around them.

'So.'

His voice broke the silence. She looked up at him again, found that he'd taken a hand from his pocket, was running it through the tangle of his hair.

'So, he showed you my letters, did he?'

She felt herself grow hot. She'd mentioned it, shortly before they left the canteen, hoping to spark a conversation about Africa. He'd looked embarrassed, had rapidly changed the subject, not mentioned John, or the letters, or Africa since.

She tried a light-hearted laugh but it came out wrong. 'Yes, but only to put me off.'

His lips pursed, but he said nothing. On his side of the corridor they drew level with a large, ancient, wooden door, studded with rivets, a heavy, ornate metal knocker hanging in its centre. Suddenly inspired, she stopped.

'Come on, let me show you something.'

She stepped round him and pushed at the door. The minimal pressure from her hand caused both the solid slab of oak and the heavy iron knocker to cleave cleanly in two down the middle. She passed through to the other side.

The heat from the gas fire was making her feel quite heady – that and the gin. She took another long sip. The ice clinked as she lowered the tumbler precipitately.

'Anyway, so there I was, scrolling through, painstakingly plotting the course of this river, when I saw –'

He was no longer looking at her. He seemed more interested in the floor.

'John? – I actually saw a herd of elephants. Clear as day, frozen for ever in this great long line, heading down to the water.'

She felt wetness on her fingers, arrested her hand in the middle of another gesticulation. Inside the glass the G&T slopped wildly.

'Careful!'

'And did they? Put you off, I mean?'

She turned to face him, trying to think how to phrase her reply. The double doors swung closed behind him with a soft thud, shutting out the Venetian canal. He stood looking directly into her eyes, his gaze making her feel strangely vertiginous, a half-smile on his lips.

She couldn't think how to explain, raised an arm, let it fall to her side. 'Let me show you what I see.'

'Oh, come on, Helen. What is it Stevens always says, about photogrammetry? It's all an illusion?'

'John! This is important to me.'

The ice sounded another warning and she saw his eyes stray again. With a heavy sigh, she rested the tumbler on the small table beside her chair.

The wine rack was some seven feet high, innumerable bottles stacked on their sides, necks and corks facing out into the small side corridor. Helen grasped a handle protruding from between the bottles, levered it down, and pushed the entire structure through the wall.

A startled shout came from somewhere. She hurriedly pulled the rack back towards her, restoring it to its rightful position, a click sounding as she did so. She looked over her shoulder at Laurance, who was regarding her with a perplexed air.

'Oops! Already engaged.'

He smiled, a little self-consciously. 'Never mind, let's go for a walk instead. I'll tell you what *I* see.'

Over at the double doors he paused, turning to see her still standing there.

'No letters. Straight from the horse's mouth.'

'I'm serious, John. It's all I think about, stuck in that cupboard all day.' She sighed, noting his expression. 'Not all I think about. But I mean it. I feel really drawn.'

He spoke directly to the fire. 'I don't see why. There must be so many things to paint in this country.'

'It's not the painting.' She raised her hands, let them fall in her lap. 'I don't know. It's about doing something with my life.'

He looked up at her, held her gaze. She drew breath, gesticulated again, let her arm drop, fell silent.

Their breath billowed in grey-white clouds. It was freezing out here, but she wasn't about to voice a protest. He appeared impressively immune to it, inclining his head towards her as he told her tales of Africa. His hands were plunged casually in his trouser pockets, whereas she had her arms wrapped round herself in an effort to keep warm. As they walked across the expanse of frosty grass, they left two trails of dark green smudges on the silvery ground, marking the spots where their feet had fallen as they made their journey.

'I don't think you've considered the practicalities. It's not all glamour, you know.'

His voice came from behind her. She made no reply, staring at the fiercely glowing grille of the fire, her face burning. Eventually, with no let-up in the sound of his rummaging, she got to her feet. On the wall above the fireplace was the RSPB calendar she'd given him for Christmas, still showing February. Only a week late. She flipped the page over, revealing Falco tinnunculus *as the bird for March 1960. On the mantelpiece in front of her, ranged on either side of his African carving, were the birthday cards he'd opened the day before. One was from his parents, another from Brigadier Hotine. The middle card was a collective effort signed by the members of the cricket club, and there was an overly flowery one from his secretary, Margaret. The fifth card was from her, though she'd signed it simply, 'Much love.'*

'Here we are!'

She turned to find him holding a sheaf of blue airmail paper out towards her.

'Go on, read it. This is what life out there's really like.'

'Giggleswick.'

She leaned against the wall, searching his face for any hint that he might be having her on. 'Seriously?'

'Cross my heart. What's so funny?'

'That's only twenty miles from where I grew up!'

'No!'

'Dunsop Bridge?'

He wrinkled his nose. 'Never heard of it.'

'Laurance!'

'No, really. I was a boarder. Couldn't tell you the name of the next village along, let alone one twenty miles down the road.'

'So where are you actually from, then?'

'Me?' He paused for a moment or two. 'Nowhere really. My parents were abroad quite a lot – my father's in the diplomatic corps. I spent more time at Giggleswick than anywhere else, but that's not home.'

'So where are they now? Is your father out in Africa, too?'

He shook his head and gave a dry laugh. 'No, he got a Foreign Office post a few years ago. They settled in Cambridge. I hardly ever see them – the odd letter, nothing more.'

'Really? Why?'

'Oh.' He ran a hand through his hair. 'I'm what you might call a bit of a black sheep. Anyway, all this stuff about me. What about you? Your folks still in Lancashire?'

Half-way down the third page she realised what she was doing. But if John had noticed her start to reread the letter, he showed no sign. He was gazing at the fire, a forefinger running round and round the rim of his tumbler, looking for all the world as though he'd forgotten that she was even there. She resumed her reading, an exhilarating swirl of images competing for attention in her mind.

'Why, what does he do?'

'Teacher. Well, he's a headmaster, actually.'

'And, what? He couldn't find a job in all London?'

'No, well.'

'What?'

She drew in a deep breath, the crisp air biting somewhere inside her chest. 'There was an – indiscretion. With another teacher. He had to find himself another post, a very long way away.'

Tucking the final page at the back of the sheaf once again, she laid the letter down and took up her drink. John, perhaps nudged out of his trance by the movement, met her gaze. They stayed like that, neither of them looking away, the soft ticking of the clock and the hiss of gas the only sounds. Eventually he cleared his throat.

'What about your family? You'd never see them.'

She sighed. 'In case it's escaped your notice, I haven't been back since I got here.'

He had to stoop a little. She had to stand on tiptoe. She could feel, could *hear*, the blood pounding in her neck. She shrank with embarrassment, desperately willing her heart to calm itself, sure that he could hear it too. His lips were warm, soft. She'd had no time to moisten her own. She felt his hand press the small of her back, pulling her towards him. His other hand stroked her shoulder. He tasted of wine. Her calves started to tremble and she clung more tightly to his neck and shoulders, fearing collapse. She was reeling, even though she was perfectly still.

A faint noise grew rapidly in intensity, rushing, drubbing in her ears. It became loud, almost palpable. Startled, they broke their embrace, looked around. She swapped an alarmed look with the woman in another couple further along the wall. Now it was deafening, filling her senses. From behind the row of trees, their bare branches rimed with silver, a train burst into view, thundering past on the embankment above.

The noise receding, she turned to face him. For a moment he stayed staring after the departing train. In that instant, her eye was caught by a flash of colour behind a pane of glass in the wall of an adjoining block of offices. The window was partially iced, reflecting back a confusion of external images. Then, a movement. And a bright red paper hat could clearly be seen behind it all.

PART TWO

Great Britain has lost an empire and has not yet found a role.

Dean Acheson, Speech to the West Point Military Academy, 1962

Thursday 6 March, Starkie Arms Hotel, Clitheroe

A marvellous surprise. I pull back the curtains to be greeted by bright sunshine, the hilly moors stretching away behind the town bathed in it. After the incessant rain which accompanied me on the latter half of my journey yesterday, it is a welcome sight, engendering a real sensation of warmth and hope. The view, particularly if one ignores the near distance, is inspiring. The hillsides appear uncultivated – earthy, deep browns and dark greens. The straggling lines of dry-stone walls are the only sign of man's encroachment.

Although my usual practice would be to get dressed in the company of the presenters of *Today*, there is no radio. The hoteliers have provided a TV instead and I have this on in the background. As I shave, a weather man confirms the good news: the country will be warm and dry, a taste of the spring to come. The spattering of water in the shower prevents me hearing full details of Boris Yeltsin's annual state-of-the-nation address in troubled Russia. As I towel myself and dress in my best suit – the shirt has creased somewhat in the journey but never mind – a special report commemorates the tenth anniversary of the deaths in Zeebrugge of 173 people aboard the *Herald of Free Enterprise.*

The television is also on in the lounge bar cum breakfast room downstairs. The agenda has moved on, the latest spat over hygiene conditions in Britain's abattoirs only slightly spoiling my enjoyment of my bacon and sausages. After eating, I attempt to settle my bill. The landlady, on learning of my plans to visit Dunsop Bridge, kindly offers to mind my suitcase so as to save me carting it around. An appealing idea, but I decline. The outcome of my visit cannot even be guessed at and I should be loath to have to return here regardless of what unfolds. She seems to interpret my refusal as a condemnation.

'Was everything all right for you –' a quick glance at the cheque in her hands – 'Mr Hopkins?'

I strive to reassure her. The hotel is pleasant enough, the bed reasonably comfortable, my meals tasty and substantial.

'Clitheroe not to your liking?'

Suddenly I understand her bemusement. Arriving, bedraggled by the unrelenting drizzle, the previous evening, suitcase and briefcase in hand, I am now moving immediately on.

'No, it's perfectly charming.'

It's true, too. Something about the name, and the monotonous urban panorama as I traversed the north by train, had led me to expect a grim, grey little town, the air polluted and suffused with depression. But, rain-soaked as they were, my first impressions of Clitheroe were all to the good. Sturdy and appealing architecture, the buildings constructed with pleasing conformity from bold blocks of a local stone. The atmosphere, cleansed by the steady downpour, was crisp and refreshing. In trying to find a hotel, I walked the length of the high street, lined with quaint one-offs: Fred Read & Co., Gentlemen's Outfitters; Orchid Designs, specialising in wedding wear; D. Byrne & Co., Fine Wines and Spirits; Harrison and Kerr, Family Butchers; Harry Garlick, from whom Clitheroe's inhabitants can evidently purchase any white goods they desire. Admittedly the national banks and building societies were well represented, and I passed a branch of Threshers. But the overwhelming impression was of unfamiliarity, as though I had stepped back to the high streets of my youth, or arrived in a foreign country.

The landlady returns my cheque card with a resigned shrug, advising me at least not to miss the castle before leaving. Not wishing to appear ungrateful, I declare I will pay it a visit before catching my bus, an assertion I'm sure neither of us believes. Still, I think she appreciates the gesture, holding open the door and sending me off with a smile.

There is no opportunity to call Mrs Bryant – the first bus leaves a little after nine-thirty and she will be fully engaged in getting her husband washed, dressed and into the sitting room. Once he is installed in front of the television, she will set off for my own house, by which time I shall be in Dunsop Bridge. I resolve to catch her then, when she will be able to open any promising-looking mail I might have received in this morning's post.

The coach is at the stop when I arrive, completely empty, its doors closed. I wait around, a little nonplussed, a cold wind biting into me despite the sunshine. After a few minutes, a man, who turns out to be the driver, emerges from Wilson's the Bakers, chewing on a pastry of some sort, and makes up for his absence by carrying my case on board for me. There is a moment of indecision when he confronts me with the choice between single and return, then I buy my ticket.

'Nice day!' he observes as I pocket my change.

'It is. Certainly better than yesterday.'

His expression indicates his disenchantment with the previously inclement conditions. In the ensuing silence the onus seems unmistakably on me to continue the fledgling conversation.

'I might try and get out for a walk.'

'Going for a walk, are you?'

'I may.'

He seems satisfied with this, closing our exchange with a nod and a turn of his ignition key. The bus starts to quiver with the throb of the diesel. I shunt my case along the aisle, choosing a seat a few rows back. A thought occurs.

'Could you let me know when we get there?' I call.

'Will do!' he shouts, glancing in his wing mirror. Then to the tick-tick-tick of the indicator we pull out and the final stage of my journey is underway.

There are some things which cannot be assessed simply in economic terms. This bus service is but a tiny example. My fare – not much more than I was required to pay for a cup of tea in the Preston branch of QuickSnack – looks to be the only income the driver will make for the duration of his outward trip. We wend our way through open, rough grassland, racing a pretty brook flowing beside us, then cut through dense forest, the road clinging precariously to the sheer hillside. Along the way, we stop at a number of rural villages and hamlets. No one gets on. I suspect the return trip will be busier, but when one considers the cost of the bus, the driver's wages, the fuel, it is clear this is a loss-making route. Nevertheless it is, I imagine, vital. I for one could never have hoped to reach Dunsop Bridge without it. Yet it is all too easy to imagine some accountant, struggling to improve the bus company's performance, itching to ditch the service. Though a city-dweller myself, I have read enough of protests about such matters – the loss of post offices, cottage hospitals, transport links, local shops – to realise that it would be one more lifeline severed.

Not that I hold a naïve view of such matters. My career in the world of map-making has left me with a keen appreciation of the difficult choices which must sometimes be made in the light of cost and effectiveness. Right from the earliest days, when part of my role was to prepare briefings on mapping requests from countries throughout the empire, I saw first-hand the struggle of the directing staff to decide upon priorities. There was only so much money in the annual Colonial Office vote. Many extremely worthwhile proposals had to go by the board – maps that would never be made, development that would never be achieved, lives of hundreds or thousands of indigenous people that would be left to continue in the same poverty-stricken vein. In the early sixties, when the Directorate was pushed out from under the Colonial Office's wing, many saw it as the beginning of the end. But in truth, the challenge – of *earning* our place in the world – was more opportunity than threat. Through my stewardship of Special Projects, I had a hand in attracting income from all manner of sources. We didn't think in those terms back then, but I suppose one could say I was a marketing man, selling the considerable expertise concentrated at Tolworth to diverse companies and governmental bodies. The money I helped to generate went a long way towards subsiding the Directorate's main function, the taming of the world, the distillation of information, its representation in the form of maps.

I was, if I say so myself, a rather effective marketing man. In part, I suppose, this resulted from the difficulties I had experienced in my personal life. When the immediate upset had settled – when Laurance had removed his belongings from Surbiton Drive, when Helen finally left the Directorate – at that point I threw myself into my work. It was the very best time to do so. Demand for the Directorate's skills was never higher, representatives from all sorts of commercial organisations beat a path to our door. I was busier and more fulfilled than ever – at least between the hours of nine and five I could forget. It wasn't just the distraction. I also recall the very real sense that I was making a difference. Not just to the finances of the Directorate, though of course that was important, but to the world around me. There were so many projects – identifying forests to be harvested for timber, pinpointing mineral reserves which could be mined – that much of my work is lost in a blur. A few examples burn brightly across the years, however. I was responsible for brokering one of the earliest public–private collaborations, between the Directorate and the Shell-BP Development Company of Nigeria, which required detailed maps of the Niger Delta for the purposes of oil exploration. Shell-BP employed surveyors to do the Tellurometer traverses. The raw data was turned over to us, and we produced the 260-odd sheets that cover the entire delta at 1:25,000. As a result, vast areas of that country were charted, regions which would otherwise have remained undefined for many years. The outcome was mutually beneficial. The Directorate produced more maps. Shell and BP went on to play a crucial role in the development of Nigeria's oil industry. And the people of that far-off land, which I will never see, found jobs, income, prosperity. Another, more quixotic collaboration was with the Meat Marketing Board, which, in the early sixties, was searching for ways of improving beef yields. Our two organisations attempted to devise a system, based on the stereoscopic photogrammetric process, for 'mapping' muscle mass in cattle, plotting contours of the beasts' bodies much as we plotted elevations in the land. In this way, it was hoped, animals could be selected for breeding and a generation of 'super cows' would result. In the event this collaboration came to naught. Science moved on. New methods of intensive feeding, the growing use of antibiotics, ensured that each and every cow realised its maximum beef production potential. Nevertheless, it was projects such as this that made my professional life so rewarding, and which, consequently, helped me to forget more personal disappointments. In this I have been extremely fortunate. I could have been in some sterile, valueless occupation, labouring on some obscure aspect of British life – standards for road signs, for example, or dealing with correspondence relating to licensing laws. As it is, I can survey the years and derive a considerable amount of satisfaction from the realisation that my life has not been entirely wasted.

I am interrupted in my reminiscences by an alteration in the engine note. Tucking my handkerchief back in my pocket, I look up to find the driver negotiating a tricky right-hand turn over a hump-back bridge, the diesel almost choking on itself in the process. I have a scattered impression of buildings, of a broad, well-kept green stretching to where trees line the banks of a stream. There's a petrol station, and a post office, outside which we judder to a stop. I see the driver's eyes find me in the rear-view mirror. I'm half-standing by the time he cries out.

'Dunsop Bridge!'

'Folly to Ignore' Nationalism

From Our Parliamentary Correspondent
Sutton, 18th March 1961

In a speech delivered at Sutton, Surrey, last night Mr. James Griffiths, M.P., said that Parliament should make it clearly understood that colonial policy in all East and Central African territories was directed towards the establishment of full democracy. Until that was achieved, authority would not be surrendered by the British Government.

The forces of African nationalism were 'spreading like a bush fire', he said. It was folly to ignore them. The task was to guide them down constructive paths.

Much of the journey was above a blanket of cloud. But from time to time there was an uninterrupted view of the ground and Helen peered avidly out of the window, feasting on a glorious, full-colour vision of the land hitherto seen only as a black and white illusion in a darkened little room deep in the Surrey suburbs. Snow-capped mountains reached up to her, endless jungle rolled beneath her. She flew over carpets of high veldt savannah. The surface of great lakes glittered in the sunshine, a million points of light twinkling their welcome. By the time the aeroplane began its descent, her mind was churning with images, excitement, anticipation.

The temperature was the first thing to hit her, a forceful wall of sheer heat into which she walked as she passed through the doorway of the Comet. Pausing at the top of the steps, surveying the airport, she felt perspiration start to spring, as though her skin had come to a rash judgement. The stewardess thanked her for flying BOAC, smiling a smile of such sympathy that Helen compounded matters by blushing, wondering whether her expression could have so comprehensively betrayed her.

It wasn't the place itself which was a shock. The stops at increasingly basic airports at Rome, Cairo, Khartoum, Entebbe had prepared her, in stepwise fashion, for the facilities on which she now gazed. Forcing herself forward, climbing gingerly down the steps, she took a more detailed look at her surroundings. The airport consisted of a single runway, concrete shimmering with haze, a few hangars and maintenance sheds, and one long low building with two doorways: Arrivals and Departures. What held her attention, the sight to which her eyes strayed helplessly again and again, was the row of military aircraft lined up on the edge of the apron, their snub snouts nosing upwards as though sniffing the air. The jets, Meteors she thought, were patterned with browns and greens. Each bore the roundels of the RAF on its wings. She could hear passengers clattering behind her. The handrail was burning to the touch; she'd stowed her gloves in her handbag. She descended the remaining steps unsupported, trusting her heels not to let her down, then planted her feet firmly, for the first time, on African soil – albeit soil buried beneath a layer of slightly crumbling concrete.

A truck, pulling a trailer loaded with luggage, overtook her on the walk to the Arrivals door. A group of African workmen was gathered around a shallow trench, watching as one of their number swung his pickaxe again, again, each impact causing droplets of sweat to fly from his face, his shoulders, his bare torso. One of the on-lookers glanced impassively at her as she passed. She jerked her head abruptly forward, staring fixedly at the airport building. Would he be here? She felt suddenly appallingly exposed. What if he failed to meet her? What would she do then, stranded in the middle of God knew where, knowing no one in the whole country, the entire, endless continent?

She nerved herself. She was being foolish. Of course he'd be there. Did she think he'd abandon her? Even so, the sands of their short-lived relationship suddenly seemed shifting, subsiding. What, beyond a couple of months of heady romance, a diamond on her finger, bound them together? What if he'd had second thoughts, had gone off the whole idea? Realised what a fool he'd been the minute he returned here to T—? She quickened her pace, eyes locked on the Arrivals door, beyond which lay safety, the smiling face, the comforting arms. She half trotted the remaining few yards, sliding the handbag up her arm and grasping the bar on the heavy door.

The distinction between Arrivals and Departures was spurious. Both doors opened on to a single large hall, nothing but an insubstantial rope to funnel newly landed passengers towards the passport desk. She scanned the people milling about. No Laurance. Nauseous, she presented her documents to the official, declared herself to have nothing to declare, and passed into the main body of the hall.

Her eyes roved increasingly wildly, catching curious looks from total strangers. A porter, his white tunic contrasting profoundly with his ebony skin, grinned hopefully, his smile fading as she brushed past. A middle-aged European, his complexion ruddy and blistered, tipped his hat. A ragged African with a bunch of bananas in hand shouted out to her. *Where was he?* She felt herself start to shake. Then she saw him: a slightly stooped African, dressed in a grey, collarless shirt which hung almost to his trouser-clad knees, gazing uncertainly past her to where she had come from, a rectangle of cardboard held in front of his chest, on which were written the words 'Miss Helen Gardner'.

As they drove along, the old Bedford jolting uncomfortably, Helen gazed out of the window, mesmerised by the colour. Of the *trees*. Vivid red leaves on one variety, the more conservative foliage of another offset by flowers, of all things, huge yellow petals forming cups as big as her head. Even the hedges were exuberant, the walls of green freckled with pinkish-purple blooms jutting out on long stems.

From time to time she would become aware of eyes on her and turn to see the driver grinning in her direction, paying disconcertingly little attention to the road, one hand resting on the gear stick, the other draped casually over the top of the wheel. She returned his smiles, trying to appear friendly. She couldn't remember his name. The unfamiliar syllables had glided straight past when he introduced himself, so relieved was she that Laurance had sent *someone* to meet her. All she could recall was his description of himself as 'Massa Laurents's dreva'. He'd asked whether she'd had a pleasant flight. Yes, but the only thought that had come to her had been: would he know the difference? She'd felt instantly ashamed. For all she knew, he might be a seasoned air traveller. Yet the thought had paralysed her mind. The exchange encapsulated all the strangeness of her situation – what, exactly, was she doing here? She'd followed him numbly, meekly deferring to his insistence that he carry her cases from reclaim out to the truck. He seemed confident he would be taking her straight to Laurance, but when she'd tried to discover why he'd not come himself, why he'd sent this man in his stead, all she'd got was a genial grin, as though the fellow hadn't the faintest idea what she was asking.

Now, the Bedford prowling through the outskirts of K—, her mood soared wildly between panicked misgiving and awful wonder. She couldn't look everywhere at once: languid pedestrians clothed in exotic prints, street stalls stacked high with pallets of fruit, crudely painted signs above shop doorways, the jumble of dusty cars cluttering the street ahead. Things were at once familiar: hoardings advertising baby food, shop windows populated by mannequins. Yet at the same time they were completely other: the shop façades were wooden; policemen had white uniforms and outlandishly large helmets, their belts sagged with holstered pistols, rifles were slung over their shoulders.

'Miss?'

She glanced at the driver, who was regarding her with an alarmed expression, and realised she'd been laughing out loud.

'Nothing!' She smiled at him, shaking her head. 'I just – oh, never mind.'

He showed her his teeth, jutting at various angles, in an

uncertain grin, then looked back at the fairway, his arms suddenly rigid as his hands gripped the wheel. She laughed out loud again.

They pulled into the kerb on a residential street. As the engine coughed to a reluctant quiet, she tried to guess which of the verandah-fronted villas, each half-hidden behind the foliage of their front gardens, would be her new home. Peering past massive fern fronds, clumps of grasses twice as tall as a man, she searched for a familiar linen-suited figure coming out to meet them. The rasp of the handbrake preceded the driver's remark, much as the clearing of a throat alerts one to an impending difficult comment.

'Over here, Miss Helen.'

She followed the direction of his nod, momentarily perplexed by the sight of the large stone building on the far side of the road, its central spire oddly squat, a single bell hanging in the open void at its apex. Her insides somersaulted as she realised.

'What? *Now?*'

His chuckle seemed both pleased and embarrassed, his eyes white and wide as he delivered his next line with all the stiltedness of an amateur actor.

'Massa Laurents said I's to tell you: he's sorry not to have sent a white Rolls.'

The small group at the altar turned as one at the sound of her steps. Laurance smiled a broad greeting. The expressions of the two men in the front pew were of amused curiosity. The priest, a kindly-looking elderly man, spread his arms and mouthed a 'Welcome.' An electric excitement coursed through her. As she reached them, Laurance leaned to kiss her, taking her hand and giving it a little squeeze.

'This is Urquhart, and Hildred.'

The men murmured their pleasure at meeting her. She gazed back at her fiancé.

'*Laurance.*'

He ran a hand through his hair, tangled as ever despite the occasion.

Dear John,

The most difficult thing about writing is the not knowing – how you are, how it will be received. I shall be brief and if I cause any offence by contacting you like this then I apologize and please just throw this away and have done with it.

A couple of new surveyors came out to join Laurance's party last month and over dinner, in amongst the usual D.O.S. gossip, we learned that you have married. Congratulations, to you both. I suppose this is what has prompted me to write. If it's a foolish hope then – well, I simply thought, what with all the water that's now flowed under the bridge, perhaps we could patch things up, that's all. I always think of you fondly – Laurance does too, come to that. It seems such a shame, this whole situation, it really does. Don't you think so too?

So much has happened here, I should love to tell you about it. Africa is everything I hoped for and more. How I should ever cope with the busy-ness of London again I don't know. It's funny, I'd imagined that once here I would paint paint paint but I've hardly touched a brush in a year. It's not that I lack subjects – scarcely a day goes by without life throwing something affecting, inspiring, into my sight. It's just that I seem at last content merely to savour, appreciate, *live* in the world. I often wonder how you're getting along back there in Tolworth. If it's not too dreadfully difficult – oh, I don't know. I suppose I'm trying to say I'm sorry, for everything, for how it all turned out. I'm terribly happy and I hope you are too.

Laurance is up-country at present, settling the new chaps in. I'm missing him dreadfully – for the past year I've been going with him, helping out where I can. I love life in the bush, rough as it can often be. But they've almost reached the Arc of the Thirtieth now, the end of the chain. Laurance is *so* excited, driving on for the finishing line. You know how long he's been working on it. The nearer he gets the slower it seems to go. The remaining country is extremely difficult, a long way from even the humblest of dirt tracks, so it's all foot safari. It's largely uninhabited, thick bush, lots of strenuous work involved in cutting through it. They're so far from base camp, they have to carry supplies for several weeks. All very frustrating and no place for a woman, so I'm told, especially not one who's five months gone. So I'm confined to the K— bungalow and I'm driving myself absolutely *mad* with worry. It's foolish, I know – something to do with my condition, I'm sure.

I've gone on long enough. Please do write with your news if you feel at all like it. Laurance knows nothing of this – I'm acting on a whim – but we'd both love to hear from you. Hopefully we shall.

Fond regards, to you and to Margaret,

Helen

P.S. I'm sending this to you at work as I have no idea whether you are still at Surbiton Drive: I should imagine you've bitten the bullet and moved by now?

Thursday 6 March, Dunsop Bridge, nr Clitheroe, Lancashire

'Where are you *now*?'

Despite myself, Mrs Bryant's question causes a smile. So alarmed, so worried.

'I'm calling from the very centre of Great Britain and its four hundred and one associated islands!'

There's a palpable pause at the other end of the line while my housekeeper digests this obliquely couched information. But it seems she's not forgotten the contents of the e-mail which set this whole journey in train.

'You've made it, then! Did you meet up with your friend all right?'

'Not yet,' I tell her. 'Has any post arrived?'

'No.'

'Nothing?'

'No, well, a pizza circular, nothing else.'

My good humour is punctured. I was *so* sure there'd be a letter. There's an awkward silence during which I can think of nothing to say.

'Is it nice there?' Mrs Bryant asks. I can detect suspicion behind her outwardly bright tone. It dawns on me that my housekeeper has finally put two and two together: my obsession with the mail, the ambiguity of my plans, the fact that I've yet to see Helen.

'Lovely, Mrs Bryant. And you were quite right about the north – absolutely beautiful.'

It was a stupid thing to say. I listen with mounting horror as I realise that the noise I can hear is her muffled sobbing. I feel completely at a loss, no idea how to comfort her.

'Sorry, Mr Hopkins,' she manages eventually. 'Things have been very difficult with Bill.'

I nod sympathetically until I realise she can't see me. 'That's all right, Mrs B. Not to worry.'

We commune quietly with each other for a while, the digital display on the payphone counting down the money remaining to us. While my housekeeper collects herself, my gaze strays out of this unusual phone box, taking in the tranquil scene. The buildings across the green are old; whitewashed stone and slate roofs. There are very few people about – none, if I'm honest. The only sign of life is the flock of ducks on the green – a motley collection of mallards, teals and pintails – which has waddled away again, having followed me doggedly from bus-stop bench to call box, quacking all the while in expectation of bread, of which I have none. I rehearse a rendition of this anecdote in my mind, trying to picture how it would sound by way of a change of subject. But I'm not sure how appropriate it would be, so I keep my counsel.

'Oh, Mr Hopkins!' Mrs Bryant sounds suddenly in my ear.

'Yes?'

'Happy birthday!'

'Mrs Bryant!' I'm genuinely pleased – touched that she should have remembered, and glad to having something to say. 'How very kind of you.'

'I hope you have a lovely time.'

This is ridiculous. I mean no discourtesy, but there's really nothing I can do at this distance. Despite the fact that the display tells me there's twenty-eight pence remaining, I cut across her renewed sobbing, thank her again and tell her my money is all but gone. We say a hasty goodbye.

The call, far from bolstering my spirits as I anticipated, has left me deflated. I linger by the phone box for a minute or two, studying the design etched into the glass of the door, a motif depicting the major conurbations of our country slewed in an irregular circle, the cities represented by dots ranged at varying radial distances from a centre point which is, of course, this,

British Telecom's 100,000th telephone box. As a map it leaves a lot to be desired, absolutely useless for navigation, route planning, or indeed any appreciation of the proper spatial relationships between the various places. As a design, an artefact, I can see it has a certain charm.

This is getting me nowhere. I must make a decision. Half an hour ago, an absolute quiet bubbling up around me as the bus trundled out of earshot, I sat on a bench in the warm spring sun, biding my time. Gradually – reading Helen's letter from my correspondence file – the minutes passed until eventually I was sure that Mrs Bryant would have arrived at my house. I was so certain that I would have finally received word from Helen. As it is, if I am to proceed I shall have to do so blindly, with no idea how my visit will be received, if indeed it is to be received at all. Helen's postscript reminds me – if I needed any reminder – that I may call at the White House only to find that she's long since gone, no forwarding address known.

Walking back across the cropped grass, the chuckling and gurgling of the nearby River Dunsop providing a soothing soundtrack, I attempt to make up my mind. There can be no harm in popping round. I can always make my excuses if I detect the wrong sort of atmosphere. And there's the convenient artifice of my stated reason for being in the area at all, my fictional involvement with a centre of Britain project. She need never know. As far as she's concerned, I haven't retired, could very plausibly be engaged in just such a scheme. The ducks, seeing my approach, waddle towards me *en masse*, chattering softly amongst themselves. Doubts assail me. What if there's a very good reason for her failure to reply? Perhaps she still harbours resentment at the way our correspondence ended. Quite possibly she has remarried. What if she feels she has left her past far, far behind? My appearance on her doorstep could quite conceivably be the most embarrassing, unwanted thing that could possibly happen to her.

I reach the village shop – post office, grocer's, newsagent, all rolled into one. A sign in the window catches my eye. Pink and white, the familiar logo, O and S separated by an upright arrow. *Linking you to the real world.* This tiny, out of the way little shop is an approved stockist of Ordnance Survey maps. The realisation decides me. Somehow I am sure – if she still lives here – that ever time she sees that circular sticker, Helen will be reminded of me, of Laurance, of the earliest days of her adult life.

The woman behind the counter, cheerily overweight, looks up as the door chime jangles.

'Morning,' she says cautiously.

I echo her greeting, then dawdle awkwardly over by the map rack, pretending to look for something. The stock is almost entirely large-scale Pathfinders, reflecting the interest in the minute detail of local geography amongst the walkers who, I imagine, are the usual sort of visitor to the area. Eventually, realising that my attire – wool suit, shirt and tie, sensible brogues, heavy suitcase – rather undermines the illusion I am trying to create, I turn and sidle over to her.

'I wonder if you could help me?'

She gives a nod.

'I'm hoping to visit a friend, she lives in a house called the White House. Could you direct me?'

The slight narrowing of her eyes does not escape me. 'What's the name?'

I nod, understanding, yet surprised by such city suspicion in this little backwater.

'Gardner, Helen Gardner.'

She seems satisfied by this, embarking on a swift outline of the route I should take through the village. It doesn't sound too complicated. Fortunately, as it transpires. I have great difficulty in concentrating on what she's saying, such is my elation. So she is here! And still a Gardner!

As I walk through Dunsop Bridge, past the tiny working-men's club, over the eponymous hump-backed bridge, admiring the early daffs peeking cautiously above ground in front of a row of pretty cottages, my thoughts return to Helen's letter. At the time of receiving it, the very last thing I felt like doing was replying. I had washed my hands of the pair of them. I had painstakingly reconstructed my life and I wasn't about to rock the boat by receiving glowing, glamorous missives from half-way round the world which might force me to consider how my lot might otherwise have been. I still recall, as if it was yesterday, the resentment I felt when reading of how 'terribly happy' she was. At the time, of course, I took the remark at face value. Since that isolated visit from Laurance's family, I had some inkling of the alternative reality barely discernible beneath the words, like a shark gliding below the surface of the water. But I could have had no idea of how quickly events would conspire to explode the myth, for the fin to break through. For Helen to realise just how terrible her happiness was. No, at the time, all I knew was she was gloriously content. She hoped I was too. I buried the letter in a drawer of my desk, intending never to think of it again.

It is the only one from her I still possess. Margaret never knew of its existence. I suppose I could have instructed Helen to continue to write to me at the Directorate, yet to do so would have been in some way disloyal to my wife. Throughout the years of our subsequent correspondence – Helen writing from Dunsop Bridge to me at Surbiton Drive – the post would invariably arrive well after I had gone to work. I would return in the evening to find an envelope positioned on the mantelpiece and I would know that the Clitheroe postmark had been carefully noted. I soon learned, for the sake of a quiet life, to make their disposal in the bin an ostentatious act. I always read and replied to them, however, though I've no doubt it would have pleased Margaret no end were I not to have done so.

Continuing to receive letters from Helen was not without its personal cost, however. It served to keep the circumstances of my marriage in the forefront of my mind. Sitting in the lounge of an evening, Margaret knitting or sewing or listening to music, me wrapped up in my newspaper, or leafing through my old maps, the pair of us sitting there, occasionally swapping the sort of airy, inconsequential conversation one might expect between perfect strangers at a bus stop, we were never *unhappy*. Always perfectly content. In fact, I can honestly say that my life with Margaret was absolutely satisfactory. Yet the ground was featureless, lacking in contours, a flat and largely arid plain. No deep rift valleys, no soaring mountain peaks either.

I would often recall the moment of our coming together. How she stumbled across me in my office one winter's afternoon, how she stole up on me such that the first I knew of her presence was the light touch of her hand on my jacket sleeve. How I turned from my bleary staring out of the window to face her, saw her features oscillating between pity and a smile. How I saw a woman, some years my senior, more or less resigned to her place on the shelf, much as my library was filled with file upon file of photographs of how the world once was before it moved on. How she reached up and took the paper hat from my head, how my eyes were drawn by the flash of red as her hand fell to her side. How, as I looked back towards her, her lips pressed against mine. And we kissed. And we contrived an awkward embrace. Each doing for the other what no one else in the world was prepared to do.

White it may once have been, but the house is now a distempered grey. It has a pleasing elegance, though. Nothing showy: a central front door beneath a simple slate porch, each of the symmetrically placed windows a collection of nine small panes arrayed in the three by three grid of the frame. A stone path bisects the front garden, which, despite it being winter, shows evidence of considerable tending. The gate squeaks appallingly loudly as I open it and suddenly I feel peculiarly exposed.

Approaching the house, my breathing quickened no doubt by the effort of lugging my suitcase all the way from the shop, I scrutinise those windows for any flicker to indicate that I am being observed. The façade of the house remains impassive. At last I am at the porch. I wipe my feet on the grill which stands in place of a mat and clear my throat. The bell push is old, substantial; the brass is a dark, mottled brown, tinged with the green of the years. The button is inscribed with the superfluous legend, 'Press'. This I do. Somewhere in the depths of the house a shrill bell is heard to ring.

Opposition Seek Government Assurances

From Our Parliamentary Correspondent
Westminster, 14ᵗʰ April 1961

Responding to the statement to the Commons on T— by Mr. Amery, Under-Secretary, Colonial Office, Mr. Callaghan, Labour M.P. for South-East Cardiff, quoted the comments of Sir Edgar Whitehead, the P.M. of Southern Rhodesia, reported in *The Times* to-day: 'If we only clean up the situation in S. Rhodesia and nowhere else, there is a risk of reinfection. I hope we shall find the other Governments follow the example S. Rhodesia has set.'

Mr. Callaghan sought assurances that Her Majesty's Government was not contemplating copying the 'panic-stricken' measures of S. Rhodesia. He asked why the visit to T— of Lord Perth, Minister of State for Colonial Affairs, had been postponed. 'Have we not yet impressed on the Government,' he demanded, 'the absolute, essential first importance of getting on with these constitutional proposals so that the people of T— know where they stand?'

In reply, Mr. Amery said that it would have been quite impracticable to hold further talks against the background of recent rioting and violence. 'We were advised by the Governor,' he said, 'that to have gone ahead with the talks now would have risked provoking further serious disturbances.' Challenged on this by Mr. Johnson, Labour member for Rugby, Mr. Amery said it was advice from 'the man on the spot'. Mr. Callaghan suggested that if Lord Perth could not go to T—, then perhaps the Governor might come to London. Mr. Amery said that was a decision for the Governor alone.

His replies did not satisfy the Opposition and at the end Mr. Callaghan suggested that he had better resign.

She woke late, alone, found him in the 10′ by 12′, poring over a mess of papers at his desk. He looked up at her approach, stretched his arms above his head and arched his back against the canvas sling of the chair. 'Darling.'

She smiled, came to stand by him. He wrapped an arm round

her hips, leaned his head against her side. She rested a hand in the nest of his hair.

'Happy?'

'Very.'

They stayed like that for a moment or two until she remembered the reason for interrupting his work.

'I know this sounds funny –' she laughed – 'but how does one have a bath in this place?'

He laughed too. 'God! Haven't I shown you?' He pushed his chair back and stood. 'Come on.'

The tub was fashioned from half an oil barrel, cut longitudinally and laid, open side up, atop a couple of curved wooden cradles, the whole contraption shaded by a tree at the very edge of camp. Beneath the bath, Helen could see blackened charcoal in a pit. Laurance peered circumspectly over the rim.

'We'll have to get those blighters out to start with.'

Helen suppressed a shudder at the sight of the snakes coiled at either end of the bath.

'They're perfectly harmless.' Laurance gave her shoulders a squeeze. 'Get trapped in there like spiders do back home.'

Seeing her hesitation, he said, 'I'll ask some of the chaps to fill it. Fire'll take a while to get going but it'll be piping hot in an hour or so.'

Helen looked around, finding several porters idly watching them from different parts of the tent village.

'Laurance?'

He raised his eyebrows.

She couldn't think how to voice it, cast a deliberate glance around again instead.

'What?'

'*Laurance!*'

He laughed, unable to keep it up any longer. 'It's all right! Once it's ready, we'll put a Whymper up round it!'

Helen dropped his loofah over the side and eased herself back again, smoothing the wet hair over her scalp, her shoulders coming to rest against the warm metal of the tub. A haze of steam rose from the surface of the water. Her knees protruded like mountain summits through cloud. Outside she could hear the sounds of camp life: a shout from a porter, the rhythmic hacking of firewood, a burst of laughter, a man humming quietly to himself as he walked by. She felt tingly. Her hand slid up to rest on her breast. The thought of those other people – men, exclusively – carrying on all around her, while she lay there, naked, flushed with warmth, hidden from sight by the insubstantial canvas walls of the Whymper. She glanced at the front of the tent, checking that the flaps were securely overlapping. Then she inhaled deeply, watched the steam eddy and swirl as she let her breath out. Whenever she moved, the water slopped and lapped, whispering the secret of what lay inside to anyone passing by.

The water took a long while to cool but eventually she climbed out and started to dry herself. More footsteps, approaching. An attempt at knocking, the canvas billowing with each tap from a hand. She wrapped the towel hastily round herself.

'Only me.' The flaps parted and Laurance ducked inside. 'Nice bath?'

By way of reply, Helen extended her arms, pulling him close when he came within reach. She stood on tiptoe, her mouth finding his, the warm breath from his nostrils tickling her cheek. Aware of a sudden internal heat, she pressed herself against him, her thighs moving to embrace his. One of his hands came to rest in the small of her back, insistent pressure drawing her further forward, fusing their points of contact. His other hand stroked her head. She felt water drip cool on her bare shoulders.

He broke off the kiss. 'Here! You haven't dried your hair!'

She smiled, adopting a gently accusatory tone. 'You only let me bring one towel.'

'Ah!'

He nodded, pursing his lips, his fingers easing their way between skin and towel, releasing the hurried tuck that held it in place.

'Well, we'll just have to use this one, won't we?'

She had many favourite moments. Striding behind him, sweat staining the back of his shirt, as they trekked through the bush, the tramping of the porters behind her the one indication that they weren't the only two people on earth. Crouching by his side as a solitary white rhino snorted and pawed the ground not twenty yards away, Laurance making theatrical shhing gestures to the rest of the party. Standing on the summit of a towering mountain, absolutely miles of empty country at their feet, as he squinted into the Tellurometer, calling out the readings, and she scribbled the observations down for him.

But the times she was most content were the evenings, the abrupt sunset of the equatorial region colouring the sky a thousand different shades of orange and red. At such times she would sit back in her chair, listen to the hiss and guttering of the Tilley lamp, the unceasing sounds of the bush around them. And her eyes would rest on him, hunched forward in his own seat, a thin trail of blue-tinged smoke spiralling up from the cigarette between his fingers, the notebook open on his lap, pencil scratching methodically as he wrote the events of the day in his monthly diary.

'I remember you mentioning him in your letters.'

As if admonishing her for the inadvertent reference to John, the Land Rover started to buck furiously. She glanced to her right, searching her husband's profile for signs of annoyance. He kept his eyes front, ramming down to first, concentrating on navigating the least injurious route through the sudden run of potholes where she presumed a stream crossed the track in the wet season.

'Yes, of course,' was all he said.

They drove on in silence for another few minutes until she saw a large boulder to one side, painted white, beyond which a narrow turning departed from the dirt road.

'Bus stop,' Laurance explained, swinging the wheel.

As they flashed past the rock, Helen glimpsed the words 'Bon Voyage' daubed in red across the whitewash.

They ploughed off left, following what was little more than a path, a screeching choir of bushes and stunted trees scraping the sides of the Land Rover as they went.

She rested a hand on his thigh and his face eased into a smile. 'Not far now.'

Sure enough, about half a mile further along, the track suddenly broadened, terminating in a grassy clearing. As they came to a halt Helen started to make out huts scattered about, partially camouflaged by the trees. Within seconds of Laurance extinguishing the engine, a different sound reached her ears: the laughter and excited gabbling of other human beings. From every direction figures materialised, mostly children, huddling together in small groups as they stared, astonished, at the Land Rover. For a long moment the soft ticking of cooling metal under the bonnet was the only sound, then the chattering and laughing started afresh. Laurance laid his hand on top of hers.

'I think you'll cause quite a stir.'

She found herself completely charmed by Medicine's wife.

'You are well-come,' Nesta kept repeating, singing the word as two distinct syllables – when she met them at the gate to the compound, as she ushered them towards one of the largest huts, as she finally persuaded the last of her excitable brood into a line, as Helen finished shaking hands with what must have been a dozen children – their names washing over her in wave after wave of unfamiliarity – every one of whose feet she noticed were bare.

'You are well-come!'

Helen smiled gratefully at her. Despite the heat, Nesta was wearing a woollen hat, alternating blue and white hoops, with a red cardigan buttoned over a simple print dress. She kept giggling, covering her face with a hand, then trying to be serious. In spite of the fact that she was being laughed at, Helen felt no rancour – this was not malicious. She caught a sense of the infectious excitement their arrival had caused.

'Nesta!' Laurance cried. 'How well you're looking!'

'Ai-ai-ai!' She dissolved again, shooing him away with waves of an outstretched hand.

Helen gazed around, drinking in her surroundings. The compound was studded with huts and the greater part of the yard was covered by a flood of maize cobs. Those nearest to them were merely husks and a sizeable mound of grain was heaped to the side. A skinny little dog was nosing among the pile of cobs awaiting threshing. She had a brief sense of interrupting, of being a nuisance, but looking back at Laurance and Nesta beaming at one another, she realised she was the only one to be feeling that way.

'And where's your husband?' she heard Laurance ask.

'With Churchill.'

There was a fleeting moment in which she saw Laurance's face still, in which the smile solidified on Nesta's. Before anyone could speak, Helen felt a tugging at her trousers. One of the girls, six or so from the look of her, was intently examining the khaki cotton.

Nesta, seeing the direction of Helen's gaze, rapped out a phrase in dialect and the daughter stepped back, head bowed.

'It's all right.' Helen beckoned to the girl again, crouching down to be nearer her height, eliciting a shy advance.

Laurance and Nesta fell into gossip about the wedding and Helen turned her attention to the little girl. She couldn't get a word out of her, finding the sober steadiness of her regard a little unnerving. Eventually the girl's eyes strayed to her wrist. Helen released the strap with a deft flick and handed her watch over for scrutiny. The timepiece, its gold plate glittering in the sun, was still being investigated, turned over and over, when a male voice boomed out above the sound of the others' murmuring.

'Massa Laurents! So you have brought a lady friend to see us.'

Helen looked up to see a broad-shouldered African striding from one of the huts, thick thighs protruding from his shorts and an unbuttoned shirt flapping at his sides. On his feet he wore sandals fashioned from lengths of old car tyre. In that first glimpse of Medicine, she was struck by the gravity of his expression, the seriousness of his face against his wife's ebullient greetings.

She leaned back against the wall of the hut, her eyes a little sore from the smoky air, but otherwise feeling wonderfully at peace. In little groups around the hut the children stood absorbed – their fascination with their trophies was endless. Nesta sat a little further around the circular wall. There seemed no compulsion to converse, no need for unnecessary niceties. Once she'd got used to the technique – rolling wads of mealie-meal into little balls, dipping them into the sauce – she'd eaten with relish, savouring the spare flavour the stew imparted to the greater blandness of the maize. She felt full and a little drowsy, what with the drive from K— and the insatiable demands of the children. Nesta seemed to know this, smiling across at her occasionally, but otherwise leaving her to her thoughts and her contemplation of the red glow from the heart of the fire.

After a short time Laurance and Medicine reappeared from their stroll and smoke. Laurance nodded to the room and Nesta sprang to life, clapping her hands and cajoling the youngsters into returning their various toys. Laurance took custody of his lighter, the keys; Helen her rings, her watch, a much depleted lipstick, and the compact, the mirror of which had caused such inventive hilarity. She stood, a smile forming on her lips in readiness for farewells, a smile which was arrested by Laurance's expression.

'Before we go? If you wouldn't mind?'

She searched his face.

'It would mean a lot to him, Miss Helen.'

She smiled at Medicine, despite being a little irritated by the implication behind their hesitancy. 'Of course. I don't mind in the slightest – really.'

Her eyes had barely accommodated to the sunlight before she was plunged back into the darkness of another hut. Blinking into the gloom, Laurance's breathing loud at her side, she began to make out the seated figure. The chair – the only bit of furniture she'd seen in the entire time they'd been there – was constructed from thick beams of wood, a simple, functional design, clumsy compared to those at home, yet the more dignified to her because of it. The young man slumped in it, skewed to one side, his head lolling, stared up at her with eyes which at first appeared sightless. Then his mouth jerked – she was shocked to see spittle drooling down his chin – and formed a lopsided smile.

She took a hesitant step, then another, eventually coming to his side. She reached out and touched his hand. Instantly, his fingers curled round hers, gripping so tightly. They stood there for an eternity – motionless – until Laurance, perhaps sensing her growing unease, walked swiftly to her side.

'Come on, old man.'

She couldn't break her gaze away from Churchill's, felt Laurance gently prising the clasped hand from hers.

He was driving too fast but she dared not admonish him. The Land Rover bounced along the narrow path; at one point he had to stand on the brakes to avoid hitting a startled deer that leapt across just yards ahead of them. In the silence, her mind busied itself with personal regrets. The devotion of Nesta and Medicine to their handicapped son had stirred a painful amalgam of guilt and anger. She resolved to write to her mother on returning to K—. The pitiful opposition to her coming out here now seemed irrelevant. She should at least let her know that she had married, was finding happiness at last. As for her father. She wondered if she could convey the feelings that the sight of Medicine, his livelihood abandoned in order to be with his wife and children, had provoked. Wondered, if she could communicate the intense love she had glimpsed between so-called savages in this tiny, out of the way African village, whether her mother might finally realise the stupidity of her situation. Realise that she should have expected more from the man who'd become her husband.

'Well, he wasn't keen – quite hostile to start with. He still feels badly betrayed – the maps and everything. But I think I persuaded him.' Laurance's words derailed her thoughts.

She rested her hand on his thigh.

'It's bloody hopeless, otherwise. I think he knows that.'

They reached the bus stop, nosed out on to the dirt road, heading back to K—.

'She's so lovely,' Helen said. 'Will she manage?'

'Have to.' He changed up a gear. 'I'll make it worth his while, of course. Advantages of being party leader. Stuff London if they think otherwise.'

Helen nodded, feeling pride swell out of the blackness of the mood. She leaned across and planted a kiss on his cheek.

'Will he be like that for ever?'

Laurance nodded, glanced at her. ' 'Fraid so. Damage to the brain.' He gave a bitter-sounding laugh. 'One of the brightest in his year, apparently. Now he can't even feed himself.'

As they rattled along she tried to imagine how Nesta would cope without her husband for months at a time, with the small-holding they farmed, with her lace-making, with Churchill, with the innumerable youngsters. She desperately wanted to do something. Eventually, as if reading her mind, Laurance spoke again.

'It's their only hope – honestly. Educate the others, hope it leads to more money in the long run. Charity will only last so long.'

Coroner's Court,
1 Marsh Lane,
Kingston upon Thames,
Surrey

9th June 1962

Your Ref:
Our Ref: mej/4169/63

Dear Mr Hopkins,

Acknowledgement of receipt of:

i) Airmail letters (five).

Thank you for submitting the aforementioned items. They will be returned to you at such time as the Coroner deems their value for evidential purposes to have ceased.

Thank you for your cooperation in this matter.

Yours sincerely,

<u>M. James (Mrs.)</u>
<u>Coroner's Officer</u>

Mr. J. A. Hopkins,
Flat A,
162 Surbiton Drive,
Tolworth,
Kingston,
Surrey

Thursday 6 March, Dunsop Bridge, nr Clitheroe, Lancashire

There is much more to Dunsop Bridge than the grey blob and the ℗ depicted on my north of England Travelmaster. This I came to appreciate during my stroll, electing to haul my luggage through the narrow lanes as the only way of occupying the interminable two hours before the next bus back to Clitheroe. In the car park, just along from the public conveniences, there is a notice-board displaying a poster with a potted description of the locality. From this I learned that there was once a thriving horse industry in the area. And not any old horses either. The village's connection with racing is commemorated in carvings and paintings in St Hubert's church. Indeed, much of the £700 cost of constructing the church itself was met by a local landed family out of the purse they received when their gelding Kettledrum won the Derby in 1861.

Nowadays, the major landowners are the Duchy of Lancaster and NorthWest Water, and livelihood is earned in a different way. The village is apparently the gateway to an area known as the Trough of Bowland. As such it is the starting point for a number of walks and, as I suspected from the map stock in the shop, is a favourite with what are termed hardy hill-walkers. Indeed, as I was reading that very passage, a car pulled up in the car park and disgorged a pair of very hardy-looking hill-walkers indeed. They gave me no more than a cursory glance before shouldering their day packs and hiking purposefully along a nearby footpath leading to the hills rising up behind the village.

I finished reading the poster and set off on my own modest stroll. Reaching the shop again, I paused to rest my case for a few moments, massaging the blood back into my aching fingers. The postbox in the wall is embossed with the letters 'GR'. Above it I found another notice-board from which I learned that even here there is the need to protect one's children from the dangers of drug abuse. Having also discovered that a Mr P. Saunders is due to give a talk entitled 'Round the World on a Push Bike' in the village hall in a little under a week's time, I picked up my case and ambled on.

At the top of the village I passed the Catholic Sch, the one where Helen received her education, and the one where – I now know – she teaches art on a part-time basis. Just along from this was St Hubert's church, of the same Roman denomination. One can only assume that Irish immigration affected the religious make-up of the area. Anyway, I spent an interesting half-hour nosing around inside, eventually locating the small statues of Kettledrum on the side pillars of the altar. St Hubert, I discovered from a leaflet at the back of the church, is the patron saint of hunters, and once preyed on stags in the royal forest of Bowland. Having been converted to Christianity, he abandoned blood sports, and soared through the hierarchy of the church, eventually being appointed Bishop of Maastricht.

The diversions of the village exhausted, I made my way back to the bus stop to await the start of my journey home, reflecting as I went upon the varied colour contained within a simple grey blob.

These days, should one wish, one could apply to Ordnance Survey for a much more personalised map of the Dunsop Bridge area. It can still be printed on paper, but if you have access to a CD-ROM, so much the better – in any case it will have been generated by computer. The user is able to specify the features they would like to see. If your interest is in walking, for example, then footpaths and terrain can be highlighted at the expense of other extraneous detail. If, however, one's main purpose is to plan a new housing development, then transport links, administrative boundaries, woodlands, educational and shopping facilities would be given prominence. Familiar two-dimensional contouring can be exploded into a three-dimensional terrain model, assisting in the analysis of flood risk, the planning of a new road. Those working in the insurance industry might like to see the area represented in terms of risk: of subsidence, car theft, burglary. Similarly, if one is hoping to target the marketing of one's products to certain subsections of the population, one can fuse one's map with one's customer database, superimposing demographic characteristics on geographical ones. Map-makers still assemble the information, but their users now decide for themselves what will be shown, and what excluded. The cartographer is dead. Long live the consumer.

Clearly, in such a climate, a hundred different versions of Dunsop Bridge are possible. If one leaves aside the initial dazzle of such technology, one realises what maps really are. Nothing but information. They have always been so. The charming charts of my youth, with their cool, thick paper, their simple colour schemes, their comfortingly consistent symbols, their received wisdom as to what it was one needed to know about the world – these maps are revealed in all their embarrassing partiality. Beneath their certainties, their authoritative veneer, beneath the contours and B roads and grey blobs and ⓒs, teem numerous other interpretations of the same reality, suppressed, hidden, because the cartographer deems them irrelevant.

And, as with all information – even that contained in an innocent-looking letter – the information presented in one cartographic version of an area can be viewed in different ways. This is the hardest lesson I have learned in my long involvement with the world of map-making. One man's convenient new motorway is another's decimated countryside. One man's oil industry is another's environmental destruction. One man's hydroelectric dam is a thousand others' displacement, their homes, their farms, the landscapes of their youth vanished beneath a vast new lake.

And it's not just the way a map is viewed. It's the use that's made of it. A tableau is preserved with stark clarity in my mind: a courtroom in Kingston upon Thames, my hands gripping the front of the witness stand, the greying, world-weary coroner leaning in my direction. A clearing of his throat, a slight hesitation before he speaks, then the question: could I throw any light on Mr Usai's counsel's assertion that the maps on which he had worked all his life had ultimately been used against his people, in the hunting down of militant nationalists during the turbulent years leading to his country's independence? And, as clear as if it was yesterday, my own voice replying: I'm terribly sorry, sir, but I really haven't the faintest idea.

Eventually, tired out, I take my seat again on the bench by the bus stop. The sun, its premature enthusiasm spent, has retreated behind some cloud and the day has become decidedly chilly. I'm hungry, too. Leaving my suitcase unguarded – I can't be bothered to carry it another yard and I really can't conceive of any harm coming to it here – I pay a second call on the local shop, purchasing a couple of bags of crisps and an orange in lieu of lunch. Thankfully, the plump woman behind the counter forbears to ask how my visit to the Gardners went.

Now that my travels are over, I want nothing but to get on my way, return to my house, to Mrs Bryant, to the tidying up of my affairs. I begin to experience the frustrations of those who dwell so very far from the major conurbations. According to the timetable, I still have some forty minutes before I can expect my bus to arrive. My snack causes considerable excitement, and not a little disappointment, amongst the local duck population. It takes only a few minutes to consume. The orange in particular is a great let-down, desiccated, fibrous, not an ounce of flavour in it.

Lunch over, I remove from my briefcase the last two unread items – separated now from the file which had been their resting place all these years – and determine to put the remaining minutes to good use.

The note from the coroner's officer takes no time at all. Even though she read them many more times than did I, I don't believe Helen ever appreciated what Laurance's letters revealed about the man, Medicine Usai, whom I never properly met. Nor indeed what they told of the feelings Laurance had for him and his blighted family. As she read them, her interest was always focused on the romance, the exotica, of the Africa Laurance portrayed. An Africa of which he was king. Given the nature of her grief, and the enormous struggle facing her, she can, I think, be forgiven for her reaction at the inquest, and for her persisting beliefs thereafter. Fortunately, the coroner, detached from the personalities, had none of her difficulty. Whereas Helen, along with the authorities in K—, always maintained that Laurance had been betrayed, that it would have been preferable for the two men to have perished together, the coroner saw things differently. No doubt in the context of our nation's changing place in the world, he was able to brush aside the accusations that Mr Usai had failed in his duty. As he said in his summing up, it is a rare man who owes allegiance to only one quarter.

Returning the coroner's officer's letter to my briefcase, I steel myself, in the remaining half-hour, to read again the final item of my erstwhile correspondence file. As I arrange the sheets on my lap, I find it immensely comforting to remind myself of Brigadier Hotine's maxim, imparted to me at the end of a discussion of what he termed Mau Mau maps many, many years ago: the map-maker bears no responsibility for the uses to which others put his maps.

Telegrams in Brief

T—, 18th May 1962. – The last seat to be decided in T—'s first general election, the Asian seat for the Southern Province, has been won by the candidate supported by T.A.N.A. – Reuter.

Hang the weather, swimming was the one thing that helped. Returning from her trip to the post office, Helen changed quickly into her costume – a tight fit and becoming really quite indecent at five months, but never mind, the pool was hardly overlooked. The garden was fragrant, a light breeze wafting the scent of frangipani from the beds across the lawn. After a temperature-testing exploration on the part of her right foot, she lowered herself rung by rung into the pool, the water rapidly ceasing to feel cold as she waded out, dipping her shoulders below the rippling surface. The minute she was floating she felt relief from the gnawing pain in her back that the medic could do nothing for. A normal part of pregnancy, so he said, with the exasperating good humour of one whose sex precludes ever having to cope with such problems. She lay there, hands wafting by her sides, gazing up at the grey hulks lumbering across the African sky, threatening further rain.

At first she thought it was something to do with the maid. But then the voice grew loud, distinct, calling her name. She righted herself, feet swinging beneath her to find the tiled floor of the pool. Turning towards the rear of the bungalow she saw Hildred, hat in hand, hurrying out of the verandah doors.

'Helen?'

His tone, his agitated manner, caused her, unbidden, to stride for the side, the water churning as she fought against its resistance. She hauled herself up the rungs of the ladder and met him by the springboard.

'There's some worrying news, I'm afraid.'

Had he never seen a pregnant woman before? She folded her arms across her breasts, shivering slightly in the breeze.

'It's Laurance.' At last he lifted his eyes. 'He's two weeks overdue. We've only just had word from the camp. No sign of his boys either.'

And the wind was cold! She hugged herself more tightly, studying his face with intense interest, the way his nostrils flared, the way the moustache mimicked the movements of his lips as he talked.

'Urquhart's setting off with a relief party. The flooding's still horrendous, though.'

She shook her head, wondering what on earth he was on about.

'Hopefully we'll have word soon.' His eyes dropped again. The costume was clinging coldly against her skin now, heavy with water. 'I thought I should let you know.'

Transcript of monthly diary, L. D. Wallace, May 1962

1ST MAY

Better day all round. Woke to complete absence of rain, hence hasty prep^{n}s and *at last* got hell out of staging camp. Rivers v. high but allowed fording of sorts. Bare minimum supplies on heads; repeat crossings too risky. Left rest in dump. Regrouped far bank, no losses to crocs, only casualties one sack mealie-meal and Isaac's right shoe. Gamely he carries on without. My boots saturated and chafing.

Headed N.W., long ridge bounding us to south, steep scree, no way over. T91 (R131 on Arc 30th) due west by my reckoning but shan't go far wrong. Heavy going in thick bush, slop underfoot, beats scrambling against scree, though.

8 hr trek, few miles at most. Camped at 5.30. Mercifully still dry. Isaac shoeless; Siqueya one leg swollen below knee; M. great help, good and steady.

2ND MAY

Threatening clouds but weather held. Reached ridge end 3 p.m. and started up narrow valley, bearing S.W. Bush thinning with climb hence better progress. Sighted T91 (or I'm Dutch), though summit lost in cloud. Barometric readings. Siqueya feverish; given Penicillin. Self could do with whisky.

3RD MAY

Struck out for peak. T89, T90 parties in place three days all being well, wondering what's become of us no doubt. Feet sore – lovely crop of blisters discovered a.m. – still, Isaac uncomplaining and he in worse position by far. Deluge p.m.; sheltered 'neath trees. Men a bit despondent, M. sent to make representations. Told him we press on. *Must* make summit, last link.

No let-up in downpour, camped under branches though little protection. Siqueya more Penicillin – several degrees better. Hope for climb tomorrow, though whether other parties have hung around for us, God only knows.

4TH MAY

Cold to core all night. Blasted rain no let-up. Groundsheet awash a.m., others' similarly. M. says hopeless. Inclined to agree, except down to drizzle by end breakfast, weak sun breaking through by end decamp. T91 mocking us; near yet far. Decided on attempt – at least we'd get above weather. Sullen looks from Siqueya, Isaac phlegmatic. M. hard to read – cracked good jokes en route. Own feet devilish sore, especially right. Said nothing – any excuse would suffice, Siqueya partic. Started Penicillin.

Got third way up but route impassable. Camp at base and try different tack in morning. Checked equipment: cases watertight. Food for six days only; send back if climb successful. Despite feet, took gun out evening. Great pity, no game. Morale poor generally. M. quiet. Turned in early, all exhausted. Hope weather holds.

5TH MAY

Fever overnight – right foot bad. S. & I. gone in night, most food too. M. knew, no doubt; nothing but shrug and weak smile. No option but turn back. Took what could carry, left rest to hyenas and wandering tribesmen of whom no blasted sign, otherwise could recruit and resupply. Limping badly late p.m. Tried raising other parties on two-way 'phone but no joy – far too low altitude. Abandoned Tellurometer and all non-essentials – D.O.S. £1,500 down but too bad, no choice but get out. Thank God Penicillin and aspirin and continued dry. Downhill much easier, reached ridge by dusk. Cosy night in store, M. and I in only tent. Stayed close to river, divided mealie-meal for three days at outside. Wouldn't keep gnat going but supply dump no more than two days' hobble away, depending on rivers.

6TH MAY

Said would have to rest – foot v. painful, red and swollen, fevers. Agreed M. press on for dump, much quicker without me, may even get there today, God willing. Return with resupply. Mercifully sunny. Ate a little but nauseous. Decided get Penicillin down at least.

7TH MAY

Some improvement, ?foot less swollen. Still painful, though. M. not returned. Waited mid-p.m. when too late for anything. Resolve set off in morning and meet him half-way. Spooked – kept gun close by. Rested except fetch water. Hot day, no shade. Tent suffocating till evening.

8TH MAY

Left kit except gun, medicines and rest food – no prospect of carrying. Foot bearing up but progress slow. No M. – despair evening. Forded first of rivers dusk. Stupid. Wet for night under tree. Chilled through. BF.

9TH MAY

Nearly came cropper in river crossing – lost gun – lucky not to get swept away in currents. Reached staging camp site 4.30 p.m. – NO FOOD. *Where* M.? Foot worse – doubled up Penicillin. Rain. Slept under tree – no strength go on. Utterly exhausted.

10TH MAY

Foot and leg in bad shape, barely move with stick, feel v. weak. Small amt. mealie-meal only. Only assume S. & I. cleaned out cache, M.

decided press on for help. Pointless trying to follow – await relief. Spent day making shelter of sorts – v. painful.

11TH MAY

Torrential rain all night. Went to higher ground to avoid flood. Last mealie-meal (dry-ish). No sign others. Try to think. Even assuming good pace, M. will reach base several days at *soonest*. Must hang on. Right foot mess – massaged and cleaned. Last Penicillin – though what good it's doing God only knows.

12TH MAY

Dry night, high fever. Grass for food, plus some rotten berries. Walked only for water – 60 ft in one hr. Maggots between toes right foot. Stench. Dug out with knife till came to grey membrane, couldn't get through. Washed with urine. Occurred eat maggots but stomach not strong. Feel if M. can reach base, should see help within the week, less if alarm raised by others. Tried making marker out of stones – 'plane could drop supplies. Sun came out.

13TH MAY

A.'s birthday. What wouldn't give, &c. Much as could do to fetch grass, water. Flesh right foot/calf spongy, red, crackling to touch. Awful smell. Many maggots – cleaned out fifty or more. Bowels, gut, urine OK. DELIGHTED hear plane at 4 . . . [indecipherable]. Little joy.

14TH MAY

Fair night, little rain, right leg intense pain, left foot swollen. Feeling v. sick. Sun pleasant but made v. drowsy. Tried clean foot but handkerchief bandage stuck . . . [indecipherable] . . . Hope others trying as hard as me. Could be M. came to grief in river. Very depressed, thinking Nesta, Churchill. How will they cope without him? Hope H. OK. Would like to make quite clear, only thing I did was try

to finish chain. S. & I. lack experience – lack discipline, loyalty. S.
especially – hope doesn't say I'm dead. Hope someone comes soon.
Hope M. . . . [indecipherable] . . .

Last aspirin. Maybe last day to write. Try to . . . [indecipher-
able] . . . for what worth,

15TH MAY

Rain a.m. Pain increase. *Maggots left foot.*
   got grass, water. *where* M.?

16TH MAY

Everything too wet . . . [indecipherable] . . . energy to write

17TH MAY

got just over pint water handful grass

18TH MAY

maybe last day to write hope get water tomorrow IF DEAD WHEN
YOU FIND THIS PERHAPS 19th LAST DAY PERHAPS 20th GO
THROUGH THIS AND DO WHAT'S NECESSARY

Jubilant Scenes in T—
Africans Welcome New Status

From Our Correspondent
T—, 23ʳᵈ June 1962

Scenes of the utmost rejoicing followed the announcement to-day by the Governor, Sir Leonard Hodge, that T— is to be granted responsible government under an interim United Nations Trusteeship Council. Several thousand Africans, many sporting the distinctive brown 'livery' of T.A.N.A., despite the proscription of political uniforms, were gathered behind temporary barriers in the grounds of the Legislative Council building to hear the proclamation.

After the Governor's departure the appearance of Mr. Robert Allohya, T.A.N.A. president and chair of the newly elected members' forum, was the signal for an outburst of cheering and singing. Garlanded, and bearing an olive branch, Mr. Allohya was hoisted on the shoulders of his jubilant supporters and carried through the wildly enthusiastic crowd to an open limousine.

Asked later at a press conference how long T— would have to wait until full independence, Mr. Allohya said, 'I and my colleagues wish to set up a momentum of economic development which will carry an independent country forward without difficulty. We must also have a minimum of local men in the Civil Service. Until these two goals are satisfied our people must remain patient.' He emphasized that he foresaw independence within the Commonwealth. Mr. Allohya was then asked whether the Governor had shown sympathy to African ideals. He replied that since Sir Leonard had been there the whole political landscape had changed.

The pace of constitutional progress had surprised many. Less than a year ago proposals were on the table for the equal sharing of power between the three races. The rapidity of the acceptance of political determination by Africans is largely attributable to the moderation of nationalist leaders. Mr. Allohya, often under great pressure from extremists in his own ranks, has stuck diligently to the task of democratic persuasion. The return of a T.A.N.A.-approved candidate in every seat – African, Asian and European – in last month's general election vindicated his strategy. His reward seems likely to be that, in a year or so's time, he will become leader of the first African Government in the country.

'But look, here's the certificate.'

Charles Gray took the document and indulged them with a minute of his time spent in studying it.

'I'm very sorry, Mrs . . . Miss Gardner, but as I say, this carries no weight whatsoever.'

He dipped his head, regarding the trio over the top of his half-moon glasses. 'As far as English law is concerned, Laurance Wallace was legally married to one –' he consulted his notes – 'Annette Wallace, née Chapman, occupation: barmaid, of 31 Long Furlong, Cambridge.'

He paused to allow the finality of his judgement to sink in. 'The validity of a marriage cemented in a dependent territory is superseded by a prior union registered in this country.'

'So, so what you're saying – so Helen's to bring up this child on her *own*?'

He tried a placating smile. 'All I'm *doing*, Mr Gardner, is giving you my opinion as to the legal position.'

'Well, we'll bloody fight it –'

'*Michael* –'

'No, we'll bloody fight it, it isn't right, it bloody well isn't right!'

'*Mister* Gardner! If you wouldn't mind?'

'Is there nothing we can do?'

He felt a sudden pity for the young woman across the desk from him, well advanced in pregnancy. Her father resumed his seat. Her mother remained as she had done throughout, sitting stock still, staring at him with barely disguised horror.

'I'm sorry, but no. Had he left a will, then his estate would have been divided according to his last wishes, which I've no doubt would have included a substantial settlement upon you. But as it is, intestate . . . Well, the law is clear.'

It was the mother who broke down, sobbing uncontrollably, her head sagging until it met her hands. The young woman remained motionless, her hands gripped tightly across her lap, her head now bowed. The father looked from one to the other, back at him, back to his daughter, back to his wife.

Charles Gray pressed a switch on his intercom.

'Ah, Miss Jenkins? If you wouldn't mind?'

Thursday 6 March, Dunsop Bridge, nr Clitheroe, Lancashire

I hear the bus a short while before I see it, the grumble of the diesel reaching my ears while the coach itself remains out of sight. I'm on my feet, suitcase in hand, when finally it rounds the bend beyond the car park.

It's a different driver, so I'm spared potential embarrassment when purchasing my single to Clitheroe. I notice little of the return trip, my mind given over to desolate thoughts as to the loneliness of Laurance's final days. I resolve, when I get back to Southampton, to burn the transcript, never wanting to read it again in my life.

One thing I remain grateful for: that he never appeared fully to appreciate the unholy mess he left behind him. In this day and age, when every third family has but one parent – or so it seems – it is easy to forget the difficulties that faced a single mother back then. Never mind the unkind gossip, the name-calling in the playground, the disapprobation of a church community committed to the sanctity of marriage – there was the sheer grinding difficulty of making ends meet. To give them their due – or at least, to give his father his due – Laurance's parents, once they were made aware of the situation, did what they could in the way of financial support. In the same way as they had cared for the poor, impressionable Cambridge barmaid to whom Laurance had taken a fancy, with such disastrous consequences, in his student days. Only they were in no position to force another marriage. Laurance had done that already, and – painful as it is to admit – I believe to this day that his betrothal to Helen was sincere. Not a union he would have subsequently tried to escape by espousing the life of the overseas surveyor.

A memory, preserved with vivid clarity. Laurance's funeral, standing there in helpless fascination at the sight of those two women on either side of his grave, Helen – heavily pregnant – perfectly pale despite her time in the African sun; Annette contrastingly calm, perhaps resolved now that the final chapter had been closed, however tragically. Hearing the dull thud of their respective handfuls of earth landing on the lid of his coffin, one after the other, Annette's first, Helen's a short while after. Making awkward eye-contact with Laurance's father, his mother's blank face. Staring at the eight-year-old girl's hand enveloped in Annette's own.

I faithfully replied to every one of Helen's letters. She was facing enough of a struggle. I had found my magnanimity.

I know she never got over it. If she had to blame anyone, it should have been Laurance. Not the wretched Annette. Not his well-intentioned father, pathetically powerless to make up for the misdeeds of his son. Not that rabbit-in-a-headlight, Medicine Usai, whose only thought was to survive, for the sake of his own family. Who had seen quite how grave Laurance's condition was. Who took what little food was left from the staging camp and walked his way out, neither willing to return to probable death nursing a gangrenous, lame surveyor in a gesture of futile loyalty, nor daring to be the one to report to authorities in whom he did not trust.

I never knew if she held me in any way responsible. Throughout our subsequent correspondence, I managed to conceal quite when it was that I had first suspected Laurance's bigamy. She never learned about the day I had a knight of the realm and his odd family to tea. As to her other question, the use to which our maps had once been put, and the insidious poison instilled in the minds of some of our African workers because of it – well, I always maintained that I'd never had the faintest idea. Quite whether I would have been able to keep up those pretences had we met face to face, I do not know. But some things are easy to do in a letter.

No, it was Laurance who should be blamed, yet I understand only too well why she could not.

Go through this and do what's necessary. The last gasp of a surveyor a few days away from completing the chain of triangulation that had come to obsess him? A conscientious appeal for the recovery of lost equipment? The death-bed plea of an abandoned man craving retribution against those who had let him down? Or the hopelessly naïve wish of a sentimental fool who believed that the mess he'd made of other people's lives could in some simple way be put right? A hundred different versions are possible.

I alight at the station, taking my case and bidding the driver farewell. On the platform, I am pleased to discover there is only ten minutes to wait for the next train to Blackburn. I contemplate ringing Mrs Bryant to tell her I am coming home, but Clitheroe station has yet to benefit from the proliferation of telephone facilities. Instead, I settle down on a platform bench and contemplate my own betrayals.

Thursday 6 March, on board the CrossCountry service from Edinburgh to Brighton

Given the fact that I didn't leave Clitheroe until well past two, I had already resigned myself to a late arrival back in Southampton. So the delay due to signal failure makes little difference to me. The same cannot be said for my fellow travellers, some of whom are looking decidedly hot under the collar the longer we sit in limbo outside Birmingham New Street. The mobile phone is clearly an important accessory to modern living and I note several calls being made. A number of other passengers leave for the buffet car when the guard announces that free use of the phonecard phone will be made available to customers wishing to inform others of their delay.

I would like to think that the majority of these calls are to loved ones, who might otherwise be facing a worrying wait at an empty station further down the line. But the rigours of travelling to which I've been subjected over the past two days have left me with something of a jaundiced view. Every respectable suit, every neatly kept hairstyle, every camel coat might very well be hiding an alternative reality. I can't help wondering how many of my fellow passengers are instead calling lovers, mistresses. How many are in fact calling their legitimate partners, but only out of fear that the delay in their return – for entirely innocent reasons – might set their loved ones wondering.

Excepting Mrs Bryant, I myself have no one to inform of the hold-up. I have only myself to blame. By the early eighties, the Directorate was in its death throes, the victim of the new dogma. Despite my best efforts in Special Projects, we had never managed fully to pay our way, always relying upon grants from the overseas aid budget to keep going. As Britain turned in on herself, becoming less and less concerned with the welfare of those countries over which she had once wielded power; as commercial companies and foreign countries developed mapping of rival quality, so the Directorate's role became increasingly marginal. Couple that with the new loathing of anything which smacked of government agency – anything whose value couldn't be measured in purely economic terms – and the death knell was sounding.

There was tremendous uncertainty. I myself had known no other career, had no idea what I would go on to do when my job ceased to exist. It was my bleakest time, my evenings dogged by memories of my father returning from another humiliating day spent touting his unwanted brushes door to door, imagining a similar fate for myself. To compound my anxieties, or perhaps because of them, life with Margaret became increasingly strained. For months, what little we had to say to one another came largely in the form of irritable snaps and barbed asides. In the end she left quite abruptly, caught up in what I later learned to have been a whirlwind romance with an insurance salesman who called while I was at work and offered her more than just a pension. Fortunately we had no children to suffer from the split. It was never that kind of marriage.

I recall writing to Helen around this time, telling her these various bits of news and wondering, through the medium of ink on page, what would now become of me. Several months passed with no word from her. Before I finally received her reply, Argentinian forces were landing on the Falklands.

For an agency under threat of extinction, the Directorate was suddenly central once again. There were no coy memos from the director's office in that day and age. Requests for assistance were channelled directly to me. As many copies as possible of 1:50,000 and 1:250,000 sheets of the Falklands to the MoD, yesterday – the day before preferably. Unpublished town plans of Stanley. Maps of the airfield. The days passed in a blur, the phone ringing hourly with new demands. Urgent clarification required of errors in the position of two small islands on sheets nineteen and twenty-five.

South Georgia, did we have anything on South Georgia? Into work over the Easter weekend for charts of Ascension. The US embassy, ABC, the BBC, the *Daily Mirror*, LWT, the *Los Angeles Times* – everyone wanted access to maps, aerial photographs, and every request had to be cleared. Everyone's, that is, except the Argentinians', who had walked into a map shop in London and purchased all the information they could possibly have required a few years before.

For a time, though, my hopes were high. Surely, after this, the Directorate – the organisation in which I'd invested my life's work – would be saved? Who could put a figure on the value of information at one's fingertips at such a time? As the war unfolded and reports came through of chaos and casualties sustained because of out-of-date depictions of fence lines, even those tragedies seemed to strengthen our hand. Information had been allowed to fall behind reality on the ground. There could be no more compelling case for increased funding, for a re-expansion of the Directorate's role. My future seemed assured, the flimsiest of silver linings to an otherwise grimly black cloud.

Once the conflict was over, the announcement was made. The Directorate of Overseas Surveys was to close. No one could comprehend it. The only concession was the survival of a handful of staff, who would be absorbed into Ordnance Survey, creating the new International Section. I was one of the lucky few.

Helen took her time replying. Her last letter to me arrived in the midst of packing for the move and was consequently hopelessly out of date. She was sorry to hear I was to be made redundant. She was equally dismayed to learn that my marriage was at an end. As I recall it, there was a bit of news: an update of her son's progress – he'd recently left home for seminary; something about her finding the days so long now she was on her own; a sentence suggesting that this could be why she found herself thinking about the past so often. She finished the letter with the suggestion that if I found I had the time, perhaps I might like to visit, might like to come and stay for a few days, see what I made of Dunsop Bridge. She thought I would love it there.

I put the letter to one side. What with the move, all the difficulties of settling into a new place, trying to carve another role for myself in a fast-changing world, endeavouring to get to grips with technology that was altering unrecognisably the work I had known, I don't remember answering it. I don't think I ever gave her my new address.

In the process of packing up Surbiton Drive, I came across two unexpected things. One was a mildewed cardboard box at the back of the shed which, when opened, proved to contain all manner of yellowing lace table wear which, I dimly recalled, would make the ideal present for someone somewhere at some time. The other was a collection of airmail paper, plus a number of other items of correspondence, all bound together with a thick elastic band. The box I forwarded to the woman I believed it had been intended for, many years before, care of a knight of the realm whose address of twenty years previously I found amongst the bundle of letters in my desk drawer. I've no idea whether it reached its intended recipient; never heard a thing. The letters I filed in what I have always termed a 'string file' and subsequently stored in the loft of my new home in Southampton.

The situation is becoming intractable. The guard makes frequent announcements over the loudspeaker system repeating the mantra: we apologise for the delay, which is due to a signal failure at Banbury. Eventually, in an effort to placate the mounting unrest all around, he informs us that a free hot drink is available for every passenger from the buffet car. Initially there is reluctance in my coach. People glance somewhat furtively at one another, wondering who will be first to break ranks. I feel it, too, the embarrassment at being seen to rush for a gratuity, even though we are all highly deserving. In the end, a couple at the far end of the carriage get to their feet and, with a mutter to those sitting nearby, they set off towards the rear of the train. Within minutes, more than half of us are following in their wake.

Shortly before I reach the head of the queue in the buffet car –

still trying to decide between a hot chocolate and a tea – the train lurches, stutters, then gets underway. A ragged, muted cheer goes up. There is a heartening atmosphere – what might be termed a blitz spirit – and I resolve to relate the story to Mrs Bryant. I hope she will be a little cheered up by it. The events of the past few months, since her husband's stroke, have thrown her into a flat spin.

I am not sure what to say to her when she asks, as she inevitably will do, about Helen. For some reason she seems to have set great store by the success of my trip and I fear that my failure to produce a happy ending will further deepen her gloom. It would be much easier were I able to write her a letter. As it is, I shall have to tell her the truth.

Helen's son is the spitting image of her, excepting his hair, which is tangled and curly. He looks a handsome fellow, though whether the years have started to take their toll in the decade and a half since the ordination photo, I have no idea. In any case, she is clearly right to feel so very proud of him. The middle-aged woman smiling and hanging on to his arm in the picture hadn't changed so very much. Even now, greying somewhat, her face rounder and a little lined, her demeanour more subdued and serious, she is not too different from the Helen Gardner I once knew.

She seemed pleased enough to see me, especially after the awkwardness of the first few minutes had subsided. She excused her failure to reply to my recent letter on the grounds of work. Speaking of which, she was due in school in a little under an hour. We filled some of the time by drinking a cup of tea and swapping pleasantries about the village, and the journey I had undertaken to get there. I had hoped to keep up my pretence of a centre of Britain project, a call on the off-chance. But my suitcase was, I realised, something of a weak point in my plan. She appeared slightly shocked to learn that I'd travelled all this way specifically to see her. I was subjected to a mild scolding, very reminiscent of the old days, for not making myself more plain in my letter. In that respect, in her opinion, I hadn't changed one bit. Had she realised the true situation, she would of course have written back and arranged a more convenient time.

There was a period of silence after that. Perhaps all the talk of letters and visits brought to her mind the matter of the last letter she had sent to me. Whatever it was, the very next thing she said was to remind me of it, to tell me how upset she'd been that I never replied. I was taken aback to say the least – I hadn't in any way prepared myself for such directness. For a moment or two I was quite at a loss. I found some comfort in rearranging the position of my teaspoon on its saucer. Eventually, the time remaining to us ticking inexorably away, I made do with a simple apology.

Although I am still uncertain, I think this was perhaps the right reply. Our conversation returned to safer ground thereafter, and I learned something of her job as part-time art teacher, which she'd taken up when someone called Mr Andrews retired from the school. Her mother, she told me, had died some years before. She didn't mention her father and I can only assume he, too, is long since gone.

After a time she got to her feet and said she must get ready to go. While she was in the loo, I occupied myself by having a nose around the room. I was surprised to find on the mantelpiece, next to the picture of her son's ordination, a yellowing photograph of Laurance. In it he stands on a verandah, somewhere in Africa, the jacket of his linen suit frozen at the moment of being flapped open by the breeze. One hand is in a trouser pocket, the other holds a cigarette. He is smiling. As I studied the picture more closely, however, my sense of surprise at it being there gradually diminished. He was, after all, the father of her son, and I could well understand her retaining an affection for him. I must have become lost in my thoughts, for her voice, when it came from close to my side, quite startled me.

'You loved him, too, in your own way, didn't you?'

I wasn't at all sure how to answer such a complex question. In the end, conscious that she would have to be off to take her class, I settled for a murmured assent.

I left his letters with her. I think perhaps I had intended to do so all along. At the very least she can show them to her son some day, so that he might better come to know the father he never had. She accepted them without a word. I plan to burn the remainder of my correspondence file on the coal fire in the lounge of my home in Southampton upon my return. I shall watch placidly as the flames flicker and the papers blacken and combust. My letter of appointment, Hotine's memo, Sir David Wallace's note, Laurance's final days – all will go up in smoke.

When we parted company on her doorstep, Helen indicated how nice it had been to see me. She promised she would write. She even suggested that I make the trip again some time, during the school holidays, or at a weekend, when we might spend a bit longer together and make a go of renewing our acquaintance.

In time, if she's as good as her word, I may very well do so. At the moment, though, I am tired by all the travelling. I am greatly looking forward to getting home, hopefully not too late to give Mrs Bryant a ring to inform her of my safe return. But, in a while, another trip to Dunsop Bridge may seem the perfect thing to do.

AUTHOR'S NOTE

Although some of the events in the book have their roots in fact, it is important to stress that the story is a work of fiction. Brigadier Hotine, Lt Colonel Humphries, Mr Gaselee and Mr Henlen are historical figures, but the character portraits within the novel are my own. All other characters are entirely fictional, and any resemblance to persons living or dead is coincidental. The newspaper extracts are fictionalised versions of letters and reports which appeared in *The Times* during the late 1950s and early 1960s. 'Ordnance Survey', 'Travelmaster' and 'Pathfinder' are registered trademarks of Ordnance Survey, the national mapping agency of Great Britain. They are used with the kind permission of Ordnance Survey, as is the phrase 'Linking you to the real world'. No inference as to the policies or actions of either the Directorate of Overseas Surveys or Ordnance Survey should be drawn from the depictions of their fictional counterparts in the novel.

I could not have written this book without the help of a number of people. The starting point for my research was Alastair Macdonald's excellent social history of the Directorate, *Mapping the World* (HMSO, 1996). I am extremely grateful to Alastair for granting me access to his research material, for his generous hospitality, and for sharing with me so many anecdotes concerning life in the Directorate. I am equally indebted to Russell Fox, who kindly allowed me access to the Directorate archive, who responded tirelessly to my requests for assistance, and whose thoughts and ideas about the history and uses of mapping proved so inspirational.

Trevor Mouncey gave me incomparable information on the

question of the centre of Great Britain. Margaret Barrett showed me many items of equipment belonging to the map-makers of the past. My fiction was supported by letters, articles and memoirs written by many dozens of people who worked for the Directorate. I cannot name them all, but would particularly acknowledge L. J. Howells' article, 'On the Road to Ibadan' (*DOS Gazette*, July 1962), and the letters and papers of Martin Hotine. Both sources played a significant part in the creation of the Africa of the novel, in a few places very directly. I wish also to record my sincere respect for Bruce Sandilands. The Public Record Office was a source of valuable material. Derek and Bridget Whitaker assisted with period detail. David and Rosemary Hannant extended much-appreciated hospitality in Southampton.

Having received such generous help with my research, I have, of course, selected and distorted material to suit my fictional purposes. In particular, I have adapted details of surveying, cartographic and record-keeping techniques. Any errors are quite probably deliberate. Even if not, they are my own responsibility and not the fault of those who assisted in the research.

A number of people critiqued drafts of the novel. Sue Whitaker, Simon Crouch, Clayton Lister, and Derek and Bridget Whitaker all made helpful comments. I would like to thank my agent, Jonny Geller, and my publisher, Maggie McKernan, for their advice, editorial input and encouragement. Thanks also to Daphne Tagg for meticulous copy editing, and to Fanny Blake for starting the ball rolling. I am particularly indebted to Martyn Bedford who, in addition to his habitual support, encouragement and criticism, dug me out of a deep hole of my own making at an early stage in the writing. Finally, my wife, Lynn, showed herself once again to possess that rare combination: the ability to provide insightful criticism while never allowing me to doubt her love and support. She remains the perfect partner.

Triangulation was inspired by a remarkable organisation. I hope it serves, in however flawed a way, as a tribute to the men and women of all nationalities who worked, with such dedication, for the Directorate of Overseas Surveys.